THE CURSE

It was the infernal Wild Bill business. The name drew all the young men who fancied themselves fast with a gun, the young unknowns so desperate to be known that they were willing to risk their lives for a chance at notoriety. His dear wife Agnes never called him Wild Bill. To her he was James, and to his family he was Jim. If he had remained just plain Jim Hickok, if Colonel George Ward Nichols had never written all that folderol about him in *Harper's New Monthly,* the path of his life might have been entirely different.

To be fair, though, the fame that had accrued to him over the years brought with it a few benefits, too. In the days before he had married his dear Agnes, there had been a number of young women who were anxious to share the presence of the famous gunman Wild Bill. He had reaped financial rewards, as well, by joining with old friends and fellow scouts Bill Cody and Texas Jack Omohundro and performing in a series of rather ridiculous stage plays that were supposed to present the true story of life in the West to a bunch of soft-handed Easterners.

The money was never as good as it should have been, though, and he hated the East with its crowds and stink and noise. The pleasures of the flesh were fleeting and left him vaguely unsatisfied.

On a morning like this, when he lay in his hotel with his face pressed into a pillow and his head pounding from the whiskey he had drunk the night before, he wished he had never heard of Wild Bill Hickok.

Tales from

DEADWOOD

Mike Jameson

BERKLEY BOOKS, NEW YORK

THE BERKLEY PUBLISHING GROUP
Published by the Penguin Group
Penguin Group (USA) Inc.
375 Hudson Street, New York, New York 10014, USA
Penguin Group (Canada), 90 Eglinton Avenue East, Suite 700, Toronto, Ontario M4P 2Y3, Canada
(a division of Pearson Penguin Canada Inc.)
Penguin Books Ltd., 80 Strand, London WC2R 0RL, England
Penguin Books Ireland, 25 St. Stephen's Green, Dublin 2, Ireland (a division of Penguin Books Ltd.)
Penguin Group (Australia), 250 Camberwell Road, Camberwell, Victoria 3124, Australia
(a division of Pearson Australia Group Pty. Ltd.)
Penguin Books India Pvt. Ltd., 11 Community Centre, Panchsheel Park, New Delhi—110 017, India
Penguin Group (NZ), Cnr. Airborne and Rosedale Roads, Albany, Auckland 1310, New Zealand
(a division of Pearson New Zealand Ltd.)
Penguin Books (South Africa) (Pty.) Ltd., 24 Sturdee Avenue, Rosebank, Johannesburg 2196,
South Africa

Penguin Books Ltd., Registered Offices: 80 Strand, London WC2R 0RL, England

This is a work of fiction. Names, characters, places, and incidents either are the product of the author's imagination or are used fictitiously, and any resemblance to actual persons, living or dead, business establishments, events, or locales is entirely coincidental.

TALES FROM DEADWOOD

A Berkley Book / published by arrangement with the author

PRINTING HISTORY
Berkley edition / November 2005

Copyright © 2005 by The Berkley Publishing Group.
Cover design by Steven Ferlauto.
Interior text design by Kristin del Rosario.

ISBN: 0-425-20675-0

BERKLEY®
Berkley Books are published by The Berkley Publishing Group,
a division of Penguin Group (USA) Inc.,
375 Hudson Street, New York, New York 10014.
BERKLEY is a registered trademark of Penguin Group (USA) Inc.
The "B" design is a trademark belonging to Penguin Group (USA) Inc.

PRINTED IN THE UNITED STATES OF AMERICA

10 9 8 7 6 5 4 3 2 1

Prologue

Dakota Territory, May 1875

S HE just lost her head, simple as that. It had happened plenty of times before and likely would again, because when an impulse hit her, Martha Jane Cannary wasn't one to stand around thinking about what the consequences might be.

Besides, the sun was so hot, and the river looked so damned cool and inviting. And everybody else was doing it, so without hesitating any longer, she shucked her duds and jumped in, too. She whooped and hollered and splashed around in the stream just like the rest of them.

And wouldn't you know it, it didn't take those troopers any time at all to notice that one of their "fellow soldiers" wasn't a fella at all. Jane had never been overly endowed in the bosom area, but they were big enough to be womanly. Nor did she have a talleywhacker and balls hanging down between her legs, and that lack was a dead giveaway, even to a bunch of old boys who'd been dumb enough to think that enlisting in the cavalry would be better than staying back home on the family farm or clerking in the family store. None of them the sharpest sabers in the scabbard, those boys, but they damn sure knew a woman when they saw her.

"Look!" one of them yelled, pointing at Jane. "He's got titties!"

Silence fell over the river, a silence as vast and encompassing as can only be achieved in the wilderness, and the Dakota Territory qualified, sure enough. Jane stood there, calf-deep in the water now as a dozen or more equally naked men gathered around to gawk at her. Their peckers stood up at attention better than they themselves ever did on the parade ground, that was for damned sure. Jane got to musing on the situation and decided that in a way she sort of liked it. All the attention was a mite flattering. But it made her a little uncomfortable, too, so she said, "What're you assholes gawkin' at? Ain't you never seen a woman before?"

"We thought you was a trooper like us," said a skinny, weak-chinned young man from Iowa who thought it would be the height of glorious adventure to go fight Injuns in the Dakota Territory.

Martha Jane Cannary, sometimes called Calamity Jane, sometimes just Calam, snorted in disgust and said, "Not hardly."

"But you been dressed like a soldier ever since we left Fort Laramie," one of the other men pointed out.

"And I reckon if push come to shove I'd be a better soldier than any o' you dumb-blasted sons o' bitches." Jane shook a finger at the encircling troopers. "Now don't none o' y'all go runnin' off to tell ol' Colonel Dodge that he's got a woman along on this here expedition, you hear me?"

Most of the men were smiling shyly, but one of them wore an outright leer on his face as he said, "What'll you give us if we keep your secret?"

Jane frowned as she thought it over. She had come along on this expedition into the Black Hills so she could be near Sergeant Frank Siechrist, her current lover. Considering that she'd been whoring for nigh onto ten years, faithfulness and propriety were not high on her list of virtues. But when she was fond of a fella, as she was of Frank, she generally tried not to fool around on him too much.

Still, it might be that the only way she could preserve her secret and remain with the expedition was to let these boys take her off in the bushes and do whatever they wanted to her. Hell, she thought, it might be fun. There were a dozen of them, so it would last for a while.

The decision was taken out of her hands. A harsh voice yelled, "You men! What's going on down there?"

The troopers were sort of bunched up around her, so the captain who had happened to see them as he strolled along this nameless stream couldn't get a good look at her. The men tried to come to attention, which wasn't easy considering that they were all naked and standing in a river.

"Spread out!" the captain shouted. "Form a line, damn it! What's so interesting that you're all clustered around it like that?"

The troopers hesitated, but they had been given a direct order. Slowly, they scattered out and formed a rough line. Jane was along about the middle of it, and she hoped that the captain wouldn't be paying real close attention as he swept his gaze along the row of enlisted men.

He would have had to be not just inattentive, but also blind not to recognize her as a woman, even with her close-cropped hair and mannish figure. The captain's eyes widened as they settled on her. He started to sputter and gasp. Finally, he was able to say, "You . . . you're a woman!"

Old habits died hard. Calamity Jane leered at him and said, "Go off into yonder bushes with me, Cap'n honey, and I'll show you just how much of a woman I be."

That was a mistake, too, just like stripping down stark naked and jumping into a river with a bunch of soldiers.

THE expedition, under the command of Lieutenant Colonel R.I. Dodge, had left Fort Laramie on May 24th. Four hundred men and seventy-five wagons, men and wagons alike belonging to the United States Army, had been sent into the Black Hills of the Dakota Territory for one reason and one reason only.

Gold.

A year earlier, back in '74, the Seventh Cavalry under the Boy General, George Armstrong Custer of the flowing yellow locks, had made a daring foray into the Black Hills to locate a suitable spot for a new military outpost. The hills, which were really a dark, dark green because of their growths of pine rather than black, were part of an area set aside and ceded by treaty to the Sioux Nation. Custer hadn't found a good site for a fort, but in the clear, fast-flowing streams his men had found small, glittering flakes of pure temptation. In '48, in California, the rallying cry had been "Gold! Gold in the American River!" Now, twenty-seven years later, the clarion call was "Gold! Gold in the Black Hills!"

Naturally, the government wanted to know what was in that supposedly worthless land they had turned over to the savages. If the find was as lucrative as it sounded like it might be, the high-ups in Washington might just have to re-think this whole treaty business.

The need for accurate information on which to base a decision had led to Colonel Dodge and his men being sent into the Black Hills. Accompanying them were a couple of geologists and mineralogists, Walter P. Jenney and Henry Newton, and a topographer, Dr. V.T. McGillicuddy, along with a dozen or so other civilians, including an astronomer so that highly accurate star sightings could be taken, and a young reporter from the Chicago *Inter-Ocean*. The expedition was charged with mapping the Black Hills and making an assessment of just how rich in gold deposits the hills really were.

So this was a serious, important business the Army was about, and from the scowl on the face of Colonel Dodge, it appeared that he didn't appreciate being saddled with a distraction like the one that faced him now in his tent.

"I didn't mean to cause no ruckus," Jane said. She wore

her cavalry uniform, since she didn't have anything else to wear. "I just wanted to come along and see the sights, and I didn't want to be parted from my fella."

"Sergeant Siechrist, sir," the colonel's orderly said, leaning in to do so.

"I know to whom the lady is referring, Lieutenant," Dodge snapped. "I've ordered him brought before me, too, but he hasn't been located yet. I almost hope, for his sake, that he's been snatched by the Sioux. Their treatment of him would probably be more kind than what I have in store for him as punishment for his part in this little charade."

Jane frowned as she thought about what Dodge had just said, and then she burst out, "Hell's bells, Colonel, don't go bustin' Frank's balls over this. It was my idea, right from the start. He didn't have nothin' to do with it."

Dodge looked at her intently. "He was not aware that you were a member of our party when we left Fort Laramie?"

"No, sir, he didn't have nary an idea." Jane wiped her nose with the back of her hand and wished she had a drink. "I figured if 'n I told him ahead of time that I was comin' along, he'd tell me I couldn't. So I didn't let him know I was anywhere about until after we'd left the fort."

"You presented him with a fait accompli, eh?"

"No, sir, I didn't bring him no presents . . . unless, o' course, you count what we done when we snuck off at night."

"Dereliction of duty on top of his other crimes, eh?"

The orderly leaned in and said, "I believe we have grounds for a court-martial, sir."

Dodge glowered at the young lieutenant. "We're in the middle of a vast wilderness, Parmalee. Even though we have not yet sighted any hostiles, there could be hundreds of bloodthirsty Sioux just over the next rise. A court-martial, if there is one, can wait until we return safely to Fort Laramie." The colonel glanced at Jane again. "Not that I don't intend to make Sergeant Siechrist rue the day that he took up with this . . . this woman."

The orderly accepted the rebuke with a meek nod. Colonel Dodge lit his pipe, shifted on his camp stool, and said to Jane, "What did you say your name was?"

"Martha Jane Cannary, sir. But they mostly call me Jane."

"Calamity Jane, isn't that right?"

She couldn't help but grin. Deep down, she really liked the name and the notoriety that went with it.

"That's right, Colonel, I been called that. Some say it's because I give a fella a case o' the clap whilst I was workin' in a house in Cheyenne, but that ain't true, not a bit of it. I got the name just 'cause I'm what you might call a calamitous person and trouble tends to follow me around, whether I want it to or not."

"I can believe that part about trouble following you around," Dodge said. He puffed on his pipe for a moment and then went on. "There is no doubt but that you must be sent back to the fort."

Jane shook her head vehemently. "No, sir! No, sir, I don't want to go."

"I have no choice! I can't carry a woman along on a military expedition. Your presence would cause a disruption among the men."

"I'll stay in one of the wagons," Jane promised. "Hell, I'll even drive one of the wagons. I can handle a team as good or better'n any o' them men you got drivin' 'em."

Dodge said, "No, I've made my decision, and I won't be swayed from it. One of the wagons is going to turn back shortly with the men who have fallen ill. You'll go with them, Miss Cannary. And you'll go in female attire, not the uniform of the United States Army."

"Ain't got no woman duds," Jane said in a surly voice, not bothering to hide the resentment she felt toward the colonel and his decision. "Ain't there nothin' I can do to change your mind, Colonel?" She paused and then went on with a sly smile. "If 'n you'd send that young pup outta this tent, I could give you a mighty good reason to keep me around."

Colonel Dodge drew himself up, his face purpling, as he managed to look embarrassed, outraged, and repulsed all at the same time.

"I'll pretend I did not hear that outrageous statement, madam. Now, leave this tent and find something to wear besides that uniform. Stay away from Sergeant Siechrist and the rest of my men until you depart. Do you understand?"

"I reckon I do," Jane mumbled sullenly.

That was twice today she had offered herself to one of these soldiers, and both times she had been turned down. Either she was losing her touch, or the Army was mighty hard up for real men. That had to be it, she decided.

After all, what fella in his right mind wouldn't want to cavort with her for a spell?

THE next day, wearing a pair of britches, a shirt, and a hat she had borrowed from various civilian members of the party, Jane sat on the horse she had been riding during the expedition and watched the wagons pull away, except for the one that was going to turn around and head back to Fort Laramie. Jane had looked for Frank Siechrist, but hadn't been able to find him. He was probably doing his damnedest to avoid her, she thought darkly. Men were a craven lot, good for one thing and one thing only.

She lifted her head and looked past the wagons and the cavalrymen to the pine-clad hills. This was pretty country, mighty pretty country, and it stirred something inside her, something deep and vital. She sensed that she would find her destiny here, though she had no idea what that destiny might be.

The damned ol' Army could kick her out of the Black Hills, but that didn't mean she wouldn't be back someday. Already the country was buzzing about gold, and whenever talk like that started, there could be only one outcome. Men followed gold just like night followed day, like moths followed flame. It was natural, and there wasn't a damned thing anybody could do to stop it. Not Washington, not the

Army, not even the Sioux. The lure of riches was just too strong.

So she would have plenty of chances, Martha Jane Cannary, also known as Calamity Jane, told herself.

There would come a day when she rode back to the Black Hills, and that would be her time to howl!

One

Dakota Territory, June 1876

IT had been the intention of Daniel Ryan, former sergeant in the United States Army, that the Black Hills would make him a rich man.

Now it appeared that the hills would make him a dead man instead.

Not the hills themselves, of course, but rather the bloodthirsty savages who inhabited the nearby plains. The Sioux regarded the Black Hills as their own personal property, even though they seldom ventured into the rough, pine-covered terrain. Indeed, the treaty signed at Fort Laramie in 1868 had given the Sioux right of possession, Dan Ryan knew. He had been posted to the fort when the damned thing was signed and had witnessed the ceremony.

So it might well be that the Indians had the law on their side. That didn't stop Dan from poking his Henry rifle out from under the wagon where he had taken cover and doing his damnedest to ventilate some of the bastards before they killed him and took his hair.

An arrow thudded into the wagon's sideboards above his head. Another whistled past him and buried its flint head in the ground beside him. Dan drew a bead and fired again, and this time one of the Sioux tumbled off his pony and flopped lifelessly to the ground.

The kid who had scrambled under the wagon with Dan when the attack began let out an excited whoop. "That's good shootin'!"

His name was Bellamy Bridges, Dan recalled. "Better do some of it yourself," Dan advised. He worked the Henry's lever, throwing another cartridge into the rifle's chamber.

Bellamy loosed a round from his single-shot rifle, but didn't hit a blasted thing as far as Dan could tell. Bellamy started to reload awkwardly.

Have to be faster than that, Dan thought, or you won't live to see Deadwood.

Of course, it was entirely possible that none of them would live to see Deadwood. . . .

The party, consisting of four wagons and eighteen men, had left Cheyenne a week earlier and had made excellent progress, covering a good distance every day and not sighting any Indians. Since Dan was the only one among the men who had been to the Black Hills before, as a member of General Custer's command, he served as the guide for the group. He remembered the route quite well and was confident that he could lead the wagons straight to the gulch where Deadwood Creek merged with Whitewood Creek. That was where the main camp in the area was located.

Deadwood was an outlaw camp. The government had put out several proclamations stating that the Black Hills were part of the Sioux reservation and were not to be trespassed on by white men. Earlier this year, cavalry patrols had even turned back several parties of prospectors bound for the gold claims. But there were too many fortune-seekers and not enough troopers, and what had started as a trickle had become a veritable flood of men who planned on striking gold and hitting it rich. By now, the Army was pretty much turning a blind eye to the miners heading into the Black Hills.

Dan had been in the Army for fifteen years, working his way up to the rank of sergeant, and he knew not only its capabilities but also its limitations. The Army would never be able to stem the tide of gold-hunters. In fact, desertion was becoming a problem as enlisted men decided to slip away from their units and do a little prospecting themselves.

At least Dan had waited until his hitch was up and he'd been mustered out properly before he turned his hand to gold-hunting. Two years earlier, he had been a member of Custer's expedition into the Black Hills, and as long as he lived—which might not be too long if those blasted savages had their way—he would never forget the thrill that had gone through him when he'd picked up a handful of gravel from the bottom of a streambed and seen the dully glittering flakes of gold scattered through it. There was something about gold, something that no man could understand until he had held it in his own hand.

He had gone from Fort Laramie to Cheyenne as a civilian. The town was full of prospectors these days, seeing as it was a prime jumping-off place for the Black Hills. It hadn't taken Dan long to hook up with the other members of this party. Stories of Sioux depredations on the trails leading to the hills were numerous. No one wanted to travel alone. And since Dan had experience in the area, he was welcomed with open arms.

Earlier today, the wagons had been rocking along easily through the foothills, following a long, shallow valley. Dan had kept a close eye on the timbered ridges that bordered the valley on either side, but he thought the cover was too sparse for a large group of Indians to hide there.

He hadn't seen the dry wash in front of the wagons until it was too late. The Sioux came up out of it like they were emerging from the ground itself, whooping and hollering and racing at the wagons on their stocky little ponies. Arrows and bullets filled the air.

There was no time to pull the wagons in a circle, no time to protect the livestock. All the drivers could do was haul their teams to a stop, yell a warning, grab their guns, and dive under the wagons. Some of the men stayed inside the vehicles, crouching among the crates of supplies. Either way, cover was scanty.

Dan had lost track of how long the attack had been going on. It seemed like an hour, but was probably closer to ten minutes. He aimed the Henry and fired again. He missed the Sioux warrior who had been his target, but judging by the way the man's pony jumped wildly, the bullet had singed some horseflesh. The Indian lost his hold and toppled off, landing hard on the ground. He rolled over and pushed himself to his feet, weaving slightly.

Bellamy fired again, and this time the young man's aim was true. The Sioux jerked backward and fell, not to rise again.

"Teamwork!" Bellamy called to Dan. "You unhorse 'em, and I'll kill 'em!"

Dan wasn't sure they had enough bullets for that, so he didn't say anything, figuring it was better not to encourage the youngster's ideas. He cranked off another shot, but with all the dust in the air, he wasn't sure if he hit anything or not.

Bellamy was from Illinois or Indiana, someplace like that, a handsome lad with a shock of blond hair and a ready grin. A farmer, he had told Dan while they were riding together. And not a very successful one, judging by the holes in his boots and the patches on his trousers. The britches were probably hand-me-downs, because they were too baggy and would have fallen off if not for the rope belt that Bellamy tied tightly around his waist.

Like all young men, he was full of hopes and dreams, and he had chattered incessantly about everything he would do once he had struck gold and was rich. Dan had stopped paying attention after a while. His ambitions weren't so elaborate. He wanted enough money so that he would never again have to say, "Yes, sir!" None of the rest of it really mattered to him. He was just tired of taking orders.

Somewhere close by, a mule screamed in pain. At first the Sioux had concentrated their fire on the men, but now they were going after the animals. That would strand the wagons here, and then the Sioux could keep the prospectors pinned down, picking them off one by one.

Most of the men realized what was happening and redoubled their efforts, throwing lead at the savages as fast as they could. The odds had been about even at first, as Dan figured there were around eighteen Sioux in the war party. Three or four of them had been brought down so far during the fighting. Dan had no idea how many of his companions had been wounded or killed. He heard a lot of gunfire still coming from the other wagons, though, so he was encouraged. The Sioux would break off the attack if they thought they were going to have to pay too high a price. If the prospectors could just pick off three or four more of them, that might do the trick.

Suddenly, he heard a swift rataplan of hoofbeats behind him. At least one of the Sioux had gotten around the wagons and closed in from that direction. Dan rolled onto his back as a shrill whoop sounded. He saw the painted face and the feathered headdress of a warrior as the Sioux thrust a rifle at him at close range. Dan struck out with his own rifle, slamming the barrels together and knocking the Indian's gun aside as it exploded. One-handed, Dan jabbed the Henry's muzzle against the Sioux's chest and pulled the trigger. He couldn't recall if he had worked the lever just before this face-to-face altercation. The Henry's firing chamber might be empty.

Luck was with him. The rifle blasted, throwing the Sioux back as the heavy slug bored a hole all the way through him. He rolled over a couple of times as blood spouted from his chest.

"You cover that side, I'll cover this one!" Dan called to

Bellamy as he scrambled up on his knees. "And keep your eyes open, damn it!"

"Right!" Bellamy replied.

Dan crawled behind one of the wheels and rested the rifle barrel on a spoke. He worked the lever and watched several more Sioux circling toward this side of the wagons. None of them had rifles, though, so that gave him a little advantage. They had to come well within range of the Henry before they could launch their arrows.

He heard Bellamy's rifle boom again. "I got another one!" the young man cried.

"Good work, kid," Dan told him grimly. "Keep it up."

A second later he heard something and glanced over his shoulder to see Bellamy scuttling out from under the wagon, dragging the empty rifle with him. What the hell! Where was the kid going?

Dan crawled backward on his belly and twisted his head to see Bellamy swinging the rifle like a club at a mounted Sioux who was practically right on top of the wagon. The Indian swung a coup stick at Bellamy at the same time and clouted him on the left shoulder. Bellamy went down, but the Sioux did, too, knocked off his pony by the rifle blow across the belly.

Bellamy's left arm dangled uselessly, probably numbed if not broken, but at least Bellamy could still move. The Sioux had had the wind knocked out of him and could only lie there gasping for air. On his knees, Bellamy lurched over to the Indian and used his right hand to slam the butt of the rifle down into the Sioux's face. He hit him again and again.

That was all Dan had time to see before he had to turn back to the other foes. An arrow clattered through the wagon spokes, barely missing him. He had let the enemy get closer than he'd intended.

He pointed the Henry at the Sioux and fired five times as fast as he could work the rifle's lever. Powder smoke bit at his eyes and nose and throat. His vision blurred, then focused again, and as the dust settled a little he saw two more buckskin-clad bodies lying on the ground not far away.

An exultant shout came from one of the other wagons. "They're pulling back! They're giving up!"

Dan wasn't so sure about the last part of that celebratory shout, but there was no denying that the remaining members of the war party were now galloping hell-bent-for-leather toward the ridge on the west side of the valley. Dan counted seven of them, which meant that the Sioux had lost a little more than half their number.

Losses on that scale were usually enough to make the Indians call off an attack. Except on rare occasions, they didn't subscribe to the theory of fighting to the last man. To their way of thinking, it was better to lose a fight one day so that they could win another day.

A few last shots sped the Sioux on their way. Dan didn't waste powder and lead. The Indians were either leaving or they weren't. He crawled out from under the wagon and hurried around to the other side to check on Bellamy.

The young man was trying to climb shakily onto his feet. Dan grasped his right arm to steady him. "Are you all right, kid?" he asked. "That bastard break your arm with his coup stick?"

"Is that what it was?" Bellamy asked between clenched teeth. "I thought it was just a club." Gingerly, he moved his left arm. "I'm starting to get some feeling back in it. I don't think it's broken."

"No, it doesn't look like it," Dan agreed. "You're lucky. The way you climbed out from under the wagon to take him on, you ought to be dead."

"He was right there on top of us, and I didn't have time to reload. I didn't know what else I could do."

There wasn't anything else, Dan thought. He squeezed Bellamy's good shoulder and nodded.

"Are they really gone?" Bellamy went on.

Dan's gaze was trained on the ridge where the Sioux had disappeared. The haze of dust kicked up by their ponies' hooves was starting to dissipate on the far side of the ridge.

"Yeah, I think they decided we were too tough a nut to crack. Better reload that rifle of yours, though, just in case. Can you handle it?"

Bellamy worked his left arm back and forth. "I think so."

Dan got a handful of cartridges from a box just inside the wagon's tailgate and thumbed them into the Henry's loading gate until the rifle carried its full complement of fifteen shots again. Load it on Sunday and shoot it all week, people had said about the Henry when it was introduced. There was a newer-model repeater now, the Winchester, but this old Henry did just fine as far as Dan was concerned.

One of his mules had an arrow sticking out of its flank, but it didn't look like the head had penetrated too deep. Dan thought he could doctor that wound and keep the mule going until they reached Deadwood. He walked back to the other wagons and saw that two mules were dead, one with an arrow through its throat, the other riddled by bullets. Only one wagon would have to make do with a four-mule hitch instead of six. That would slow them down anyway, since they could only move as fast as their slowest vehicle.

Still, it could have been a lot worse, mule-wise. "Anybody hit?" Dan called.

"Cartland's dead," replied one of the prospectors, a tall, raw-boned man named Cromwell. "Took an arrow right through the throat, just like that mule."

"So's Bentley," added another man. "One of those red devils shot him right between the eyes."

Dan's mouth was a grim line under his dark, heavy mustache as he nodded. He had hoped that none of the men had been killed, but such good fortune was too much to expect. The fight with the Sioux had not been a long one, but it had been furious while it lasted.

"We'll bury them here and then move on," he said. The group of prospectors had not elected a captain before leaving Cheyenne, but since Dan was their guide they looked to him for leadership. He knew it and accepted the responsibility. "Still time in the day to make a few more miles."

"What about the Indians?" a man asked.

"We'll post guards. The rest of you . . . break out some shovels."

Two

Cheyenne, Wyoming Territory, June 1876

"IT was a diamond, my friends, a diamond as big as a man's fist, can you believe it, and when a stray beam of sunlight came slanting down through a small hole in the cavern's roof, it struck the gem I held in my hand and set up such a scintillant explosion of light that the entire cave was illuminated."

The crowd gathered around the man who stood at the bar in the Metropole Hotel *ooh*-ed and *ahh*-ed. The speaker swept them with his intent gaze and continued. "Nor was this the only such gem to be found there. The floor was littered with them, as if they were nothing but marbles tossed around by an angry child."

"What did you do?" one of the onlookers asked eagerly. "Did you bring out a fortune?"

The storyteller hooked his thumbs in the red sash that went around his waist. "How could I do that?" he said. "As I explained before, the cave-in had utterly sealed the only tunnel that led in and out of the place. I sought refuge there from a band of marauding Indians, as you will no doubt recall, but I found only an impregnable tomb . . . though one festooned with riches, to be sure."

One of the drinkers scratched his head, looked confused, and said, "But . . . you're standin' right here. You must've gotten out. And if you did, you could've put some o' them diamonds in your pockets, anyway, even if you couldn't carry all of 'em out."

"Your logic is impeccable, my friend, save for one small point. . . . I didn't make it out of that cave."

"But . . . you're here!"

The storyteller shook his head solemnly, which made his long, light-brown hair brush the shoulders of his coat.

"No, sad though it is to relate, I died there in that diamond cave, amidst such splendor as would put a maharajah of India to shame."

The rapt onlookers stared at the storyteller for a long moment, and then several of them began to laugh. At a nearby table where several men sat, one of them shook his head, chuckled, and said, "That Bill."

An angry voice burst out, "I never heard such a load o' horseshit in my life!"

Silence fell over the hotel bar as the men who had been laughing over the storyteller's tall tale turned to see who was responsible for the harsh comment.

A broad-shouldered man swaggered forward. He was something of a dandy, like the storyteller and one of the men at the nearby table. Whipcord trousers were tucked into high-topped black boots. He wore a gray wool shirt with a cowhide vest over it, and a gray hat with a Montana pinch. A gun belt was strapped around his waist, but there was nothing uncommon in that. Nearly every man in the Metropole's bar was packing iron.

With the forefinger of his left hand, the storyteller brushed his mustache away from his lips. "Did you say something to me, friend?" he inquired mildly.

"I said that story of yours is a load of horseshit," the stranger said. "You never found no cave full of diamonds, and even if you did, you didn't die in it. That's just stupid!"

"A good yarn shouldn't be taken too literally, friend," the storyteller said. "You have to allow for a certain amount of embellishment, just as you allow the cook to add a bit of salt and other spices to the stew pot."

"I wouldn't let no cook dump a load of shit in the stew pot, and that's what you've been doin', mister. You're just lyin' your ass off so's you can cadge drinks from a bunch o' simpleminded gents who swallow that line o' bull you're handin' out."

One of the three men at the table spoke up, the one who had chuckled earlier at the conclusion of the story. He was smaller in size, but if anything he was dressed in an even gaudier, flashier fashion than the storyteller at the bar.

"Listen, mister, we're just having a few drinks and a good time here. Why don't you move along and don't interrupt it?"

The stranger sneered at him. "Why don't you go fuck a mule?"

"Because the mule wouldn't enjoy it and neither would I." The little dandy started to get to his feet. His face was hard with anger.

The storyteller sauntered forward, skillfully insinuating himself between the two men. "Now, Charley, there's no need for you to get involved in this unpleasantness. It's me that this fellow seems to have an unreasonable grudge against."

"I don't have a grudge against you," the stranger said. "I just think you're a lyin' sack o' shit."

Men all around the barroom started to move away, trying to get out of the line of fire. The problem was, in relatively close quarters like this, it was hard to tell exactly where the line of fire was going to be. When gunplay broke out in a saloon, usually the pistoleers were just as likely to hit an innocent bystander as they were their intended target.

The three men at the table didn't budge, though. They weren't going to desert their friend, even though he hadn't asked for, and indeed didn't seem to want, their help. One of them, a young man with an unusual physical feature—the brow over his left eye was pure white, rather than dark like the rest of his hair—said, "Mister, I've got to believe you don't know who you're talkin' to."

The stranger shook his head. "I don't know and I don't care. I know bullshit when I hear it, no matter who's spoutin' it."

The third man at the table said in a soft British accent, "His name is James Butler Hickok. Just so you know."

The stranger's eyes widened slightly, but if he was shaken, his pride would not allow him to show it any more than that. "I don't care," he said stubbornly.

"Well, then, it's your funeral," said the little dandy called Charley.

"Oh, hell," James Butler Hickok said in a hearty voice. "There ain't gonna be any funeral. Hasn't been anything said here that can't be passed off as jollity between a couple of old friends, or even a couple of new ones." His thumbs were still hooked in the red sash, quite near the butts of a pair of new .38 Colt revolvers, in fact.

The stranger swallowed hard and said, "I'm not lookin' to run, damn it."

"To tell you the truth, neither am I," Hickok said. "Running tends to work up a sweat in weather like this, and I'm not overly fond of it myself."

"Well . . . what are we gonna do? The way I see it, we got to fight."

"Seeing is a delicate matter," Hickok said. "You may have heard rumors about my eyes going bad on me."

The loudmouthed stranger seized on that. "Is it true? Are your eyes goin' bad, Wild Bill?"

Hickok smiled. "If it were true, then I could hardly engage you in fair combat, now could I? Why, a gentleman such as yourself wouldn't even issue a challenge to a man who found himself at such a disadvantage."

"Uh . . . that's right. I reckon I wouldn't."

"So all you have to do is walk away," Hickok said quietly, "and this whole unpleasant incident will be forgotten."

"You think?"

"If anyone speaks of it, it will only be to mention your honor in refusing to fight a man with bad eyes."

The stranger hitched his gun belt up and nodded. "Yeah. Yeah, I reckon you're right, Wild Bill."

"Then we're done here, correct?" Hickok asked, his voice so soft it was almost a whisper.

"Uh . . . yeah. Done." The man turned and walked toward the arched entranceway between the barroom and the hotel lobby. He looked back once at the tall man standing beside the bar and then walked a little faster.

Once the would-be gunman was gone, Hickok sighed and reached for his long-neglected drink sitting on the bar. He took a sip and sighed again, this time in satisfaction.

"You're a better man than me, Bill," Colorado Charley Utter said from the table. "If I was you, I'd have blowed that fool's head off."

"You heard it yourself, Charley," Hickok said. "My eyes are bad."

Charley snorted. "You just gave him an excuse, that's what, so it wouldn't look like he was slinking off with his tail between his legs."

"That's right, Bill," White-Eye Jack Anderson said. "I've seen you shoot lately. You never miss what you're aimin' at."

Hickok shrugged. "At twenty-five paces or less, perhaps."

"Considerably less than twenty-five paces between you and that bastard," Dick Seymour countered.

"Let's just say I didn't feel like killing anybody tonight and let it go at that, shall we?"

"Sure, Bill," Charley said. "Anyway, you've killed your share of fools. Let somebody else take up the chore for a while."

"Yes," Hickok murmured as he looked down into the amber liquid remaining in his glass. "I've killed my share. . . ."

* * *

IT was that infernal Wild Bill business. The name drew them out of the woodwork, all the young men who fancied themselves fast with a gun, the young unknowns so desperate to be known that they were willing to risk their lives for a chance at notoriety. His dear wife Agnes never called him Wild Bill. To her he was James, and to his family he was Jim. If he had remained just plain Jim Hickok, if Colonel George Ward Nichols had never written all that folderol about him in *Harper's New Monthly,* the path of his life might have been entirely different.

To be fair, though, the fame that had accrued to him over the years brought with it a few benefits, too. In the days before he had married his dear Agnes, there had been a number of young women who were anxious to share the presence of the famous gunman Wild Bill. He had reaped financial rewards, as well, by joining with old friends and fellow scouts Bill Cody and Texas Jack Omohundro and performing in a series of rather ridiculous stage plays that were supposed to present the true story of life in the West to a bunch of soft-handed Easterners eager for some vicarious excitement.

The money was never as good as it should have been, though, and he had hated the East with its crowds and stink and noise. The pleasures of the flesh were fleeting and left him vaguely unsatisfied. As the years passed, what had come to matter most to him were good friends, and of those he had only a few. Charley Utter—good old Colorado Charley—was perhaps the best of those.

On a morning like this, when he lay in his hotel room with his face pressed into a pillow and his head pounding from the whiskey he had drunk the night before, he wished he had never heard of Wild Bill Hickok.

Someone pounded on the door. Perhaps in reality it was a light knock; to Hickok's ears it was a violent pounding. Without lifting his head from the pillow, he called a muffled, "Go away, God damn it!"

"Bill? You awake, Bill?"

That was Charley's voice. Even through his hangover,

Hickok recognized it. Since he had just been thinking about how Charley was his best friend, he supposed he ought to get up and open the door so that Charley could come in. Either that or find one of his pistols and fire a warning shot through the panel.

No, it wouldn't do to go around shooting his friends. He had done that once already in his life.

He pushed away thoughts of Mike Williams and Phil Coe and that night in Abilene, that unholy night when he had first realized the full extent of his failing vision. The White-Eyed Kid and Bloody Dick Seymour were right—in good light, at a short distance, he was as deadly with his Colts as ever. But at more than twenty-five paces, or at night . . . well, that was a much different story.

Charley was still hammering away on the door. With a groan, Hickok rolled over, ran his fingers through his long, tangled hair, and swung his legs off the bed. He stood up in his long underwear and walked over to the door.

"What is it, the crack of dawn and you're the Angel Gabriel?" he demanded as he jerked the door open.

Charley looked a little surprised. "It's not that early, Bill," he said. "The sun's up and everything."

Hickok went back and sat on the edge of the bed, motioning for Charley to come in. He did so, closing the door behind him. He wore a cream-colored hat this morning and a fringed and beaded buckskin jacket. He was resplendent at an hour when no man had a right to appear so.

Turning a chair around, Charley Utter straddled it and sat down. "Word around town is that that young bastard from last night is saying he backed down Wild Bill Hickok."

"Let him say whatever he pleases," Hickok said with a wave of his hand. "It's nothing to me."

"I know that. You got nothing to prove to anybody, Bill. Folks know about you from one end of the country to the other."

"Yes, but is what they know the truth?"

Charley snorted. "You think they care about that? You think anybody does?"

"A few might."

Charley shook his head. "Let's face it, Bill, if any of us frontiersmen are remembered at all, it'll be for the dime novels writ about us, and the stage plays and the Bill shows, and you know there's about as much truth to any of them as there is to a big steamin' pile o' buffalo turds."

"On the contrary," Hickok said with a grin. "A pile of buffalo turds is *more* authentic."

"Yeah, you're probably right about that. You want to go get some breakfast?"

Hickok groaned again.

"Maybe a little hair o' the dog, then," Charley suggested. "We got to talk, seriouslike."

"Talk about what?"

"You been sayin' you want to go to the Black Hills and look for gold. Well, I got the perfect opportunity for you."

Hickok sat up a little straighter, and his bleary eyes opened wider with interest. "What are you talking about, Charley?"

"You know my brother Steve. . . ."

Hickok nodded.

"Him and me have been talkin' about setting up a freight line between Cheyenne and the Black Hills. There are so many miners heading up there to look for gold, we figure we can do a mighty fine business hauling supplies to them."

"I expect you could," Hickok agreed.

"Not only that, but I plan on putting in a mail service, too, along the same lines as the Pony Express."

"I worked for Russell, Majors, and Waddell, did you know that?" Hickok said. "Bill Cody rode the Pony Express for them, but I never did. I drove a wagon instead."

"Yeah, I've heard about them days," Charley said with a distracted nod. He was eager to get back to what he had been saying. "Anyway, time Steve and me get the freight business and the mail runnin', we ought to have a pretty good operation."

"I would certainly think so."

"But first we got to go up to the Black Hills, find the best routes, scout out the lay of the land. You know what I mean."

Hickok nodded. "Indeed I do."

Charley leaned forward and grasped the back of the chair he was straddling. "So why don't you come with us?" he said. "It'd be a fine trip, Bill."

Hickok used the balls of his hands to rub at his eyes. "Where did you say you were going?" he asked.

"To the Black Hills," Charley replied, a touch of impatience in his voice. "I told you that."

"Yes, but the hills cover quite an area. You must have a more specific destination in mind."

"Oh," Charley said, understanding now. "Yeah, we're going to the biggest mining camp up there. I know you've heard of it. Place called Deadwood."

Three

NOBODY knew for sure when white men had first come to the Black Hills. The ruins of at least one cabin, apparently decades old, had been found, along with ancient picks and shovels and other implements, so maybe people had come there searching for gold in the past. The first white men to venture into the hills had probably been fur trappers, maybe Frenchmen who had come down from Canada seeking their fortune in pelts. But it was certain that white explorers in the area had been few and far between until the discovery of gold by Custer's men in '74. 1875 had seen a few parties of prospectors make their way into the hills despite the Army's efforts to turn them back. Among these fortune-seekers was Annie Tallent, the first white woman to set foot in the Black Hills, at least as far as anybody knew.

Also in 1875, the Army had sent an expedition into the hills to map the area and gauge the amount of gold that could really be found there. More prospectors came, too, defying the Army's ban and risking danger from the Indians.

One group that made its way into the hills in the fall of

1875 included a man named Frank Bryant. While panning for gold in a narrow, fast-flowing creek that had cut a deep gulch between several thickly wooded hills, Bryant found abundant color and along with his partners staked a claim that ran for three hundred yards up and down the stream and from rimrock to rimrock on either side. Since the miners had no legal right to be there in the first place, the legality of such a claim was questionable, but as long as it was respected by the other prospectors who entered the area later, that was all that really mattered.

Word of the discovery got around, as word always does, and by the spring of '76, every gulch along every creek in the vicinity was dotted with claims. The heaviest concentration of gold, and therefore the heaviest concentration of claims, seemed to be along a stream that somebody had dubbed Whitewood Creek. At the head of a long, twisting gulch formed by Whitewood Creek, another stream merged with it, and when the prospectors looked up at the hills looming above the two creeks, they saw a broad stretch of dead timber, evidently killed by a forest fire. With all that dead wood around, it seemed only natural that the second creek, and the gulch formed by it and Whitewood Creek, be called Deadwood. The name was hung on the mining camp that sprang up at the head of the gulch, as well.

And so an outlaw town with no right to be there was born.

EVEN though he had been to the Black Hills before, Dan Ryan had never seen Deadwood. The inrush of miners had come after he left the area with Custer's cavalry. He knew that since then, thousands of men had converged on the hills in search of gold, but he was still surprised to see so many figures swarming over the timbered hills and gulches. Canvas tents seemed to be pitched anywhere and everywhere there was a level patch of ground. And Dan and his companions hadn't even gotten to Deadwood itself yet.

Since the battle with the Sioux a week or so earlier

when two of their number had been lost, the party had not encountered any more trouble. The four wagons had rolled on steadily until now, when late on a gorgeous summer afternoon, they topped a rise and the miners saw the gulch and the town spread out before them.

There was only one main street that paralleled Whitewood Creek, although from this height Dan could see a couple of rough paths that might also become streets in time. The floor of the gulch had evidently been heavily wooded, because tree stumps stuck up everywhere. Main Street, which was just north of the creek, was lined with hastily erected log buildings. Some of them had false fronts constructed of raw, rough-hewn planks. Some of the buildings were just big tents, but many of them had false fronts, too, despite the rather ridiculous appearance that gave them. Even from a distance Dan could hear the sound of hammering going on, as new buildings were thrown up. Dan saw several places under construction, the frameworks looking like raw pine skeletons in the sun.

Men scurried everywhere like ants. Deadwood was a busy, booming camp. As Dan started his wagon down the hill toward the town, he saw restaurants and stores, saloons and gambling halls and theaters, laundries and tailor shops and shoe shops. Anything a prospector might need, someone had come to Deadwood in hopes of providing it to him . . . at a healthy profit, of course.

Beside Dan on the wagon seat, Bellamy Bridges let out a low whistle to show how impressed he was. "Looks like quite a place," the young man said.

Before the Indian attack, Dan had gotten along all right with Bellamy. Fate had them fighting side by side that day, and that shared combat had made them closer friends. Bellamy had told Dan all about life on the family farm back in Illinois, and had proven to be a receptive audience as Dan spun yarns about his time in the cavalry. Bellamy seemed to think that was just about the most dashing life possible, even though to tell the truth, it had mostly been sweltering drudgery in the summer and freezing drudgery in the winter and bullshit from the officers all year round as far as Dan was concerned.

"Yeah, it's a hell-roarin' camp, from what I've heard," he agreed with Bellamy. "Don't let that suck you in, though. Folks down there just want to take away whatever gold you're lucky enough to find."

"Oh, I'm sure they're not all that bad." Bellamy paused and then asked in a lower voice, "Dan, you think there are any women in Deadwood?"

Dan kept a firm hand on the reins and another on the brake lever as the wagon descended the steep trail toward the camp. "Painted ladies, you mean? Whores?"

"You don't have to be crude about it," Bellamy said uncomfortably. When Dan glanced over at him, the kid was actually blushing.

Dan grinned despite the effort he was putting into driving the wagon. "I'd be willin' to bet there are women in Deadwood, Bellamy."

And probably quite a few of them by now, he thought. The camp had been in existence for a couple of months, and any time a lot of men swarmed into a place, the whores were never far behind. That was one thing the Army had taught him. An outpost had to be mighty damned isolated before at least a few soiled doves wouldn't turn up in short order after the fort was established.

Bellamy started to say, "I never—" but Dan stopped him.

"That's your business, kid, and none of mine, but I can tell you right now . . . just about anything you want, Deadwood's gonna have it."

The trail reached the bottom of the slope. Dan glanced back to see that the other three wagons were following him without any trouble. He hauled on the reins to veer the team around some tree stumps and started along the main street.

The wagon hadn't gone very far before a man stepped out from the side of the street and hailed Dan. He was tall and thin, with longish dark hair and a close-cropped beard.

A hammer was in one hand, and he wore rough work clothes. A half-finished building was behind him.

"Welcome, brothers!" he called up to Dan and Bellamy as Dan hauled back on the reins and brought the team to a halt. "Welcome to Deadwood, the fairest city in the Black Hills!"

"Looks like it'll have to grow a ways before it can really be called a city," Dan commented.

"Growth is constant," the man said. "Blink your eyes once, and a new building has sprung up. Blink them twice, and a whole new block has come into existence. The Lord has blessed Deadwood and its inhabitants with an uncommon enthusiasm." The man switched the hammer from right hand to left and reached up with the right. "I'm Pastor Smith, the shepherd of this rough flock. The sky pilot, they call me."

Dan took the preacher's hand. He had already spotted a Bible sticking halfway out of a pocket in Smith's trousers, so he wasn't surprised when the man introduced himself as a minister.

"Dan Ryan's my name. This fella with me is Bellamy Bridges."

Bellamy leaned over to shake hands with Smith, too. The preacher said, "I'm pleased to meet you, brothers."

Dan jerked a thumb over his shoulder at the other wagons, which had come to a stop behind his. "That's Cromwell at the reins of the second wagon, Burke behind him, and Tompkins bringing up the rear." He supplied the names of the other miners, who were all perched on the boxes and bags of supplies that filled the vehicles.

"Are you freighters," Smith asked, "come to sell these goods to the miners? Or do you seek riches from the earth itself?"

"We're after gold, if that's what you mean," Dan replied. "Reckon you could point us to somebody who might be looking to sell some claims?"

Smith smiled and shook his head. "I'm afraid such things

are out of my purview, Brother Dan. I store up my treasures in Heaven, rather than here on Earth."

"But you're working as a carpenter, looks like," Bellamy pointed out.

"So did our Lord, when He walked among us. Man must work for his bread. But don't take my comments the wrong way. I see nothing wrong with searching for gold. I simply fill my time with other things. You won't have to go far, however, before you're sure to encounter someone with a claim for sale. I know there's a brisk trade in such things."

Dan nodded. "Obliged, Pastor." He flapped the reins and got the team moving again. The wagons rolled on past the beatifically smiling minister.

Up ahead on the left was a sturdy two-story building, one of the few in the camp built of planks rather than logs. A sign on the front proclaimed it to be the Grand Central Hotel, Charles H. Wagner, Proprietor. CLEAN ACCOMMODATIONS, it added. A well-dressed man with a thick, sandy beard and a hat set at a rakish angle nodded to Dan and raised a hand in greeting. He didn't come out into the street and offer to converse the way Pastor Smith had.

Dan drove on past the hotel, looking to right and left, but not with the fervid interest that Bellamy displayed. The young man's eyes were wide with astonishment. They passed a large building on the right that had been erected simply by tacking huge sheets of canvas to a log framework. A sign attached to a stick pounded into the ground announced that this was the temporary home of the Langrishe Theater. Dan supposed that the theater owner would build a more permanent structure when he had the chance, but for now, canvas would do fine for walls and roof. The miners would be starved for entertainment and would fork over some of their hard-won gold dust for the privilege of seeing some singing and dancing and emoting. Mostly, though, the businesses lining Deadwood's Main Street were saloons. Contrary to what Dan had told Bellamy to expect, he hadn't seen any women so far. He supposed all the painted ladies were indoors at the moment.

That they were here, though, he was sure. He had already driven past several more "theaters" and "academies for young ladies." Whorehouses, Dan thought, pure and simple. Well, simple, anyway, he amended. Those places, and the women who worked there, would be far from pure.

As the wagons approached the far end of the settlement, Dan saw that many of the men on the street wore little caps and had pigtails hanging down their backs. Chinamen, he thought. He had seen plenty of them working on the Central Pacific Railroad a few years earlier, as the CP and the Union Pacific built toward each other from west and east, respectively, to form a transcontinental rail link. Chinese coolies had performed most of the back-breaking labor of extending the Central Pacific over the Sierra Nevadas. Many of them had died in the process . . . but like soldiers and Irishmen, Chinamen were expendable.

"Where are we going, Dan?" Bellamy asked.

"We'll find a place to park these wagons on the edge of town and leave a couple of the boys to guard them. The rest of us will walk back in and have us a look around. Ought to be somebody in one of these saloons or theaters who's looking to sell a claim."

"I thought we'd be able to find our own claims and file on them."

"Well, that's what I thought, too," Dan said. "I didn't reckon on there being quite this many people here already."

"Dan . . . what if we don't find any gold?"

"Don't be thinkin' like that. But if it comes to it . . ." Dan shrugged. "Well, we've had ourselves a fine adventure, haven't we?"

He didn't point out that adventure wouldn't buy a cup of coffee or even a crust of bread.

A moment later, Dan spotted the first woman he had seen in Deadwood. She was walking along the street toward the center of the camp, carrying a large wicker basket. She wore a simple but tasteful dress and high-topped shoes and had her dark hair pulled into a bun at the back of her head. Dan put her age somewhere in the thirties, much like himself. What was surprising was that her skin was a rich brown. For some reason, Dan hadn't expected to see any Africans here in Deadwood, let alone an African woman.

She must have sensed him looking at her, because she raised her dark eyes and met his gaze squarely. Given her age, she had probably been a slave at one time, before the war, although it was remotely possible that she had been born free. If she *had* been a slave, she didn't show it now. Her face held no defiance, but neither did she appear subservient. She looked at him unflinchingly.

Likely that was why she didn't notice the pair of miners reeling toward her, obviously a little drunk. The one on the right bumped heavily into her, then cursed and said, "Watch where the hell you're goin', nigger!" His hand slashed at the basket, knocking it out of the woman's grip. As the basket fell, what looked like clean sheets spilled out of it, falling in the street.

Dan hauled back sharply on the reins, bringing the wagon to a halt, then reached over to set the brake lever. "Wait here a minute," he said to Bellamy.

"Dan?" the young man said. "What are you—"

"Just wait here," Dan said again as he stepped down to the street. "This shouldn't take long."

Four

DEADWOOD'S Main Street was muddy. With so many horses, mules, and oxen traveling up and down it all the time, relieving themselves whenever and wherever they felt like it, the street couldn't be anything but a stinking morass, especially in the center. The edges were not quite as bad, but the sheets that had fallen out of the basket were already dirty and would have to be washed again, probably in one of the Chinese laundries down the street.

Dan stepped carefully around the sheets and said to the miners, "Hey! You two!"

They had started to move on, but now they stopped and looked around at him. The eyes of both men were bleary with drink.

"Sir, you don't have to—" the woman began.

"It's no problem, ma'am," he assured her. "When I was a youngster, I worked on a hog farm in Ohio, so I'm accustomed to dealing with swine like these two."

The miners squinted at each other and then glared at Dan. "Did you just call us pigs, you son of a bitch?" one of them demanded. He was the one who had knocked the laundry out of the woman's basket. He was tall and broad-shouldered and had a dirty thatch of hair the color of straw under a stained cap. His companion was shorter and stockier, with a barrel chest and a bristly black beard.

"That's right," Dan said in reply to the angry question, "but I think I may have done a disservice to the pigs." From the corner of his eye, he saw the woman reaching down to retrieve the sheets. He put out a hand toward her and said, "No need for that. These two will pick those up, take them back to the laundry, and pay to have them cleaned again."

"The hell we will!" exclaimed the black-bearded miner. "That nigger wench run into Rodney. It was her fault, not our'n."

"That's not the way I saw it," Dan insisted. "Now do as I said, or there'll be trouble."

Rodney snorted and said, "Hell, you ain't even carryin' a gun!"

"Don't need one to take care of the likes of you. My bare hands will do for that."

This confrontation seemed to have sobered up the two miners. Narrow-eyed with anger, they moved toward Dan. Their hands clenched into knobby fists.

"I swear!" the woman said as she moved suddenly between the men. She bent and grabbed up the fallen sheets before Dan could stop her. "Are all you men natural-born idiots? Fightin' over some muddy sheets! I never saw the like."

Dan reached up to tug on the brim of his felt hat. "Ma'am, these ruffians insulted you—"

"You reckon I never been insulted before, mister?" she asked him in a quiet but intense voice as she straightened. "You ever hear about what it was like in the South 'fore the war?"

"I heard about it," Dan said. "I fought to help bring about an end to such things."

"Well, then, you done your duty, didn't you?" She pushed the sheets down into the basket, her movements brisk and almost angry. "You don't have to go out of your way to fight for me no more."

"Listen," Rodney said impatiently as he glowered at Dan, "we gonna go round and round or not?"

Dan ignored him. He looked instead at the woman, and he saw the fierce pride burning in her eyes. Her words had confirmed that she had once been a slave, but that ordeal had not broken her spirit.

"I meant no offense, ma'am," he said quietly. "I just saw an injustice being done and wanted to correct it."

"I've seen plenty of injustice in my life. It ain't killed me yet."

She started to turn away, obviously willing to put this behind her and get on with her business. If that was the way she wanted it, Dan supposed he was willing to go along with her wishes.

They weren't the only ones involved, however. Rodney stepped toward the woman, thrusting his jaw out belligerently, and said, "Wait a minute, nigger. You ain't apologized for runnin' into me."

"Way you was staggerin' around, Mr. Rodney, if I hadn't been in your way you might've fallen flat on your face in the street. Might've drowned before anybody could pull you out of that muck."

"You think you're so fuckin' smart, but you're just a dumb nigger bitch," Rodney said with a hate-filled grimace.

"Oh, now that tears it, boyo," Dan said under his breath. He stepped around the woman before she could stop him and launched a punch at Rodney's head.

The black-bearded man prevented the blow from ever landing. He tackled Dan from the side, and both men sprawled to a muddy landing in the street. Dan was on the bottom, though, and his opponent's weight kept him pinned down.

"Get off him, Stubbs!" Rodney yelled. "I'll stomp the shit outta him!"

Dan spit some of the foul muck out of his mouth and wrestled with Stubbs. He got a hand under the bristly beard and closed it on the man's throat. Stubbs tried to drive his knee into Dan's groin, but the ex-sergeant twisted his hips so that the vicious thrust landed on his thigh. Grunting with effort, Dan heaved himself up and rolled to the side, taking Stubbs with him.

Stubbs outweighed Dan, but not by much. Not enough to keep him from winding up on the bottom. Dan got his other hand around Stubbs's throat and bore down on it.

He was in reach of Rodney now, however, and the man snarled a curse and stepped forward to swing his leg in a kick at Dan's head. At the same time, Bellamy dove off the wagon seat and plowed into Rodney, knocking him over backward. More mud splashed in the air as they landed and slid for several feet. Bellamy started swinging wildly, looping punches that didn't seem to have much effect on Rodney. Rodney grabbed Bellamy and flung him aside.

By that time, the lack of air getting through Stubbs's windpipe was beginning to affect him. As Stubbs's struggles grew weaker, Dan let go of the bearded man's throat with his right hand and balled it into a fist. He smashed it down twice, fast and hard, into Stubbs's face.

"Look out, Dan!" Bellamy yelled.

Dan twisted his head, blinked mud out of his eyes, and saw Rodney charging at him like a maddened bull. Letting go of Stubbs, Dan came to his feet and ducked under the punch Rodney swung at his head. He sledged a right and a left into Rodney's midsection. Dan's punches had more effect than Bellamy's had. Rodney turned pale under the coating of mud on his face and doubled over in pain. Dan gave him a hard shove that sent him tumbling off his feet again.

By now all four men were covered with muck. The other prospectors who had come into town with Dan and Bellamy had climbed down from the wagons and crowded closer to watch the fight. Quite a few of Deadwood's citizens had gathered as spectators, too, and as Dan stood over Rodney, waiting to see if the man was going to get up or not, he became aware that a loud hubbub from the crowd filled the air. A few angry shouts went back and forth between the newcomers and miners who were obviously friends of Rodney and Stubbs. The argument showed signs of turning into an all-out brawl. All it needed to set it off was another punch or two thrown.

That didn't happen, because a booming voice suddenly ordered, "All right, get back there! Step back, I say! Break it up, you men!"

Dan turned around to see the dapper, sandy-bearded man who had been on the porch of the Grand Central Hotel when the wagons rolled into town. Instantly, Dan recognized the tone of authority in the man's voice and the confidence with which he carried himself. This was a man accustomed to command.

"Stubbs! Rodney! Get up, you two. I saw what happened. You're lucky no one takes a horsewhip to you, the way you treated Aunt Lou."

Stubbs was spitting mud out of his mouth and Rodney was gasping for air as they helped each other shakily to their feet. Rodney scraped some of the mud off his face and said, "Hell, General, why you takin' up for a damned ol' nigger?"

The General glared at him and said, "Lucretia Marchbanks is a fine woman and without a doubt the best cook in the entire Dakota Territory, you idiot. As for the matter of her race, we fought a war to insure that she and all the others like her would be free. You ought to remember that, Rodney."

"Damn right I remember. I fought in it, didn't I? Killed me a mess o' them fuckin' Johnny Rebs, too." Rodney leaned over and spit. "But just 'cause I fought to take the slaves away from them damn Rebels don't mean I want anything to do with niggers myself."

The General shook his head. "Sometimes I fear all our efforts were for nothing."

"Don't say that, General," Dan put in. "We preserved the Union, didn't we?"

The General turned to him and asked, "You served in the war, sir?"

Dan fought against the impulse to come to attention. "Yes, sir. Sergeant Daniel Ryan, late of the Seventh Cavalry." He looked down at his muddy hand. "I'd shake with you, sir, but under the circumstances . . ."

"Quite all right." The General grunted. "Custer's command, eh? I'm General A.R.Z. Dawson, United States Army, retired, now collector of federal revenue for Deadwood and the surrounding district."

"Federal revenue?" Dan repeated. "I figured the government wouldn't even admit that this place exists."

"Breaking a treaty with the Indians is one thing," General Dawson said with a twinkle in his eye. "Ignoring a potential source of revenue is entirely another." He looked at the wagons. "I take it you fellows have come to Deadwood to get rich, just like everyone else."

"That's right, sir," Bellamy said. "I'm Bellamy Bridges, from Illinois."

"And straight off the farm, unless I miss my guess. I saw a lot of fresh-faced lads like you during the Great Conflict, my boy. Unfortunately, most of them died horrible deaths on the battlefield."

"Oh. Well, I don't intend to die, General. I figure on getting rich."

"Then perhaps fortune will smile upon you, young Mr. Bridges."

Dan looked around. Rodney and Stubbs had slunk off like the dogs they were, he thought, and the crowd was dispersing now that the fight was over. He didn't see any sign of the black woman, either.

"What happened to the lady?" he asked. "Aunt Lou, I think you called her. Or is it Miss Marchbanks?"

"Miss Lucretia Marchbanks is indeed her name, but most folks here in Deadwood call her Aunt Lou," General Dawson explained. "She works for Charles Wagner over at the Grand Central."

"As the best cook in the Dakota Territory," Dan said with a muddy grin. "I remember what you said."

"Indeed." The General chuckled. "Aunt Lou rules the

roost, Sergeant. Out of the goodness of her magnificent heart, she helps out with other duties at the hotel, such as fetching laundry from the Chinese washerwomen. But make no mistake about it. Any woman who can cook a peach cobbler like Aunt Lou could go anywhere in this territory and get a better job than most white men have."

"I'll make a point of eating there at least once."

"You'll enjoy yourself, I guarantee it." The General took a pipe out of his pocket and clenched the stem between his teeth. "Why don't you and your friends go find a place to leave those wagons and get cleaned up. Then come down to the Grand Central and have dinner with me. I suppose you're looking for some good claims?"

"That's right, sir," Dan said.

"Perhaps I can point you in the direction of some worthwhile ventures. I keep my ear pretty close to the ground, you know."

Dan was willing to bet that was true. The General struck him as a shrewd sort, the type who would know everything that was going on up and down the gulch.

"Thanks, General. We'll do that. You're being generous. You can't have a very high opinion of Bellamy and me, the way we were brawling and rolling around in the mud the first time you saw us."

"On the contrary, Sergeant," Dawson said with a laugh. "In Deadwood, you fellows are going to fit right in!"

Five

JOSEPH Anderson, sometimes called White-Eye Jack, sometimes the White-Eyed Kid, had narrowly escaped a prairie fire at one point in his life. During the conflagration, however, a blazing buffalo chip that had been picked up by the strong wind fanning the inferno struck Jack squarely in the left eye, singeing off that eyebrow. Miraculously, the sight in the eye had not been impaired, but when the eyebrow grew back in, the hair was pure white, rather than black like the rest of the hair on Jack's head. That gave him the distinctive appearance that led to his nicknames. He didn't really mind. Everybody needed something to set him off, to make him different from other folks.

Jack had known Wild Bill Hickok for several years, having first run into him at Fort McPherson, over in Nebraska. That is, Jack had been acquainted with Hickok for that long. It was Jack's opinion that nobody really *knew* Wild Bill unless it was Charley Utter or Hickok's wife, that Thatcher woman who owned a circus. Wild Bill was the sort of man who would talk and smile and talk and smile but seldom give away anything of who he really was.

That was all right with White-Eye Jack. Hickok was good company, and more importantly, he was on his way to the Black Hills, where there was all that gold just for the taking, according to the stories Jack had heard.

Hickok circulated. Though he was staying at the Metropole Hotel and often drank in the bar there, he ventured out frequently to other watering holes in Cheyenne. One was a narrow little saloon on a side street called Red Mike's. Jack walked in there one afternoon and found Hickok sitting at a table with Colorado Charley Utter and another man Jack thought was Charley's brother Steve. Wild Bill's chair was leaned back against the wall directly behind it, and his broad-brimmed black hat was tipped forward over his eyes. He appeared to be asleep, but Jack would have bet against that. He thought it more likely that Hickok was keenly aware of every detail of everything that was going on in the saloon.

Colorado Charley raised a hand in greeting. "If it's not the White-Eyed Kid," he said. "Sit down, Kid, sit down." He nodded toward the other man at the table. "You know my brother Steve?"

"Yes, sir, we've met." Jack shook hands with Steve Utter, who was stockier and not as much of a swell dresser as his brother. "Howdy, Mr. Utter."

"Jack," Wild Bill intoned gravely from under that big hat, "how are you?"

"Doing fine, Bill," Jack replied. There was something about Hickok, maybe that ease of manner, which prompted folks to greet him familiarly like that. As long as you were his friend, it was all right. "I hear you're going to look for gold."

Slowly, Hickok raised his left hand and thumbed back the hat so that his face was revealed. "Charley here has persuaded me to accompany him and his brother on a journey to Deadwood," he said. "I expect to do a little prospecting once I get there, if the circumstances suit me."

Jack took a deep breath and plunged right in. "I was wonderin' if it would be all right with you for me and my brother to come along on the trip." He glanced at Charley Utter. "My brother's name is Charley, too."

"Is that so? Small world, ain't it?"

Jack looked back at Hickok. "How about it, Bill? We'll pull our freight; you don't have to worry about that."

"You're asking the wrong man," Hickok replied with a faint smile. "Charley's in charge of this expedition, not me." He tipped his hat forward again and relaxed. "I'm just along for the ride."

"All right," Jack said nervously. He looked at Charley again. "What do you say, Mr. Utter?"

"If Bill don't care, I don't care," Charley said. "The more men we have along with us, the less likely the Sioux will jump us."

"All right, then." Jack shook hands with Charley and Steve on it. He added, "You really think there's a chance we might run into some savages?"

"When it comes to redskins, you can't never tell," Charley said. "What's the matter, Kid, you scared of a few Injuns?"

"No, sir," Jack answered honestly. "Way I see it, it's all an adventure, ain't it?"

A hollow chuckle came from somewhere under Wild Bill's hat.

THEY set off from Cheyenne on June 27th, 1876. Hickok and the two Anderson boys, White-Eye Jack and Charley, were on horseback, while the Utter brothers had themselves a wagon with a four-horse team hitched to it. Since the object of the trip for Colorado Charley and Steve was to assess the feasibility of setting up their proposed freight line and Pony Express service, they were taking along a wagon load of supplies to sell. Dipping their toes into the water, as it were.

Hickok held the reins in his left hand while his right strayed to the butt of one of the Colts at his waist. He had borrowed twenty bucks or so from an old pard, Doc

Howard, the night before, so that he could buy some ammunition and a few other essentials. He'd been running low on bullets, and his funds had been more severely depleted than he'd thought. But Doc had a steady job on the police force in Cheyenne and could afford a little touch.

Charley Utter would have staked him, of course, Bill knew, but somehow he didn't want to borrow money from Colorado Charley. It seemed degrading somehow to borrow money from a close friend; better to get the dough from a more casual acquaintance.

Their route carried them almost due north out of Cheyenne. After they had gone that direction for a few days, they would swing a bit more to the east, and that would carry them toward Dakota Territory. The Black Hills were in the southwest corner of that territory, about two weeks' journey from Cheyenne when there was a wagon involved. Hickok and the Anderson boys could have ridden on ahead and left Colorado Charley and Steve behind, but Bill would never do that. He had never deserted a friend and didn't intend to start now. He wasn't *that* anxious to get to Deadwood and start prospecting for gold.

The truth of the matter was, he thought as he rode along at an easy pace beside the wagon, he wasn't that anxious to look for gold in the first place. Oh, it would be nice to find a fortune of the stuff, no doubt about that, but in a boom camp like Deadwood, there would be an abundance of places where a man could sit and drink and gamble, and something inside Wild Bill warmed at the thought of spending his days engaged in such leisurely activities. He had spent enough of his life in violence and frenzy. A little of such things went a long way.

Ah, but there was Agnes to think of, he told himself. Dear, sweet Agnes . . .

Not a beautiful woman in the classical sense, but handsome, oh, yes, definitely handsome, and her years spent as a dancer and a horseback rider in the circus owned by her late husband had given her body a lithe strength, the memory of which even now brought a smile to Hickok's lips under the drooping mustache. As a young woman Agnes had run away to join the circus and to marry a clown . . . a clown who happened to own the enterprise in question. Several years later, when he was shot down by a disgruntled customer, Agnes had inherited the circus, and the performers had stood by her, vowing to continue. Under her management, the circus had become more successful than ever and had traveled extensively.

In 1871 it had visited Abilene, Kansas, where the marshal was a man named Hickok, already famous as Wild Bill.

Right away, Mrs. Agnes Lake Thatcher had set her cap for the dashing lawman. At that stage of his life, Bill had been flattered but not all that receptive to the idea of matrimony. He had dodged the circus widow's cleverly laid traps, and for the next few years the two of them had drifted in and out of each other's lives. Bill enjoyed their times together, but he always managed to emerge from the encounters with his bachelorhood intact.

Financial reverses finally forced Agnes to sell the circus. It had been a big part of her life, but she was ready to move on. The years had changed him some as well, Bill knew; he was more aware of his age and of the passing of time. A man ought to settle down sooner or later. Maybe a reasonably attractive, reasonably well-to-do widow was just what he needed. . . .

Earlier in the year, when he found himself in Cheyenne at the same time as Agnes, it all seemed preordained somehow, and Hickok was tired of fighting against fate. On March 5th, he and Agnes were married by a minister named Warren in the home of Bill's friend S.L. Moyer. Word of the union got out, and the newspapers proclaimed that Wild Bill had been tamed at last.

Nothing could be further from the truth, of course. He was still wild, he told himself as the little group traveled north from Cheyenne. He was riding along fully armed, in the company of dangerous men, risking the wrath of the Sioux and the United States government to penetrate into the rugged Black Hills, bound for an outlaw camp on the trail of a fortune in gold. Nobody could say that he wasn't still wild.

If he was lucky enough to find that fortune, *then* he could settle down at last. Take the money, invest it, maybe start a business of some sort, and spend the rest of his days in a quiet, pleasant life with Agnes. Hickok realized he was smiling as those thoughts ran through his head while he rocked along in the saddle.

He just had to keep his eyes fixed on the goal and not allow himself to get distracted. That meant no ruckuses, no gunfights. When young jackasses challenged him, as young jackasses were wont to do, he would continue turning them away with quiet words and self-mockery. His killing days were over. They had to be.

THREE days into the trip they passed through the Hunton ranch near the settlement of Bordeaux. As the wagon creaked along the trail, flanked by the three riders, Hickok saw several men on horseback approaching them. He raised a hand in greeting as he recognized Jack Hunton, the owner of the ranch and another old acquaintance. That was one good thing about leading a wildly varied life: A man wound up with friends all over the place.

"Mornin', Jack," Hickok greeted the rancher as they all reined in and Steve Utter hauled back on the leathers to bring the wagon team to a stop.

"Where are you bound, Bill?" Hunton asked with a friendly smile. "Goin' up to the Black Hills to hunt for gold?"

Hickok grinned. "How did you know?"

"That's what ever'body else and his dog seem to be doin' in this part of the country." Hunton threw a glance over his shoulder at the two men with him. "It's all I can do to keep my hands from gettin' gold fever and takin' off. Truth to tell, I've thought about it myself."

"You've got a good ranch here," Hickok told him. "No need for you to seek your fortune elsewhere."

"Don't I know it. Who's that with you?"

Hickok quickly introduced the Utter brothers and the Anderson brothers. "We're headed for Deadwood," he added. "Hear anything about the Sioux being out between here and there?"

Hunton shook his head. "There are probably some war parties out, but with Fort Laramie between us and the hills, we don't have any problems with them down here. You'd best ask at the fort."

"I intend to," Wild Bill said with a nod. "Well, we'd better get moving. No use letting the grass grow under our feet."

"I don't reckon much grass ever grew under yours, Bill," Hunton said as he pulled his horse aside to let the wagon and the riders pass. He and his men waved as the pilgrims continued on their way.

The party had gone only a couple of miles when Hickok suddenly reined in sharply. "Damn it!" he muttered under his breath.

"What's wrong, Bill?" Colorado Charley called over from the wagon.

"I left my cane stuck in the ground where we camped last night," Hickok explained. "I always put it at the head of my bedroll, and I forgot to pick it up this morning when we pulled out. I just now remembered it."

"I'll ride back and get it for you, Bill," Jack volunteered without any hesitation.

"I hate to make you do that. . . ."

"It's no trouble. I don't mind at all. And I ought to be able to catch back up without any problem."

Hickok frowned. "No, it was my error, so it's up to me to rectify it. You boys go on. I'll retrieve the cane."

"We could stop here and wait for you, Bill," Colorado Charley offered.

"No, that's not necessary."

Before Hickok could start back south, though, Charley Anderson drawled, "Rider comin'."

The men all looked around to see a lone figure on

horseback coming toward them. The man wore a tall hat and range clothes, and as he came nearer they were certain he was a cowboy, probably one of Jack Hunton's riders.

He rode right up to them and reined in. "Howdy," he said in a forthright manner. "I reckon you fellas know you're on Hunton range?"

"We do," Hickok replied. "Jack Hunton and I are old friends. My name is Hickok."

The young cowboy's eyes widened. "You mean Wild Bill?"

"That's right."

"Well, hell, I heard o' you, Mr. Hickok. I know you ain't a rustler, so I guess your friends ain't, either."

"Thanks," Colorado Charley said dryly.

"I take it you ride for Hunton?" Hickok asked.

The cowboy bobbed his head up and down. "Yes, sir. Name's Waddie Bacom."

"Well, Waddie, would you do a favor for me?"

The head-bobbing became even more emphatic. "Yes, sir, I'd be glad to, Mr. Hickok!"

"We camped about two miles south of Hunton's ranch house last night, and I accidentally left my cane there. If you'd ask Jack Hunton to retrieve it and send it on to me at Deadwood in the care of someone he trusts, I'd be much obliged."

"Camp . . . two miles south o' the ranch . . . find the cane . . . send it to Deadwood." Waddie nodded to himself as he repeated the instructions. "I'll sure do it, Mr. Hickok. Don't you worry, you'll get that cane o' yours back."

"Thank you. There's no hurry, of course. Just whenever Hunton gets around to it is fine."

"Yes, sir, I'll tell him. Anything else I can do for you, Wild Bill?"

Hickok smiled indulgently. "No, I think that's all."

With an excited whoop, Waddie Bacom wheeled his horse and galloped off to the south, toward the ranch head-quarters.

"You made that young fella's day, Bill," Colorado

Charley said. "Hell, for the rest of his life he'll probably tell folks about the time he met Wild Bill Hickok."

"That's fine, as long as I get my cane back." Bill lifted the reins. "Let's get moving, shall we?"

THEY rolled into Fort Laramie a couple of days after that. The fort was spread out, a wide-flung compound of log and sod buildings arranged around a parade ground. Nearby was a scattering of teepees where blanket Indians lived, mostly squaws and old men who had given up the fight against the whites, willing to take the food and the blankets that the Indian agents passed out in return for behaving peacefully.

There were also about thirty wagons parked near the fort, and when Hickok saw them his eyes narrowed with surprise. "Looks like an immigrant train," he commented as he dismounted. "I wonder if they're bound for Deadwood, too."

Before he could speculate any more, a loud voice exclaimed, "Oh, my God! You're Wild Bill Hickok!"

And then, Hickok thought later, it was like a fury in buckskins descended upon them.

Six

HE looked just like the pictures she had seen of him on the covers of dime novels, tall and strongly built, and she could just imagine what it would feel like to have those long arms of his wrapped around her. His hands were big, too, with strong fingers made to close around the butt of a gun. But she knew just by looking that they could be gentle hands, too.

And Lordy, talk about handsome! That long hair falling to his shoulders, the thick, impressive mustache, the piercing eyes that seemed to have seen it all in their time, seen the elephant, the creature, and so much more, all of it added up to just about the prettiest fella Calamity Jane had ever seen.

She couldn't stop herself. She bounded up to him and grabbed his hand to shake it. He looked a mite walleyed, like a horse that was ready to bolt, so she went ahead and flung her arms around him to give him a hug before he could run off.

"Don't you know me, Bill?" she asked, her enthusiasm

bubbling over. "I'm Martha Cannary. They call me Calamity Jane, but you can just call me Calam."

Wild Bill managed to get those big hands on her shoulders and move her back a step, but as he did it he was as gentle as she had thought he would be. "I'm honored to meet you, Miss Calamity," he said in a deep voice that went perfectly with his appearance. "I don't reckon it's very decorous to be embracing at the edge of a parade ground, though."

"Well, fuck decorum," she said with a broad grin. "Gimme another hug."

Wild Bill extricated himself after a moment. Jane went on. "You don't remember me, do you?"

"I know the name, of course," Bill began politely.

"Naw, that ain't what I mean. We met in Cheyenne. At Miss Hattie's place. Don't you 'member, Bill?" She leered and wiggled her eyebrows up and down. "You an' me went upstairs together, and . . . whoo-eee!"

Wild Bill got that walleyed look again. "I'm, uh, sorry, Calam, but I just don't . . . uh . . . I can't recall. . . ."

She balled her right hand into a fist and punched him on the shoulder. "Aw, hell, that's all right. I reckon a handsome son of a bitch like you is bound to've been with so many women, you can't be expected to remember 'em all . . . even the really good'uns like me."

The truth of it was, she had never even spoken to Wild Bill Hickok before today, let alone shared a bed with him, but she was pretty sure she had seen him a time or two in the past. She couldn't be certain because she'd been a mite skunk-faced on those occasions, but she considered Wild Bill an old friend anyway. She didn't read much, but she had looked at a bunch of them dime novels with his picture on the covers.

Now Wild Bill nodded weakly and turned to wave a hand at the fellas with him. "Allow me to introduce my companions."

They all looked a little like they wanted to be somewheres else, Jane thought, but it was too late for them to escape now. She knew Colorado Charley Utter's name and knew she had almost crossed paths with him several times in the past, down in Cheyenne. He wasn't a bad-looking little gent and dressed even spiffier than Wild Bill, but he would never escape from the long shadow cast by the Prince of Pistoleers. His brother Steve looked to be the plodding sort, but good-natured. One of the younger fellas was silly-looking, with a stark white eyebrow over his left eye. "I've heard of you," Jane said. "You're the White-Eyed Kid."

He nodded and tugged on the brim of his hat. "Yes, ma'am. Name's Jack Anderson." He jerked a thumb at the other young man, who had normal eyebrows. "This is my brother Charley."

"Pleased to meet all of you," Jane said distractedly, already turning back toward Wild Bill as she did so. "Whatcha doin' here, Wild Bill?" Her voice rose with excitement as a thought occurred to her. "Hell, are you on your way to Deadwood?"

He hesitated before answering, which might have made her suspicious if she hadn't known that he was Wild Bill Hickok and much too honorable to ever lie to a woman.

"Yes, we're going to Deadwood," he finally said. "Plan to do a little prospecting."

"God damn it, why didn't you say so? I'm headed for there, too. Don't know that I'll do any prospectin', though. Seems too much like hard work to me. I might just raise a ruction or two instead."

"I wouldn't be a bit surprised," Wild Bill muttered.

Jane turned and pointed toward the wagon train parked nearby. "I'm goin' with those folks. They's mostly prospectors, but there's a bunch o' whores with 'em, too, headin' up there to work for a fella name of Swearengen who's got him some sort o' theater. I been talkin' to 'em. I ain't in that line o' work myself no more, of course. I'm done with whorin'. I did some scoutin' with Gen'ral Crook up on the Rosebud, and I been workin' as a bullwhacker here an' there. Only times I let a fella have a poke now is when I want to, God damn it. Why don't you and your pards join up with us, Bill? We can all go to Deadwood together." Her eyebrows did that trick again as the words rushed out of her in a rolling, tumbling river. "Might make the trip a heap more interestin', if you know what I mean."

Wild Bill blew out his breath so that his mustache fluttered a little. "Well, I don't know. . . ."

"Safety in numbers, remember, Bill?" Colorado Charley said. Steve nodded in agreement as Colorado Charley went on. "No war party would jump a band of wagons that big."

The Anderson boys nodded, too, with eager looks on their faces, and Jane knew why. They were less concerned about the danger from the Sioux and more interested in traveling with several wagon loads of soiled doves. They figured that during the trip they'd have a chance to sample Big Dollie, Smooth Bore, Tit Bit, and the rest. And they were probably right.

Faced with the eagerness of his companions, Wild Bill had little choice but to go along with their wishes. He nodded and said, "All right, Miss Calamity. Since we're all going the same direction, we might as well travel together."

She would have punched him on the shoulder again in her excitement, but he drew back before she could do it.

"You won't regret it, Wild Bill," she said. "We'll have us a bang-up time, you'll see. I almost hope road agents or Injuns *do* jump us. I crave to see Wild Bill Hickok in action. Lordy, I'll bet that's a sight nobody would ever forget!"

THE White-Eyed Kid had never before seen anybody quite like Calamity Jane. She wore boots, buckskins, and a beat-up old hat like a man. She had a gun belt strapped around her waist with a holstered revolver attached to it, and she carried an old Sharps carbine. The bagginess of her outfit concealed most of her figure, and Jack would have been willing to bet that it wasn't very womanly to start with. She cussed like a man, too, and even if Jack had been trying to count during the day or so they all spent at Fort Laramie, on the North Platte River, he would have lost track of how many times Calamity Jane spit and scratched her crotch.

And yet, despite her lack of femininity, she looked at Wild Bill Hickok with big ol' calf eyes, like any other lovestruck gal. Clearly, she admired him. Clearly, she felt even more than admiration for him. She followed him around like she was a cat in heat and he was the biggest tom on the block.

Bill, for his part, did a manful job of ignoring her without being overly impolite about it. Whenever he spoke to her, he made a point of mentioning his wife and how devoted to her he was. The problem was that Calam wasn't the sort to take a hint. Jack began to think she was like an old mule that had to be walloped over the head with a stick just to get its attention.

Not that he was going to do the walloping, mind you. He figured that would be a good way to get dead, because Jane was always threatening to pull out that hogleg of hers and blast any son of a bitch who annoyed her. Whether she'd actually do it or not, Jack didn't know, and he didn't intend to find out. He thought the world and all of Wild Bill, but Bill was just going to have to deal with his woman troubles—loosely speaking, since they involved Calamity Jane—himself. Jack had other things on his mind.

Like Silky Jen.

She couldn't have been a whore for very long, not as young and pretty and fresh-faced as she was. She had long brown hair that came halfway down her back, and when she shook her head that hair rippled like silk. That was how she'd gotten her name. Her real name was Jenny, but it had been changed to Silky Jen because of her hair. All the whores had names like that, ones that described them somehow. There was one called Tit Bit because she was so small. Jack had thought at first the name meant something else, but Silky set him straight on that.

The post commander at Fort Laramie had ordered his soldiers not to go near the wagon train, but that was like

issuing orders for the sun not to come up in the morning.
The more daring of those randy troopers snuck over to the
wagons anyway, and from what Jack heard, some of the officers did, too. The women didn't see anything wrong with
earning a little extra money before they moved on to Deadwood and settled down in their jobs there. Some of them
were already set up, with jobs waiting for them at a place
called the Gem Theater. Others would look around when
they got to the camp and figure out then where they wanted
to work.

Jack wasn't sure why the Army had let the wagons stop
here and resupply for the last leg of the journey to Deadwood. It was supposed to be illegal, after all, for whites to
even be in the Black Hills, since it was part of the Sioux
reservation. In the past, the Army had stopped parties of
prospectors headed into the hills. Jack supposed that there
had been an official throwing up of hands, an admission
that there was no way the Army could stop all the prospectors so there wasn't really any point in wasting the time trying to stop any of them. Pragmatism, Jack thought it was
called, or something like that.

He laid eyes on Silky that first evening at the fort,
watching as she sat on the high driver's seat of one of the
wagons and brushed her long brown hair in the shifting
light from a cook fire. Her arms were bare and smooth, and
when she raised them to brush her hair her breasts lifted under the thin gown she wore. Something twisted and broke
inside Jack when he saw that, and he knew he would never
be the same. It was like the bursting of some previously
unguessed-at knowledge in his brain, the flowering of a
brand-new species of bloom in his heart. It was love, he
supposed, or one hell of a powerful case of lust, anyway.

He spent the next day hanging around the wagons, luxu-
riating in every glimpse he caught of her. His brother
Charley wanted him to come over to the sutler's store and
get in on a poker game that was going on there, but Jack
sent Charley on by himself. Cards no longer interested him.
Colorado Charley and Steve were closeted with the post

commander, discussing the Indian situation, and Wild Bill was busy trying to find new places to hide from Calamity Jane. That left White-Eye Jack free to concentrate on his new discovery.

Along around noon, Silky smiled at him and motioned for him to come over to the wagon she shared with a couple of other whores. They were inside at the moment, doing a little business with a pair of cavalrymen, but Silky was just sitting on the wagon tongue. She patted it beside her and said, "Sit down, boy. My, you're an odd-looking one, with that eyebrow like that."

Jack didn't take any offense at being called odd. He knew he looked a little strange. Besides, she could have called him a mud-wallowing, snake-licking, coyote-humping bastard and he wouldn't have cared, as long as she was talking to him.

"What's your name?"

"Jack Anderson, ma'am."

She laughed. "Oh, you don't have to call me ma'am. I'm just a whore. They call me Silky, or Silky Jen."

She went on to tell him how she'd gotten the name, and he wanted to ask her how in the hell a girl as pretty as her had wound up on a whore wagon at Fort Laramie, Wyoming Territory, but he figured that might be bad manners. So he kept his mouth shut and let her talk. She seemed to like that. She didn't mind the way his gaze caressed her face and sometimes grew bold enough to dip down to her breasts.

Eventually, she said, "You must like my titties, the way you keep lookin' at 'em."

Jack swallowed hard, feeling embarrassed and terribly excited at the same time. This was the first time he had ever heard a woman say the word "titties."

"Yes, ma'am, I mean Silky," he managed to say. "I think they're really pretty."

"You want a better look?"

Without waiting for him to answer, she slipped her gown down off her shoulders and slid it off her breasts, leaving them bare. They weren't overly large, but they were firm and creamy and had pale brown nipples on the ends of them. Jack's eyes got so big he felt like they were going to pop right out of their sockets.

Silky put her hands under her breasts and used her fore-fingers to stroke the nipples until they grew hard. "Want to feel 'em?" she said to Jack.

His pulse was like the ringing of a sledgehammer inside his head. He had lived through a couple of Indian fights and that prairie fire, which he had thought at the time was the most terrifying experience a man could ever go through, but now he knew there was something even scarier: a woman you had convinced yourself you were in love with holding onto her breasts and sticking them out at you.

"Maybe . . . maybe later," he said.

Silky laughed again. "Hell, honey, you don't have to worry. They won't bite you." She leaned closer to him and whispered, "Now, my pussy just might, though."

He fell over backward off the wagon tongue.

By the time he'd picked himself up, his face flaming with embarrassment, Silky had pulled up her gown and climbed back into the wagon, still laughing. Jack felt a surge of anger, some directed at her but most of it aimed right at himself. He had acted like a dumb kid, and he didn't make any allowances for the fact that in truth he wasn't that old and really hadn't had all that much experi-ence with women. Regardless of any of that, he should have known what to do. Now, because he'd acted like a scared rabbit, Silky Jen probably wouldn't have anything else to do with him. He had missed his chance with her, and it would never come again. He never even stopped to think that money would buy him more chances with a gal like that. He was devastated.

But as he walked off, shaking his head ruefully, he re-minded himself that he and his companions would be trav-eling with this wagon train. Surely in the days to come he would have a chance to redeem himself in her eyes and make her see that he wasn't just a callow youth. That thought put a little spring back in his step. He wasn't going to give up.

After all, it was still a long way to Deadwood.

Seven

ONCE Dan and Bellamy got all the mud washed off them—not an easy task; they had to jump into White-wood Creek in order to accomplish it, and despite the season being summer, at this altitude in a stream fed largely by melted snow, the water was damned cold—they dressed in clean clothes and gathered with the other members of the party to discuss what General Dawson had said.

"You've always been sort of in charge of this expedition, Dan," Cromwell said, "and I think we all trust you." He looked around at the other men. "Don't we, boys?"

Nods and mutters of agreement came from them.

"So you talk to this here general for all of us, why don't you?" Cromwell continued. "You know what we're all looking for: just a good claim and a fair chance to find color."

Dan rubbed a hand on his jaw and frowned. "I don't know, boys. That's a lot of responsibility to put on a man's shoulders. If some of us struck it rich and the rest didn't . . . say in particular if Bellamy and I did pretty good . . . it wouldn't really look right, now would it?"

Cromwell stuck out his right hand with the thumb pointing up and wagged it back and forth between Dan and Bellamy. "The two of you are partnerin' up, are you?"

They hadn't really talked about that, Dan realized. The comment had just come out of his mouth without him thinking about it. He looked at Bellamy and asked, "What do you say, kid?"

Without hesitation, Bellamy nodded. "Sure, Dan. That sounds fine to me. I'll be honest with you, I don't know a lot about mining, but I'll sure work hard and do my share."

"Yeah, I figure you will, too." They had fought side by side twice, first against the Sioux and then the brawl with Rodney and Stubbs, and that was what made them partners. The words just made it official.

Dan rubbed his nose. "Back to what we were talkin' about, I don't want anybody thinking that they got cheated somehow—"

"That's not going to happen," Cromwell said. "We all know what the chances are. Maybe we'll strike gold and maybe we won't. I won't be holding any grudges either way."

Dan looked around at the circle of weary, unshaven, yet eager faces. They all seemed to agree with Cromwell.

"All right," he said. "We'll talk to the General and try to line up claims for everybody. No guarantees, though."

Before they headed down to the Grand Central for their meeting with General Dawson, Dan went back to his wagon and rooted around in the crates and bags of supplies until he found the small carpetbag where he stored his personal belongings. He reached inside and drew out a holster with a flap that fastened down over the butt of the revolver it held. He unbuckled his belt, slipped the holster onto it, and fastened the belt again. He settled the holster on his left hip with the gun butt turned forward.

"What's that?" Bellamy asked, having come up behind him. "A handgun?"

Dan unfastened the flap with his left hand and reached across his body with his right to grasp the revolver's walnut grips. He drew it out of the holster and held it up so that Bellamy could see it.

"Colt Single Action Army," Dan said. "Forty-five caliber. The finest short gun ever made. Never jams or misfires if you care for it properly, and it has plenty of stopping power. Give a man one of these, and a Henry rifle or a Winchester, and he's ready for just about any trouble that might come along."

Bellamy's eyes were big as he looked at the gun. "Can I hold it?" he asked.

Dan started to hand it over, then abruptly paused. "You ever handle a gun like this before?"

"Never."

Dan grunted and said, "Wait a minute." He opened the loading gate and ejected the cartridges in the cylinder.

"You don't trust me?" Bellamy asked with a frown.

"Nothing personal, kid. When we get a chance, you can practice with it some. We find some color, you can maybe buy one of your own." He put the now-empty Colt in Bellamy's hand.

Bellamy's fingers closed around the grips. He breathed shallowly in his excitement. "That feels . . . strange. Wonderful."

"I feel an army in my fist," Dan said.

Bellamy looked up at him, puzzled. "What?"

"Some German fella named von Schiller said it. I don't reckon he was talking about a Colt's revolver, but it sure fits, don't it?"

Bellamy nodded slowly as he hefted the gun. He said, "Yeah, it does. An army in my fist. I like that."

He gave the revolver back to Dan, a little reluctantly, and Dan replaced it in the holster. "Why'd you decide to wear it?" Bellamy asked.

"Just seemed like it might be a good idea in a place like this. We've already seen that trouble can crop up without a whole lot of warning."

They walked down the street toward the Grand Central Hotel. Dusk was beginning to settle over the Black Hills.

Dan had spent enough time camped in various mountain ranges during his cavalry days to know that when night fell, it would land in a hurry. Once the sun dipped below the surrounding peaks, full darkness closed in almost immediately in gulches such as the one where Deadwood was located.

Nightfall wouldn't do much to slow down the activity in the camp, though. The saloons, theaters, and bordellos would continue to do a booming business until quite late in the evening. The more respectable enterprises, the restaurants and the stores, would close down sooner, but even they would remain open for a while after dark to give miners who had been working all day a chance to spend some hard-earned gold dust.

They had parked the wagons east of the camp, past the Chinese quarter. As they walked back through the area, with the singsong chatter of the Celestials filling the air, Bellamy looked around in wonder. He was hearing things, seeing things, even smelling things, since the Chinese women had their cook pots bubbling, that he had never encountered before back in Illinois. Dan saw the awe-filled expression on the boy's face and thought there were probably a lot of things in Deadwood that Bellamy would run into for the first time in his life.

After they passed the Chinese quarter, at the far eastern end of Main Street, they came to a two-block-long area crammed full of businesses, some large and impressive, others no more than narrow holes-in-the-wall, but all devoted to sin in one form or another. The Bella Union Theater, the Gem Theater across the street, the Red Top, the Silver Dollar, the Palace, magnificent names for enterprises that would be considered magnificent only in rough surroundings like these. Nuttall and Mann's No. 10 Saloon, with no mention of where the other nine might be located. Miss Laurette's Academy for Young Ladies. Dan hadn't seen any ladies, young or old, in Deadwood, with the notable exception of Lucretia Marchbanks. The students at Miss Laurette's academy would do all their studying indoors, he thought, likely on their backs. And they wouldn't graduate until every bit of appeal had been worn out of them by the life they led.

"Deadwood's a more cultured place than I thought it would be," Bellamy commented.

"What the hell makes you think that?"

Bellamy waved a hand to indicate their surroundings. "Well, just look at all the theaters and academies and such-like they have here." He lowered his voice a little as he went on. "I figured it would be mostly houses of ill repute and gambling dens and places like that."

Dan chuckled. "That's exactly what they are."

"What are you talking about?"

"Those places are whorehouses and saloons, no matter what the signs say."

Bellamy didn't sound convinced. "Are you sure about that? I mean, the Gem Theater sounds positively elegant." He slowed down and turned to look across the street at it.

Dan put a hand on his shoulder and steered him on toward the more respectable part of the camp. "Kid, this down here, this is the bad end of town. The Badlands, you might say. Everything wicked you can think of is for sale down here. *Everything.* But if you ever buy it, you may find that you don't really want it after all."

"How do you know about this?"

Dan shrugged. "I've seen other mining camps and boom towns. I saw end-of-track, what they call Hell on Wheels, when the railroads were being built. I saw cattle towns down in Kansas. They're all the same, doesn't matter where they are or what caused the boom. Deadwood's no different than any of the others."

"There's one thing different about Deadwood," Bellamy insisted.

"What's that?" Dan asked tolerantly.

"Deadwood's where I'm going to get rich."

ONCE they left the couple of blocks of the Badlands behind, they came to a better part of the settlement. They walked past a hardware store and the Langrishe Theater, which appeared to be an actual theatrical venue instead of a whorehouse. Men were lined up to get in, and through the open entrance flap in the big canvas-sided building, Dan saw them settling down on makeshift seats composed of posts pounded into the ground with a circle of rough-sawn wood nailed to the top of each post. That was one way to keep the audience still, Dan thought. If a fella shifted around very much on one of those crude seats, he'd wind up with splinters in his ass.

The Grand Central Hotel was on the other side of the street, a short distance farther west past Langrishe's. It had a good porch, which was a relief after slogging through the muddy street. Dan and Bellamy wiped their boots off on the edge of the porch as best they could before they went inside.

The small lobby was to their right, the dining room to the left. The air was a little smoky from the oil lanterns that gave light. A man standing behind the desk in the lobby asked, "Can I help you gentlemen?"

"We're supposed to meet General Dawson here for supper," Dan said.

The hotel proprietor—Wagner was his name, according to the sign outside—swept a hand toward the dining room. "Go right on in. I believe the General is waiting for you."

The dining room was fairly small, only about a dozen tables, and all of them were occupied. Dan spotted General Dawson at one of the tables at the same time as the General raised a hand and hailed him.

"Over here, Sergeant," Dawson said, half-rising from his chair.

Dan and Bellamy went across the room to the table. Another man waited there with the General, both of them standing now as Dan and Bellamy came up. The second man was heavily built and well dressed, with an intelligent, inquisitive gaze.

"Boys, this is A.W. Merrick, editor and publisher of our local journalistic organ, the *Black Hills Pioneer*," Dawson said in introduction. "A.W., meet Sergeant Daniel Ryan, late of General Custer's command, and his young friend, Mr. Bellamy Bridges. They've come to Deadwood to seek their fortune."

"Nobody comes to Deadwood planning to go broke," the newspaperman said as he shook hands with Dan and Bellamy. "It sometimes works out that way, though. And by the way, holding the lofty titles of editor and publisher also means that I sweep out the place."

"I'm pleased to meet you, Mr. Merrick," Bellamy said. "I never met a real journalist before."

"I have," Dan said. "Quite a few reporters have gone out on patrol with the cavalry."

Merrick nodded as the four men sat down. "Indeed they have. Military correspondents for newspapers and illustrated magazines have done sterling work, Sergeant, in informing the public about what life in the field is really like."

"Yes, sir. By the way, I don't use my rank anymore. I'm just plain old Dan Ryan now."

General Dawson laughed. "Then that makes you an oddity in Deadwood, son. We have a multitude of captains, majors, colonels, and generals in town, most of whom are officially no longer entitled to use those ranks. We even have a lieutenant or two, although why anyone would want to hold on to such a dubious honorific is beyond me. I'd rather sit down to dinner with a sergeant any day."

"Well, sir, tonight you're sitting down to dinner with a couple of civilians."

"And glad to do it." Dawson turned to Merrick and went on. "I told the lads I'd attempt to help them locate some good claims they might purchase."

Merrick nodded and looked at Dan and Bellamy. "The General's your man. He knows more about what's going on around Deadwood than anybody else. Hell of an orator, too. He's writing a speech that he's going to give in our upcoming Fourth of July celebration. I've seen an early draft, and it's very good. Very patriotic and stirring."

"Save the effusive praise for your columns, A.W.," Dawson said. "Let's eat."

At the General's signal, a couple of young women garbed in black dresses and white aprons began bringing platters of food and glasses of beer to the table. They were plump and rather plain, but Bellamy watched them intently anyway, since they were the first females he had seen in quite a spell other than Miss Marchbanks.

Dawson noted his interest and chuckled. "Don't get your hopes up, son. They're not like the waiter girls at the Gem or the Bella Union. By that I mean that they're not for sale."

"No, sir," Bellamy said, blushing. "I didn't think they were."

"If you're interested in that sort of thing, you can find plenty of it in the Badlands," Merrick put in.

"The Badlands," Dan repeated. "That's what it's really called?"

Merrick nodded. "Why shouldn't it be? Have you seen the area, Mr. Ryan? The name seems appropriate."

"Yeah, it fits real well," Dan agreed. "I was just a little surprised because I called it the Badlands a while ago when we were walking up here from our camp. I didn't know that was the name everybody else uses, too."

"Some of the respectable citizens—and there are more than you might think there would be in a boom camp like Deadwood—would like to see all those places torn down and their denizens run out of town." Dawson shook his head. "I can sympathize, I suppose, but it seems to me too idealistic a view. It seems to me that good and bad are both so deeply ingrained in man that you can't have one without the other."

"You don't believe in a utopia, General?" Merrick asked.

"Utopia? What's that? The name of another mining camp?"

The men laughed and started in on the meal. The fried chicken was surprisingly juicy and delicious, Dan thought, but it paled next to the biscuits, which were light and fluffy and as good as anything he had ever tasted. He poured a little molasses onto one of them, ate it, and thought for a moment that he had died and gone to heaven.

The General saw his expression and laughed. "Aunt Lou's biscuits have that effect on everybody when they eat one for the first time. You won't find better food anywhere this side of San Francisco . . . and to tell you the truth, I'm not sure that anything you'd find there would even equal it."

"This is mighty good grub, all right," Dan said. "I wouldn't mind telling her so."

Dawson shook his head. "Aunt Lou's not interested in compliments. She just wants to do her job and be left alone."

"That's a good way to be."

Dan found himself wanting to see the woman again, though. He'd been impressed with her during their brief encounter, and he was even more so now after eating her cooking.

The talk turned to gold claims, and he forgot about Lou Marchbanks for the time being. Dan explained about the men who had come to Deadwood with him and Bellamy. There were several partnerships among the group besides the newly formed one between the two of them. They were looking for approximately a dozen claims.

Dawson shook his head. "There won't be that many available right here in the vicinity of Deadwood. I know of four or five, though, that are for sale, and I'd be glad to speak to the owners of them on behalf of you and your friends, Dan. I'm speaking now of good claims that have the potential for production, you understand, not ones that have already proven to be worthless."

"We appreciate anything you can do, General."

"As for the rest of your party, if they have no objection to spreading out, say down toward Lead or over toward Gayville and Central City, I'm sure we can locate suitable claims for them, too. There are a dozen or more camps up and down the gulches. Admittedly, Deadwood is the largest and best known, but there's potential for wealth all over the Black Hills, gentlemen."

Dan nodded. "That'll be fine. Those boys didn't come up here to pal around. They came to find gold and get rich."

"A laudable ambition," Merrick said. He picked up the glass of beer beside his plate. "Here's to getting rich!"

The four glasses clinked together. It was a nice sound, Dan thought, sort of like what you got when you tapped a couple of gold nuggets together.

Eight

BY the time they started back to the wagons, Bellamy was a little tipsy. He'd had only one glass of beer with dinner, but he wasn't accustomed to drinking any alcohol. His folks thought it was sinful. Of course, his folks thought *everything* was sinful, except for praying and reading the Bible and working like a dog from dawn to dusk.

But of all the vile iniquities, drinking and fornicating were the worst. He'd done the drinking already tonight, Bellamy thought with a laugh. That just left the fornicating.

"What's funny?" Dan asked.

Bellamy shook his head. "Nothing. I was just thinking. Why don't we stop at one of those saloons and have a real drink, Dan? Something to celebrate what we've accomplished so far in Deadwood."

"What we've accomplished?" Dan repeated. "We got in a fight, and we ate supper. Somehow that don't seem like a lot that needs celebrating, kid."

"We made friends with a couple of influential men," Bellamy pointed out. "The General's going to help us find some good claims. I'd say that's pretty damned impressive considering we've only been in town a few hours."

Dan shrugged. "I guess if you look at it like that . . . But the rest of the boys are waiting for us back at camp. Don't you think we ought to go tell them how it went?"

"You can go on." They were approaching the Badlands, and the sounds of laughter, loud talk, and banjo music filled the air. "I think I'll poke around here for a while."

"Not by yourself," Dan declared. "A kid like you, these places would chew you up and spit you out."

Bellamy stopped short, not noticing that he was standing in a puddle. Dan stopped, too, and Bellamy poked a finger against his chest. "I'm not a fucking baby," he said, feeling a little thrill go through him as he said *that* word, the word that would have gotten him such a terrible hiding if his pa had ever heard him use it that he wouldn't have been able to sit down for a week or more. "I can take care of myself, Dan. Didn't I kill some of those Injuns?"

"Those Sioux were coming straight at you in broad daylight. It's dark now, and in the Badlands, trouble comes at you from behind."

"We're partners. I don't work for you. And you're sure as hell not my pa."

Dan sighed. "Yeah, I know. I guess one drink wouldn't hurt. But just one, and it'd better be quick."

"That's all I want," Bellamy said with a nod. "Just one to celebrate."

That brought the conversation back around to where it had started. They walked on down the street, and Bellamy pointed to the Gem Theater. "There. That's where I want to go."

"One of these places is the same as all the others to me," Dan said. "Come on."

The Gem, like the Grand Central Hotel and the Bella Union across the street, appeared to have two actual stories, not just a two-story false front. A narrow balcony with a latticework railing ran along the front of the second floor.

There was a boardwalk out front. The entrance was at the left-hand corner of the building. A couple of signboards separated by shuttered windows were spaced along the front exterior wall, advertising the name of the place and proclaiming that dancing and theatrical exhibitions could be found inside, along with games of chance—"Always a Square Deal"—the finest liqueurs and spirits west of the Mississippi, and good food—"Always a Square Meal"— served by pretty waiter girls.

"See," Bellamy said. "It's a nice place."

Dan grunted as if to say he wasn't so sure about that, but he stepped inside along with Bellamy.

The air was thick with smoke. Bellamy coughed a little before he got used to it. There was a smell in the air besides tobacco, too, an unwholesome blend of stale beer, human sweat, piss, shit, and vomit. Sawdust and pine shavings littered the floor to soak up whatever happened to be spilled on it and attempt to combat the stench, but it didn't do a very good job of the latter task. Bellamy wrinkled his nose. He told himself to ignore the smell. It was the scent of sin, after all, and that was what he wanted to explore.

The Gem was doing a booming business. Men stood two-deep at the bar on the left-hand wall, and all the tables scattered around the main room were occupied. Off to the right were several rows of empty chairs facing a small stage that wasn't in use at the moment. Men and women moved up and down a central staircase leading to the second floor, and Bellamy's eyes widened when he saw how scantily dressed the women were. They wore thin shifts that left their arms and shoulders bare and ended about halfway down their stocking-clad thighs. Bellamy lifted his gaze to the second floor and stared even harder at several women who stood there leaning over the railing. Their bosoms were completely bare. The women laughed and called crude comments to some of the men sitting at the tables below them.

"There's the only 'show' you'll ever see in this theater, kid," Dan said over the raucous noise in the room.

Bellamy gulped. The smoke and the smell were making him a little queasy, but he was determined to go through with this. One reason he had left Illinois, besides the hope of getting rich, that is, was to get out from under the thumb of his parents. They would die of shock if they ever saw him in a den of iniquity like this, he thought.

"Let's get that drink," he said as he started toward the bar.

Along the way they passed a table where one man sat alone with a bottle of whiskey and a glass. He wore a suit and a shirt with a stiff collar, but no tie. His face was dark and mottled with dissipation. He glanced at Bellamy and Dan as they went by, but other than that paid no attention to them.

They had to shove their way up to the bar, where a burly man with long dark hair and a beard took their orders. "Whiskey!" Bellamy said as he smacked his palm on the hardwood.

"Don't get impatient, kid," the bartender said. He looked at Dan. "What's for you?"

"Whiskey, I suppose," Dan said. "And if you could get it from the bottle that has the least amount of gunpowder, strychnine, and rattlesnake venom in it, I'd be obliged."

The bartender grinned. "Now there's a fella who knows which end is up." He stuck a hand across the bar. "Dan Dority's the name."

"I'm Dan, too, Dan Ryan."

"Pleased to meet you." The two men shook, and then Dority reached under the bar for a bottle. "Al ain't lookin'," he went on as he pulled the cork and splashed whiskey into a couple of glasses that weren't too badly smeared. "I'll give you a taste of his private stock."

"Who's Al?" Bellamy asked.

"Al Swearengen." Dority nodded toward the table where the dark-faced man sat alone. "He owns this joint. You don't wanna cross him. Meanest fucker in the whole Dakota Territory."

"I'll take your word for it," Dan said. "I don't intend to have trouble with anybody." He picked up his glass and tossed back his drink. He caught his breath, made a face, and shook his head. "This is the good stuff?"

"Tells you just how bad our run-o'-the-mill Who-hit-John is, don't it?" Dority said with a grin. He looked at Bellamy and added, "Go ahead, kid, drink up."

Trying not to show how apprehensive he felt, Bellamy picked up his glass and lifted it to his lips. The smell of the whiskey was almost enough to make him pull away from it, but he suppressed that impulse. Having seen how Dan drank his, Bellamy supposed that was the best way to go about it. He opened his mouth, tipped his head back, and threw the rotgut down his throat.

It was like swallowing liquid fire, and when it hit his stomach, the explosion felt like it was going to rip him apart. He dropped the glass and slumped forward against the bar, luckily catching himself with both hands before he could fall and smack his face against the hardwood. For a long moment, the world spun crazily around him, as if the entire planet had stopped in its tracks and suddenly started twirling the other way. Tears flooded his eyes. He couldn't see a thing, and all he could hear was the thunderous hammering of his own pulse inside his head.

Gradually, Bellamy's senses began to return to him. His vision was still blurred, but he could make out Dan Dority standing on the other side of the bar, a big grin on his bearded face. Dority held up an empty glass and said, "I figured that stuff 'd hit you pretty hard, kid, so I was ready to catch your glass when you dropped it. You better thank me. I'd'a had to charge you for it if it fell and busted."

Dan took hold of Bellamy's arm and helped him straighten. "You all right, Bellamy?" he asked.

Bellamy tried to talk, but his scalded mouth and tongue and throat wouldn't form any words. All he could do was gasp and mutter incoherent sounds.

"Don't worry about him," Dority said. "It'll pass in a spell. And then he'll be ready for another one."

Bellamy still couldn't talk, but he managed to shake his head vehemently.

"Is that little fucker gonna pass out?"

The question was rasped by a voice that sounded like it could have come from a grave. Dority looked past Bellamy and Dan and shook his head. "No, Al, the kid's all right. Leastways he will be in a minute."

Al Swearengen, the owner of the Gem Theater, had gotten up from his table and moved over to the bar. He said, "Good. But if he takes too long orderin' another drink, move him the hell outta here. We don't make any money from snot-nosed little bastards just standin' around."

Swearengen seemed to be drunk. He weaved a little as he made his way to the stairs and climbed them to the second floor, clutching the bottle in one hand while holding on tightly to the stair rail with the other.

"Don't mind Al," Dority said to Bellamy and Dan. "He ain't as bad as he sounds. Well, yeah, maybe he is. You boys ready for another?"

Dan shook his head. "We just came in for one. Let's go, Bellamy."

Bellamy still had his hands flat on the bar. He leaned over and slowly shook his head back and forth. The world was turning the right way again, and the inferno in his belly had settled down somewhat. He found that he could talk again as he looked up at Dority and asked, "The girls here . . . can a fella hire them?"

"Why, you sure can, partner!" Dority waved toward the balcony where several half-naked women still leaned over the railing. "You can have your pick of any o' them up yonder, or I'll call one of the gals who's down here over for you."

"Bellamy . . ." Dan said warningly. "I don't think that's a very good idea."

"Yeah, well, you're not . . ." Bellamy had to shake his head again as he tried to regain his lost train of thought. "You're not a goddamn virgin."

Dority chuckled. "Hell, kid, you're a virgin? We can take care o' that, sure enough. The gals upstairs'll likely fight over you, to see which one gets to introduce you to the pleasures of the flesh."

Bellamy slapped the bar again and said thickly, "That's what I want! The pleasures of the flesh!" He jerked his arm out of Dan's grip and started to turn toward the stairs. "Lemme at 'em!"

He had taken one step before he pitched forward, out cold by the time he hit the floor.

DAN grimaced in disgust as he bent over to pick up Bellamy. The youngster's clean clothes weren't clean anymore. The floor of the Gem wasn't covered with muck like the street outside, but it was far from pristine. Dan took hold of Bellamy's left arm.

"Let me give you a hand," a man said as he bent over to take Bellamy's right arm.

Dan glanced at him, saw a young man only a few years older than Bellamy, dressed in a black suit, white shirt, black string tie, and flat-crowned black hat. He was no prospector; that was obvious from his outfit. The long, slender fingers that he wrapped around Bellamy's arm weren't covered with calluses, either. Dan pegged him right away as a gambler, a gunman . . . or both. Dan had seen his ilk in dozens of towns, all across the frontier.

Still, a helping hand was a helping hand. "Much obliged," he said, and then he grunted as he hauled up on the deadweight that was currently Bellamy Bridges.

With the stranger's help, Dan lifted Bellamy and draped him face-first on the bar. Dority frowned and said, "You can't leave him there. He's takin' up space that could be used by a payin' customer."

"I'm not going to leave him there," Dan said as he dropped a coin on the bar to pay for their drinks. "Just let me get a good hold on him so I can drag him outta here. . . ."

"I'll help you," the stranger offered. "By the way, my name's Fletcher Parkhurst. Fletch to my friends."

"Pleased to meet you," Dan said, "even though it ain't the best of circumstances." He slipped an arm around Bellamy.

"Come on, you damned fool. Wake up enough to walk a little bit, why don't you?"

Fletch Parkhurst laughed as he supported Bellamy from the other side and together he and Dan began to drag the unconscious youngster toward the front door of the Gem.

"Once you've passed out from that panther piss Swearengen sells. you don't come to in a hurry," he said.

"Yeah, but it was only one drink! Fool kid," Dan muttered.

They wrestled Bellamy's limp form onto the boardwalk in front of the saloon. Dan looked around and asked, "Is there a horse trough around here that we can dump him in? I don't want to have to drag him all the way back to our wagons. Maybe that'd wake him up."

"Or finish the job of poisoning him," Fletch said. He grunted from the effort of holding Bellamy up. "Listen, we can take him over to Miss Laurette's. I have friends there. We can dump him in a room and let him sleep it off."

Dan frowned. "I saw that place earlier. Whorehouse, ain't it?"

"They call it an academy for young ladies."

"Same thing," Dan said with a snort.

"Well, yes, that's true, but as I said, I have friends there, and I can vouch for your friend's safety. He won't be bothered. You have my word on it."

Dan wasn't sure why he should take the word of somebody like Fletch Parkhurst, but the alternative was hauling Bellamy all the way back to the wagons. Maybe he could leave Bellamy at the bordello for a little while, he thought, just until he could borrow a wheelbarrow or something like that he could use to take Bellamy back to camp.

"All right," he said grudgingly. "Let's go."

Nine

MISS Laurette's Academy for Young Ladies was across the street from the Gem, next to the Bella Union. It was a log building with a plank false front and only one story. The inside was finished out nicely, though, Dan saw as he and Fletch Parkhurst dragged Bellamy into the place. It hadn't taken them long to get there, and Dan was grateful for that. Bellamy felt like he weighed a ton.

The academy wasn't a saloon, although drinks were available. It was set up more like someone's house, with a foyer just inside the door opening into a large parlor. There were rugs on the floor and overstuffed divans arranged around the room. A pianoforte that must have been hauled out here in a wagon from St. Louis or Cheyenne sat in one corner. Brocaded curtains hung over the windows and gave the room a slightly shabby elegance. For Deadwood, it was a pretty fancy place.

And the woman who met Dan and Fletch in the foyer was pretty fancy for Deadwood, too. She wore a gray, long-sleeved gown that buttoned up high on her throat. Just above the top button of the dress, a narrow ribbon of black silk encircled her throat. The ribbon had a small gem set on it. Probably not a real diamond, Dan thought, but it sparkled in the light and looked pretty. The woman's hair was red, and the small touches of gray here and there seemed to indicate that was its natural color. The hair was piled high on her head in an elaborate arrangement of curls. Her eyes were strikingly green. The dress clung to her figure, which was very good. Dan thought she was around forty years old. He knew without being told that this must be Miss Laurette.

"Fletcher, what are you doing?" she asked crisply, proving that Fletch was indeed known here. "Is that young man dead?"

Fletch grinned. "Nope, just dead drunk. On one shot of Al Swearengen's hooch, at that."

"In all fairness," Dan said, "he had a beer with dinner at the Grand Central, too."

Miss Laurette said, "Young men have a great capacity for a great many things. Unfortunately, whiskey is not always one of them."

"I thought maybe he could sleep it off in one of the back rooms," Fletch said.

The woman hesitated only a second and then nodded. "Of course. Take him on back."

Fletch seemed to know where he was going, so Dan let him lead the way. They went down a hallway leading from the foyer toward the rear of the building. Along the way they passed half a dozen closed doors on either side of the corridor. Dan figured that was where the young ladies did their "studying." All of them must have been occupied at the moment, because there hadn't been any gals in various stages of undress lounging around in that front parlor. That was the usual arrangement in places like this: The girls waited in the parlor, the customers came in and picked out which one they wanted, and then they moved to one of the private rooms to conclude the transaction.

The hall ended in a door. Fletch opened it while still supporting Bellamy. There was another hall beyond the door, running at right angles to the main one. The office, the kitchen, and the madam's quarters would be back here, Dan guessed, along with a few extra rooms if they were needed.

Usually there was also at least one bruiser around to handle trouble in case a customer got too rambunctious. Dan hadn't seen anybody like that, but he was confident some big gent would show up in a hurry if there was a problem. He had wondered briefly if Fletch filled that role at Miss Laurette's, but then he'd discarded that idea. Despite being fairly strong, Fletch was too slender and clearly not a brawler. More likely, he was a regular customer. If he was a gambler, he might have a poker game here from time to time and cut Miss Laurette in on the take.

Fletch opened another door into a small room furnished only with a bed, a chair, and a chamber pot. It was dark in the room, but some light spilled into it from the oil lamp hanging in the rear hall. They dumped the senseless Bellamy onto the bed.

Dan straightened and rubbed his back where a muscle ached. "I'm startin' to wonder if that fella Dority slipped knockout drops in his drink. He sure went out like a light."

"I wouldn't put much past Dority or his boss," Fletch said, "but I don't see how doping your friend would have gotten them anything. Swearengen and the people who work for him don't do anything unless there's a profit in it for them."

"Maybe they planned to rob him."

Fletch shook his head. "The Gem makes money hand over fist without having to resort to such tactics. And since this isn't the Barbary Coast and the nearest ocean is probably a thousand miles away, I don't think anybody intended to shanghai him."

"Been to the Barbary Coast, have you?"

"I've been a lot of places," Fletch said with a smile. "Don't let my apparent youth fool you. A man can pack a lot of living into a few years."

"Don't I know it," Dan muttered. Bellamy had started to

snore. Dan gestured toward him and went on. "How long can I leave him here?"

"All night, if you want. No one will bother him. If you're worried about someone cutting his throat and emptying his pockets, I can promise you that won't happen. But you can stay here with him if you want. That's fine, too."

Dan shook his head. "I got to go back and talk to the rest of the bunch that came in with us. I can bring some of them back here with me so we can carry him to camp."

"Whatever you want."

"You're an agreeable young cuss," Dan said.

Fletch grinned. "Agreeable men live longer, don't you think? Getting the blood all hot and stirred up isn't good for a fellow."

Dan grunted. "Yeah, I reckon." He looked down at Bellamy and rubbed his jaw. "You sure he'll be all right?"

From the doorway, Miss Laurette said, "I'll add my word to that of Mr. Parkhurst, sir. I'm in the business of making men happy and comfortable."

Dan turned toward her and out of habit took off his hat. "Yes, ma'am, I'm sure you are. And I wouldn't doubt your word. If it won't be too much trouble for you, I'll just come back and get this young idiot in the morning."

"That will be fine, Mister . . . ?"

"Ryan, ma'am. Daniel Ryan."

"You're new in Deadwood, aren't you?"

"Yes, ma'am, just got in late this afternoon."

Miss Laurette's full red lips curved in a smile. "You're the man who stepped up to defend Aunt Lou and got in a fight with Stubbs and Rodney."

"That's right." Dan pointed his thumb at the bed. "Bellamy was the other fella in the ruckus."

"Lou Marchbanks is a fine woman in spite of her color. I'd hire her to cook here in a minute if she'd consider such an offer." The redhead's lips quirked bitterly. "I'm afraid she wouldn't lower herself to be employed here, though." The smile came back, the momentary flash of bitterness disappearing. "I'm glad to see that Deadwood is finally starting to attract some true gentlemen."

Fletch had his left shoulder propped against the wall. "What about me?" he drawled. "Don't I qualify?"

Miss Laurette's smile didn't budge, but her green eyes glittered with some emotion that Dan couldn't read. "I'm afraid your lineage precludes that, Mr. Parkhurst."

Dan would have expected a veiled insult like that to anger Fletch, but the dapper young man just laughed. "I'm sure it does," he said.

Bellamy let out a particularly loud snore.

"I gotta be going," Dan said. He nodded to Fletch. "Thanks for your help." He looked at Miss Laurette. "And for your hospitality, ma'am. If you'll just tell me how much I owe you for the bed . . ."

"No charge," she said. "But don't expect to ever hear those words come out of my mouth again."

Dan put on his hat and tugged on the brim. "No, ma'am." He glanced one more time at Bellamy. "He's gonna have a mighty bad headache when he wakes up in the morning . . . and I reckon he'll deserve every bit of it."

AWARENESS crept in slowly around the edges of Bellamy's brain. He had no idea where he was or even what had happened to him. The last thing he remembered clearly was having dinner at the Grand Central Hotel with Dan Ryan, General Dawson, and that newspaperman, Mr. Merrick. After that . . . nothing.

All he was sure of at the moment was that he hurt. Bad.

The ache seemed to cover his entire body, but after a while he realized it originated in his head. It was a pounding, throbbing, screaming bastard of a pain, too. He wanted to open his eyes, but he couldn't. All he could manage to do was flutter his eyelids a little. He groaned.

That was when a voice whispered in his ear, "Oh, you're waking up." Soft fingers closed around his penis and began to stroke up and down on it.

Bellamy's eyes opened then. Opened wide.

His head and shoulders jerked up off the pillow that was under them. He tried to sit up, and pain exploded in his head so fierce that it overwhelmed even the feeling of having his penis caressed. He squeezed his eyes shut, groaned again, and flopped back down on the pillow.

During that second his eyes had been open, however, he had caught a glimpse of a lovely, heart-shaped face surrounded by a mass of dark curls. That image persisted in his mind, even through the thundering agony, and as the pain gradually began to ease, he forced his eyes open to see if he had just imagined such loveliness, or if it might be real.

She looked down at him with a worried frown and asked, "Are you all right now, sweetie?"

Bellamy felt sweat running down his forehead. It trickled into his eyes and made them sting. He blinked several times, and each time he expected the girl to vanish. She stayed right where she was, though, leaning over him.

He made his mouth work, despite the fact that it was dry as a bone and tasted like a skunk had crawled in there and died. "Do what . . . you were doing . . ." he rasped.

The frown on her face went away and the smile reappeared. "You mean this?" she asked as she reached down to grasp his organ again.

Bellamy closed his eyes. That shut out the light and made his head feel better. He concentrated on what she was doing to him. He couldn't believe that a girl—a *girl!*—was playing with his talleywhacker. It felt even better than when he touched it himself, which hadn't been very often because the one time his pa had caught him at it, he'd gotten a brutal whack on the head and a stern lecture about how he'd go crazy and blind if he kept performing such a vile, despicable act on himself, not to mention the fact that the Lord would probably be so angry and disgusted that He would send down a judgment on the whole family, just because of what Bellamy was doing. So if there was a drought— and with that Bellamy's pa clouted him again—or a plague of locusts—another clout—it would be Bellamy's fault, because he was so evil he couldn't keep from touching himself.

Was it as big a sin, he found himself wondering, if a gal did it for him?

"Well, you may be sick," she said, "but you ain't dead. You got a real nice one, you know that?"

Bellamy couldn't answer. His chest rose and fell more rapidly now. He wondered vaguely how come he wasn't wearing his britches, but he wasn't going to waste a lot of time pondering that question.

"Yes, sir, that's just fine," the girl said. "We don't want to waste it, though. You just hang on a minute."

He heard a rustle of clothing, and then the thin mattress underneath him shifted a little. Was she getting into bed with him?

Where in blazes was he, anyway?

He felt her straddle his hips, her thighs warm and soft against his skin as she lowered herself. Then the most incredible heat he had ever felt enveloped him. It was slick and hot, and instinct made him thrust his hips up and penetrate even deeper into it. Moving like that made his head throb and his stomach a mite unsettled, but the other sensations he was experiencing for the first time in his life were so overwhelming that he couldn't pay attention to anything else.

"There you go," the girl said softly. "That's it. That's good, honey. You just lay there and let Carla do all the work."

Carla? Was that her name? It suited her, Bellamy decided as she began to move on top of him, rocking back and forth. She took hold of his hands and lifted them, and he felt his palms filled with something silky smooth and soft. Curiosity overcame him, and he had to open his eyes and have a look.

He was holding her bosoms. She wore a thin shift of some sort that she had pulled up around her hips, but it still covered the upper half of her body. He felt her hard nipples through it.

He lifted his gaze from her breasts, up over the round-ness of her shoulders, the clean lines of her throat, and the slight jut of her chin to the rest of her face. She was as pretty as he remembered. Prettier, with that curly dark hair bouncing a little around her face as she rode him. She caught her full lower lip between her teeth for a moment.

"Pinch 'em," she gasped.

"Wh-what?"

"My nipples. Pinch 'em."

Bellamy did the best he could to oblige her, but he knew he was fumbling around quite a bit. After a while she said, "Wait a minute," and reached down to grab the bottom of the shift. She pulled it up and over her head, peeling the garment off and leaving her naked.

Never in his life had Bellamy seen a completely naked woman. Until now the closest he'd come had been the whores in the Gem Theater. Now Carla didn't have a stitch on, and his hands were filled with her soft bosoms, and his thing was inside her and she was bouncing up and down on him so that he felt . . . he felt . . . he didn't know what he was feeling, but it was sure good and Lord, Lord, it was about to get a lot better—

"Damn it, Carla, I told you to watch him, not fuck him."

The voice belonged to a woman and sounded annoyed, but Bellamy wasn't sure where it came from or who the woman was. All he knew was that if there was a point where he could have stopped what he was doing, he had sure as hell passed it. He let out a yell and grabbed Carla's bosoms in a tighter grip as he heard her say in a strained, breathless tone, "We're . . . almost done, Miss Laurette . . . almost there . . . oh, yes!"

Bellamy let go then. He might not have much experi-ence, but he knew what was happening. His insides buck-led and jumped and surged, and the wet heat surrounding his penis grew even wetter and hotter. Carla's thighs clamped hard around his hips as if she didn't intend to ever let him go.

"All right," the other woman said patiently. She sounded

amused now, instead of angry. "I guess if I needed any proof that young fella was going to live, you two just gave it to me."

Carla was out of breath, too, but she managed to turn her head toward the door. "I'm sorry, Miss Laurette," she said. "I just thought I'd take this poor young man's mind off his troubles."

Bellamy looked toward the door, too, and saw an older woman with red hair standing there. Her painted lips were curved in a smile. Bellamy knew he ought to feel embarrassed that the woman had stood there and watched him and Carla as they finished what they were doing, but he couldn't find it in himself to get too upset. In fact, he wasn't feeling much of anything at the moment except utterly drained.

"That's all right," Miss Laurette said. "You did fine, Carla. Now get off of him and go on back to your room so you can get some rest before this afternoon. I'll get Fletch to take our young friend home."

"Yes, ma'am." Carla swung off Bellamy and stood up beside the bed. She picked up her shift but didn't put it on, draping it over one shoulder instead. She leaned over Bellamy, which gave him a good view of her small breasts, and patted him on the shoulder. "You take it easy, honey," she told him. "I hope I see you again sometime."

With that she straightened and sashayed out of the room, ducking her head as she passed Miss Laurette.

Bellamy realized he was lying there in front of the older woman with his bottom half uncovered. He tried to reach for the sheet so that he could pull it over himself, but she said, "Oh, shoot, you're not showing me anything I haven't seen more times than you could ever count." She tilted her head to the side for a second, as if appraising him, and added, "You're built pretty nice, though. I can see why Carla gave in to temptation."

"Ma'am, I . . ." Bellamy's mouth was so dry he had to swallow a couple of times before he could go on. "Ma'am, I'm sorry . . . I don't know who you are . . . or where I am . . ."

"You're at Miss Laurette's Academy for Young Ladies, and I'm Miss Laurette. You've already met one of my young ladies."

Bellamy nodded weakly.

"Evidently you had too much to drink last night at the Gem."

"I only had . . . one drink . . . that I remember . . ."

"Sometimes one is too many, with the sort of liquor that Al Swearengen serves." She came a step into the room and crossed her arms over her breasts. "Your friend Mr. Ryan left you here last night to sleep it off. You were safe here. Nobody would ever bother someone in my house who's under my protection."

That sounded odd to Bellamy, a woman talking about protecting him. It was always supposed to be the other way around. He could see himself protecting that girl Carla. Just thinking about it made him feel a little better inside.

"You lay there and catch your breath," Miss Laurette went on. "I'll get somebody to help you go back to your wagons."

"Thank you . . . ma'am." Bellamy closed his eyes. "I'll just . . . lay here."

"Don't you go back to sleep. This isn't a hotel."

"No, ma'am."

Miss Laurette started to turn away, and something made Bellamy say, "Ma'am . . . this was the first time I ever did that . . . what I did with Miss Carla, I mean."

"Really?" Miss Laurette laughed and shook her head. "Well, I guess that just goes to show you that you can find almost anything in Deadwood . . . even a virgin."

Ten

DESPITE Miss Laurette's warning, Bellamy dozed off for a few minutes as he waited there in the little room. But then the door opened again, and a man Bellamy had never seen before stepped inside. At least, Bellamy didn't recall ever seeing him.

The newcomer was in his twenties, not that much older than Bellamy, and dressed mostly in black. Nobody would ever mistake him for a preacher, though. He reached down, picked Bellamy's trousers up off the floor—Bellamy had wondered where they'd gotten to—and tossed them on the bed.

"Get dressed," the man said. "You've about reached the limits of the house's hospitality, friend. By all rights, Miss Laurette ought to make you pay for the sporting you did with Carla."

Bellamy sat up, still feeling dizzy but not too bad. He swung his legs off the bed and started trying awkwardly to get his feet into his britches.

"You know Carla?" he asked.

"I know all the girls who work here. You might say I'm

a regular. My name's Fletcher Parkhurst, but you can call me Fletch."

Bellamy stood and pulled his trousers up. As he buttoned them, he introduced himself. "I'm Bellamy Bridges. From Illinois."

Fletch Parkhurst leaned a shoulder against the door-jamb. He looked like the sort of young man who usually had a casual air about him. "Yes, I know your name," he said. "Dan Ryan told me about both of you and how you came to the Black Hills to find gold, along with some other men. Deadwood's only been in existence for a few months, but it's already an old story."

Bellamy looked around for his boots. Fletch pointed them out where they sat in a corner. Bellamy got them and sat down on the edge of the bed to pull them on.

"I'm going to find gold," he said confidently. "I'm sure of it."

"I hope you're right. You'd better stay away from Swearengen's place, though, if you want to live long enough to pan some color."

"Swearengen?" Bellamy asked with a frown.

"Al Swearengen. He owns the Gem Theater. You and Ryan went in there last night. You guzzled down one glass of whiskey and went pie-eyed. Fell flat on your face, Ryan said."

Bellamy closed his eyes for a moment and massaged his aching forehead. "I don't remember that. . . . Well, I'm starting to recall a little of it, maybe, I should say. . . . I remember going in somewhere with Dan. . . ."

"Yeah, that hooch Swearengen sells is potent enough to wipe out some of your memories, all right," Fletch said with a grin. "It'll all come back to you in time, more than likely. Unless you're lucky enough that you really forgot it for good."

Bellamy stood up, trembling a little. "I won't go there again. I can promise you that."

"Don't promise me. I don't care whether you pickle your insides."

"But you helped bring me here," Bellamy said, calling up more fuzzy images in his brain. "You must care some."

"I just didn't want to see a poor helpless case like you get stepped on in Swearengen's place."

"Well, I appreciate your help. I'm all right now, though. I can get back to our camp by myself."

Fletch straightened from his negligent pose. "I'll walk with you. It's a pretty morning. Besides, I feel sort of responsible for you."

"You don't have to."

"Let's just go," Fletch said, pointing down the hall with a thumb.

They went out through the front of the house, and it was all new to Bellamy. "Miss Laurette's Academy for Young Ladies," he read off the sign out front. "I remember this place. When we walked past it yesterday evening, Dan told me it was a bordello."

"That's what it is, but don't let Miss Laurette hear you call it that. She likes to think of it as a little higher-toned than that."

"Putting on airs doesn't make a place into something it isn't."

"I wouldn't be talking about putting on airs if I was you, friend," Fletch said, his voice cooler now. "Remember what happened between you and Carla."

Bellamy felt his face burning. "Does everyone in there know about that?"

"Probably by now they do. But nobody really cares, Bellamy. That's what those girls are there for."

"Do you know Carla . . . well?"

Fletch chuckled. "Not as well as you do, if that's what you mean. I haven't had the pleasure."

"Do you know her last name, or where she's from?"

Fletch shook his head, but it was a warning gesture, not a negative reply to Bellamy's questions. "You don't want to be asking things like that about a whore, Bellamy. None of that matters."

"It might."

"No," Fletch said emphatically, "it doesn't."

Bellamy didn't feel like arguing. He looked around instead.

Deadwood's Main Street was crowded with wagons, horses, mule teams, oxen, and men, and a constant hubbub filled the air. Bellamy thought that it wasn't quite as busy as it had been the previous afternoon. The explanation for that was fairly simple: A lot of the men who had been in camp later the day before were now out at their claims, searching for gold. They would return once they had done their day's work.

The level of activity in the Chinese quarter was just about the same, however. Most of these particular immigrants hadn't come to Deadwood to prospect for gold. They ran restaurants and laundries and worked as servants. As Bellamy and Fletch walked by, Bellamy wondered if there were joss houses and opium dens hidden behind some of those innocuous facades, like in the occasional dime novels he had read when he was able to sneak one of the lurid, yellow-backed tales into the barn and steal a few minutes away from the never-ending chores. Dime novels were sinful, too, of course, just not on the same level as drinking and fornication.

They came within sight of the wagons. Bellamy saw Dan and the other men standing and talking to General Dawson. The discussion was an animated one, and Bellamy felt his pulse quicken. The General might have already found them some good claims.

He might be panning for gold before the day was over, Bellamy told himself.

"I reckon you can make it the rest of the way by yourself," Fletch said as he slowed.

Despite his eagerness to get in on the discussion with the General, Bellamy stopped and said, "Thanks for your help, Fletch. I'll try not to be such a bother in the future."

"Everybody deserves a chance to be saved from their own stupidity at least once," Fletch said with a grin. "Just don't push your luck, pilgrim."

"I won't. I think I'll be going back to Miss Laurette's place, though."

"Because of Carla?"

"I never met anybody like her before. I've got to see her again."

Fletch shrugged. "She'll be there, I reckon. But it won't be on the house next time."

"That doesn't matter."

"Whatever you say." Fletch turned away with a small wave of his hand. "So long, Bellamy."

Bellamy nodded and said politely, "Good-bye."

Then he hurried toward the wagon, his headache forgotten in his eagerness to find out where his claim was located and how soon he was going to be rich.

DAN saw Bellamy coming and said, "Hold on a minute, General, if you don't mind. My partner's about to join us."

General Dawson nodded. "Of course." He reached inside his coat and drew out a rolled-up piece of paper. "I'll get this map spread out so you boys can gather round and take a look at it."

Dan stepped away from the group for a moment and went to meet Bellamy. "I was just about to come lookin' for you," he said to the young man.

"I was right where you left me, at Miss Laurette's academy."

Something about the boy's voice sounded odd. Dan frowned and said, "Nobody bothered you there, did they? Or tried to pull any funny stuff? That fella Fletch swore you'd be all right."

"I'm fine, Dan," Bellamy assured him. "Nobody bothered me."

"Well, good." Something still struck Dan as being a little off, but he wasn't going to press the issue. Not with the General ready to talk to them about claims. "Come on over. The General's got some news for us."

They joined the other men gathered around the rear of

the wagon where General Dawson had spread out his map on the lowered tailgate. With a soldier's eye for such things, Dan looked at the map and recognized Deadwood Gulch and the other gulches formed by the creeks in the area.

"I have ten claims located," Dawson began, "where the owners are willing to sell. There's color on each of these claims. I've seen the assayer's reports, and I'm as certain of that as I can be without having walked the claims myself. Now, how much color there might be is an entirely different question. There might be a fortune still there, or the gold might be just about played out. The only way to discover which is to work the claims and let fate proceed at its own pace. Take a look at the map, gentlemen, and see what you think."

Dan bent closer to study the map. He saw that several of the claims were located fairly close to Deadwood, while others were more scattered and distant from the camp. Personally, he didn't mind being farther away. He figured he and Bellamy could live right on the claim and just come into the settlement occasionally, when they needed supplies. That would give them more time to work on finding gold. Some of the other men could take the closer claims.

Beside him, Bellamy leaned forward. His finger pointed at a spot on the map, the claim closest to Deadwood, and said, "That's the one I want."

"Number Eight above discovery," the General said. Dan knew the claims were numbered according to their location in relation to the first discovery of gold in the gulch. "Not as lucrative so far as some of the others, but handy to town, no doubt about that."

"Wait a minute," Dan began, and then stopped abruptly as he realized what the General had just said. If Dan protested now and said that he was interested in one of the other claims, it would look like his objection was based on the lower amount of gold that Number Eight had produced so far. He frowned at Bellamy, wishing the youngster had kept his mouth shut.

Of course, he could break up their newly formed partnership, Dan told himself. He and Bellamy sure as hell weren't joined together permanently. He wasn't sure Bellamy would make it out here on his own, though.

"Problem, Dan?" Cromwell asked. "I thought we said we'd just all take our chances. You never know, that Number Eight claim could turn out to be the richest one in the Black Hills."

"Yeah, I reckon it could," Dan said with a shrug. He didn't seem to have much choice in the matter. "All right. Bellamy and I will take Number Eight, if we can settle on a price with the owner."

"I suspect you can," General Dawson said, and that made Dan worry even more. It sounded like the owner of Number Eight was anxious to get rid of it. That couldn't be good.

Ah, well, he thought. He hadn't come to the Black Hills thinking that a fortune would jump up out of the ground into his pockets. He would have to work for it, just as he had everything else he had ever gotten in his life. And Bellamy certainly seemed happy about it. He was nodding eagerly.

The discussion went on for another half hour, as the rest of the men talked about the claims, asked questions of the General about them, and eventually settled on who would work which claim. Several of the men were going in together on some of the pieces of ground. The group that had come to Deadwood would soon be scattered far and wide.

"You'll all want to take a look at the claims you've picked out, I expect," Dawson said as he rolled up the map. "When you're satisfied and ready to make an offer to the current owners, come down to my office on Sherman Street."

"I didn't think there was but one street in this camp," one of the men said with a laugh.

"Well, it's not much more than a muddy path right now, but we call it a street." The General told them how to find the log hut that served as his office and living quarters, and then added, "One of these days, and soon, I suspect, Deadwood will be an actual city, with gaslights and paved streets just like back East."

"No offense meant, General," Dan said, "but we're in the middle of an Indian reservation, a hell of a long way from anywhere. What makes you think real civilization is ever gonna come calling out here?"

"Because we have the two things that always fuel the growth of civilization, Sergeant Ryan: wealth, and the men who seek it."

Eleven

THE wagons had gathered at Fort Laramie from several different places of origin, Hickok learned during the couple of days he and his friends were there at the outpost on the North Platte. Most of them belonged to gold-seekers who were on their way to the Black Hills to prospect, but others carried supplies that their owners hoped to sell for a tidy profit, much like Colorado Charley and Steve Utter. Some carried whores bound for the bordellos of Deadwood. The women were of varying stages of age and attractiveness, but all of them had a distressing tendency to flutter and simper whenever Hickok was around. In a way, it was a curse to be so damned handsome, he had declared self-mockingly in more than one saloon, but at its core there was some truth in the gibe.

On the second evening at the fort, Bill and Colorado Charley and Steve sat in the rear of the sutler's store at a table made from a barrel and played cards with a couple of sergeants and a major. Rank meant little or nothing in circumstances such as these; once the pasteboards came out, a sergeant and a major with an itch to play found themselves willingly on the same level. Bill wasn't sure where the Anderson boys were. Probably off sniffing around the whores, if he was any judge of young men, and having been one himself at one time, he thought he was qualified. White-Eye Jack was especially taken with the one called Silky, Bill recalled. And she *was* a pretty piece of baggage, he mused, especially for a soiled dove.

Hickok had his back to the wall, as usual, as he studied his cards. His mind tended to wander some at moments like this. He had been a gambler for so long that deciding how to play a poker hand no longer required his full attention. His gaze flicked around the dim, smoky room. At the first sign of trouble, he could drop his cards and whip out his Colts in the blink of an eye. His hands were as steady and swift as ever. The question was, could he see what he was shooting at if gunplay ensued?

"I'll take two," he said as he discarded.

Steve Utter was dealing. "Two to Mr. Wild Bill Hickok his own self," he said with a grin as he flipped the cards across the table.

Bill picked up the cards and suppressed the flash of annoyance he felt. Steve didn't mean anything by it. He was a good fellow, although Hickok had never been as close with Steve as he was with Colorado Charley. Colorado Charley was just about the best friend a man could ever want.

"Three," the major said. Steve gave him his cards.

Colorado Charley asked for one card. Steve said, "Must be a good hand, brother."

"Shut up," Colorado Charley growled good-naturedly.

The deal went on around the table. Bets were made. The stakes were small in this game; soldiers never had a lot of money. Hickok didn't care. He didn't play cards for the money he won but for the companionship, the sense of camaraderie and good fellowship. Too much of his life had been spent alone in recent years. His reputation was a lodestone that drew people to him, but in a way it also served as a barrier. When someone looked at him, they thought about the men he had killed. They might not mean to, but they did it anyway. And when they spoke to him, often their eyes darted nervously from side to side, because you never knew when some fledgling shootist might swagger up, issue an obscenity-laced challenge to the great Wild Bill, and slap leather. No one wanted to be in the line of fire if that happened. And since that night in Abilene, the night of the showdown with Phil Coe, when footsteps had suddenly thudded on the boardwalk behind him and he had turned to see a shadowy form coming at him, gun in hand . . .

No one had blamed him, at least not to his face. Mike Williams had been not only his friend but also a night watchman paid by the city. He should have known not to run up behind Wild Bill Hickok in the dark, especially when Hickok already had his Colts drawn and had just gunned down a mortal enemy. Williams's sheer carelessness was responsible for his death, nothing else.

But there were still moments when Hickok wished he could somehow go back and ease the pressure of his fingers on those triggers. When the sound of the sharp reports and the buck of the guns in his hands and the acrid bite of burned powder were the stuff of nightmares . . .

"I call," Wild Bill said, and laid down his cards.

Everybody else had dropped out of the hand except the major. He looked at Bill's cards, shook his head disgustedly, and tossed his cards on the stack facedown. "The pot's yours again, Mr. Hickok," he said.

Bill pulled the small pile of coins to him. He wondered on occasion if everyone who lost to him at cards really lost, or if they just let him take the pot because they were afraid of him. But any time he had the urge to reach over and turn those thrown-in cards so that he could see their faces, he suppressed it. For one thing, to do that would be something of an insult. For another, he didn't really want to know.

Steve passed him the deck, saying, "Here you go, Bill. The deal's yours now."

Since it was after hours, the door was locked. The sutler had left the key with them, trusting them to lock up again when they left. Before Bill could gather up all the cards, shuffle, and deal, an urgent knocking sounded from the store's entrance. A voice Bill recognized as belonging to Charley Anderson called, "Mr. Hickok? You in there? There's trouble!"

Bill sighed. Sooner or later, there was always trouble.

Colorado Charley said, "Keep your seat, Bill. I'll see what's goin' on. Probably nothin'."

He got up, taking the key with him, and went to the front door of the store. Whatever was going on, Hickok hoped it didn't have anything to do with that Cannary woman. She was rather likable in a crude way, he had found, possibly because she was so honest. She always spoke her mind, and Hickok admired that in a person. But he had no amatory interest in her, none whatsoever, and she seemed to have concocted some sort of romantic fantasy about him that led her to follow him around like a lovestruck calf. Though he hated to admit it, even to himself, one reason for this poker game tonight was so that he could hide out from Calamity Jane.

Colorado Charley swung the door open and confronted Charley Anderson. "What the hell's goin' on?" Colorado Charley demanded. "What's all the ruckus about?"

"It's my brother," Charley Anderson said, his voice filled with both excitement and worry. More worry than excitement, Hickok decided, and it might very well be justified, because the young man rushed on. "I think he's about to get himself killed!"

Wild Bill sighed again, squared up the deck of cards, and set them aside. The White-Eyed Kid was his friend and a good young fellow, so he would have to go see about this.

He just wished it wasn't night. Night, so full of shadows . . .

JACK had been waiting for his chance ever since he'd talked to Silky on the wagon tongue the day before. He had seen her a couple of times during the day, and she had smiled and said howdy to him each time. That gave him hope that she didn't consider him an irredeemable buffoon. He just had to wait for the right time and place to approach her.

That had come this evening, when he saw her standing beside one of the supply wagons, staring out over the prairie as dusk settled down. There had been something about the way she stood there, something lonely and poignant, and he wondered what she was thinking. Was she remembering her childhood, or something else in her past? Pondering the choices she had made, the turns in the trail she had taken that had brought her here? Knowing that he wouldn't find a better time to talk to her, he took a deep breath, squared his shoulders, gathered his courage, and walked up to her.

"Evenin', Miss Silky," he said. He tugged on the brim of his hat.

She jumped a little, startled by his greeting. She must not have heard him coming toward her. He had a habit of moving quietly, he supposed. The frontier instilled that in a man.

"Oh, hello, Jack," she said. She smiled. She wore a sleeveless brown dress this evening, with a lace shawl draped around her shoulders. Jack thought she looked mighty pretty in the fading light.

He gestured toward the prairie and said, "I saw you lookin' out there. Seemed like you were thinkin' some mighty deep thoughts."

"Me?" She shook her head. "Oh, no. I was just wondering what it'll be like in Deadwood. I'm going to work in a theater, you know. The Gem Theater. I hope I'll get to sing and dance some instead of just sportin' with the gents."

"You like to sing and dance, do you?"

"I always did. My mama told me that when I was a tyke, I'd always put on a little show for the customers at the house where she worked. A lot of times when the men found out that she was the mama of that cute little girl, they'd slip her a little extra money."

"So your ma was a . . . a . . ."

"A whore?" Silky Jen laughed. "You can say it, Jack. Of course she was. How'd you think I got into this business?"

He shook his head. "I never gave it much thought."

"She took right good care of me, too. I didn't start entertainin' gentlemen in the upstairs rooms until I was fourteen. The lady who owned the house was after her to start me out when I was twelve, 'cause she was already gettin' some high-priced offers from the gentlemen for my favors. But Mama wouldn't hear of it. Said it wasn't proper."

All Jack could do was nod and say, "I expect not." He thought hard and asked, "How old are you now?"

Silky laughed again. "Didn't anybody ever tell you you're not supposed to ask a lady her age, Jack?"

Fear shot through him. He had mortally offended her. He said hurriedly, "No, ma'am, they never did. I'm sure sorry—"

"Oh, hell, don't worry about it," she said lightly. "I ain't a lady anyway, so I guess it don't matter. I'm eighteen. Been at it four years."

"It must be . . . awful."

"You think so?" She frowned. "Not so's you'd notice, at least not that I've seen. Most of the men I've been with have treated me pretty nice, to tell you the truth. Almost like they're a mite scared of me, like I might break or something if they handle me too rough. It does get a little tiresome from time to time, but shoot, any job does, I expect. What do you do?"

"Oh . . . a little of this and a little of that, I suppose," he said with a shrug. "I've cowboyed some, drove a freight wagon for a while, and right now I'm on my way to the Black Hills to do some prospectin'."

"Are you gonna strike it rich?" she asked with a smile.

"Well, I don't know. I sure hope so."

"When you do, are you gonna go back wherever you came from and marry your childhood sweetheart?"

"I . . . I don't reckon I have one. I never liked gals much when I was a boy."

She reached out and rested a hand on his arm. "You like girls now, though, don't you, Jack?"

"Oh, yes, ma'am," he answered as he leaned closer to her. "I like 'em just fine."

After that it just seemed natural for him to kiss her. He put a hand on her shoulder and bent his head toward hers, and she tipped her head back and looked up into his eyes, the shadows of evening on her face, and then her lips were warm against his and he had never tasted anything sweeter in his life.

Silky moved closer to him and molded her body to his. Jack put both arms around her and held her tightly. He tried not to think about the hundreds, maybe thousands, of men she had kissed in the past. Or maybe she *didn't* kiss them, he told himself. Maybe they had their way with her body, but she kept her kisses to herself and bestowed them only on somebody who actually meant something to her. That sounded to him like something that a girl in her line of work might do. That meant she might really like him, and as he kissed her and the shadows thickened and the dusk turned to night around them and the stars shone overhead in the big Western sky, he told himself it must be that way until at last he believed it with all his heart.

Finally she whispered, "Jack, do you want to . . ."

"Not yet," he heard himself saying, and he was sort of surprised at the answer even though it was a truthful one. "I'd rather just kiss you some more, and hug you, if that's all right."

"Well, sure, honey, that's fine. You just go right ahead and kiss and hug me all you want."

Jack lost track of time again. All he knew was that it was night and there was a warm breeze blowing over the prairie and he had the most beautiful girl in the world in his arms. What else did he need to know?

With the taste and smell and feel of Silky Jen filling his

senses, it's no wonder that he didn't hear or see anyone else approaching. He didn't know anybody else was around until a big hand fell heavily on his shoulder and jerked him back. "What the hell are you doin' with my gal?" a deep, angry voice rumbled.

Being pulled around sharply like that had thrown Jack off balance. He caught himself before he could fall and looked up to see a tall, burly figure looming in front of him. "Who're you?" he demanded.

"They call me Cougar," the man said. "But that ain't any o' your business. Now get the hell outta here so's I can see my gal."

"She's not your gal," Jack snapped. "She's not anybody's gal." *Unless she was his.* That thought was already in his head.

Cougar gave a gravelly laugh. "She's anybody's gal who's got the money, you damn fool, and right now that's me." He turned to Silky and held up something that glittered dully in the moonlight as he went on. "Got me a gold piece right here, gal. You want to bite it and make sure it's good, so we can get down to some fuckin'?"

That was all Jack could stand. He hauled off and hit Cougar in the mouth as hard as he could.

Jack didn't weigh nearly as much as the bigger man, but he had worked hard all his life and possessed plenty of wiry strength. His fist caught Cougar flush on the mouth and knocked the man back a couple of steps. Cougar gave a shake of his head that made black drops of blood fly from his lips.

"Oh, dear Lord," Silky said in a half whisper. "You shouldn't have done that, Jack."

"I'll kill you, you bastard!" Cougar bellowed in a voice loud enough to carry all over the wagon camp and the adjoining fort. With an inarticulate shout, he lunged at Jack, his arms outstretched.

Jack knew if those massive hands ever closed around his throat, he was done for. He darted quickly to the side and hooked a punch into Cougar's midsection as the man stumbled past him. It was like hitting the trunk of an oak tree. Jack almost yelped from the pain that shot through his hand. He moved quickly a few steps away as Cougar caught himself and swung around for another charge.

Cougar was still yelling. It seemed that the only way he knew how to fight was at the top of his lungs. That brought a lot of attention from the occupants of the wagons and everyone who was still out and about in the fort. As people began to run up to see what all the commotion was about, Cougar came at Jack swinging sweeping roundhouse blows, any one of which might have knocked Jack's head off his shoulders if it had connected. Desperately, Jack ducked the punches and peppered Cougar with blows of his own, but none of them did any good, even the ones that landed solidly. Cougar just ignored them.

Jack was vaguely aware that Silky Jen was screaming for them to stop fighting. He would be glad to, he thought. Cougar was the one being damned stubborn about it. Clearly, the big man didn't mean to stop until he had beaten Jack to within an inch of his life . . . or beyond.

Cougar was pretty quick for such a hulking bruiser, too, but Jack was faster and might have been able to avoid him until Cougar had worn himself out with those wild punches. Unfortunately, luck was against him, and his foot slipped on a pile of horse droppings. "Shit!" Jack yelled, appropriately enough, as he felt himself falling. Cougar roared in triumph and pounced like his namesake.

A tremendous weight slammed down on top of Jack, knocking the breath out of him and pinning him to the ground. His head spun as he tried to drag some precious air back into his lungs, but the weight pressing down on him kept him from being able to do so. Red sparks began to dance around on the edges of his vision.

Then what he had feared all along happened, as Cougar's hamlike hands latched on to Jack's neck. The fingers clamped down like iron bands and began to squeeze.

The lack of air got even more desperate, and those red sparks turned into bright pinwheels of flame.

So this was what it was like to die, Jack thought.

And all he had done was kiss the girl. He hadn't even—

Darkness closed down, ending that thought.

Twelve

HICKOK and his companions strode across the parade ground, Charley Anderson hurrying a little ahead and motioning impatiently for them to come on. Bill heard a lot of yelling over by the wagons. The commotion had to be because of the fight Charley Anderson had told them about. Evidently Jack was clashing with some huge bruiser from the wagon train who bid fair to kill him.

If that proved to be the case once he had sized up the situation, Bill knew he would have to intervene, even though Jack might resent him for it later. A frontiersman put great stock in fighting his own battles, and some of them would rather die than accept help. Bill wasn't going to stand by and watch, though, while a friend was beaten to death.

A stocky figure came hurrying up out of the dark, and a familiar rough voice said, "Howdy, Bill! Where you goin'?"

"To see what all that ruckus is about," Hickok replied as Calamity Jane fell in step beside him. A pungent scent wafted from her, a mixture of whiskey, tobacco, unwashed flesh. and old, greasy buckskins.

"Oh, that ain't nothin'," Calamity said. "Just a couple o' fellas squabblin' over some whore. Prob'ly fightin' over which one gets to fuck her first. I took a gander at it, but decided it weren't interestin' enough to stick around and watch."

"One of the combatants is a friend of mine," Bill explained.

"Yeah? Come to think of it, I think you're right. That kid with the white eyebrow. I recollect him now. Saw him with you yesterday when y'all came in. Hell, if he ain't dead already, he soon will be. That's ol' Cougar he's tusslin' with."

Bill walked a little faster. He had no idea who Cougar was, but he trusted Calamity's assessment of the man's brawling abilities. She had been around the frontier long enough to know who to steer clear of.

"Say, Bill," Calamity went on, a rough purr in her voice. "You wanna come by my wagon later? I can be real hospitable, if you know what I mean."

"I doubt that my wife would be very happy if I were to do that," Hickok said.

"Well, whereabouts is she?"

"With her family back in Cincinnati."

"Then she'd never know about it, would she? Unless somebody was damn foolish enough to tell her."

"I appreciate the offer," Bill said, "but I have to deal with this altercation first."

Calamity Jane put her hand on the butt of the big revolver holstered at her waist. "Hell, if it'll speed things up, I'd be glad to ventilate both those varmints for you, Bill. That'll stop 'em from fightin' right quicklike."

"No, I don't want them killed—" Hickok began, but then he stopped and drew a deep breath. "Just let me handle this, all right?" he said with a note of exasperation creeping into his voice.

"Sure, sure. No need to get all touchy about it."

Hickok heard a chuckle, and glanced over to see a grin on Colorado Charley's face. He might have made some comment, but then they reached the wagons and moved quickly to where a large ring of spectators surrounded the two combatants. Some of the bystanders carried torches and lamps, which cast a garish, flickering red light over the scene, as if Fort Laramie had somehow become an adjunct of Hell.

"Step aside!" Hickok boomed in the voice that had dispersed more than one mob back in the days when he'd worn a lawman's badge. "Step aside, I say!"

The crowd parted like the Red Sea before Moses, and Hickok strode through the opening just as proud and upright as that old prophet. In the gaudy light, he saw White-Eye Jack Anderson lying on the ground, pinned beneath a ginger-bearded behemoth in buckskin trousers and a homespun shirt. The big man, who had to be Cougar, had his hands around Jack's throat and was attempting to strangle the life out of him. A few feet away, the pretty young whore called Silky Jen danced around nervously making scared faces, clearly wanting to interfere but at the same time afraid to do so.

"Stop that!" Hickok ordered Cougar, but the big man ignored him. Hickok saw that Jack was still flailing around, but his struggles seemed to be weakening. His eyes bulged from his head and his tongue protruded from his mouth.

For a second, Hickok thought about just shooting Cougar. That would put an end to the struggle in a hurry, as Calamity Jane had suggested. That would be cold-blooded murder, however, and Bill had never before stooped to such a tactic, even in defense of a friend. Tonight he wore a more sober outfit than usual, a buckskin jacket over whipcord trousers and a white shirt. Instead of the red silk sash around his waist where he often carried his Colts, he wore a gun belt with a holster on each hip, turned so that the revolvers were reversed and carried butt-forward. With a twist of his wrist, Hickok smoothly palmed out the right-hand gun as he stepped forward.

The Colt rose and fell, and when it descended the barrel slammed hard against Cougar's skull behind his left ear.

No one was more skilled than Wild Bill Hickok at buffaloing a man like that. But Cougar's head was so hard that Bill had to hit him twice before the big man slumped down on top of Jack, unconscious at last.

Hickok holstered the gun and bent down, calling to Colorado Charley and Steve, "Give me a hand here, boys."

Cougar's fingers were still locked around Jack's throat. It took the combined efforts of Hickok and the Utter brothers to pry them loose. Jack immediately began to gasp for air like a drowning man who has come unexpectedly to the surface. Hickok, Colorado Charley, and Steve rolled Cougar's deadweight to the side while Charley Anderson got hold of his brother under the arms and dragged him off a few feet. Silky Jen hovered over Jack, saying, "Don't be dead, please don't be dead."

Hickok straightened and told her, "The boy's not dead, miss. That fellow may have squeezed most of the life out of him, but not all."

Silky and Charley Anderson knelt beside Jack, lifted him into a sitting position, and held him while he tried to catch his breath. Charley pounded him some on the back, as if that would help somehow. Hickok kept an eye on Cougar, who was already starting to stir. The man was a monster, Hickok thought. Those blows to the head should have left him unconscious for a quarter hour, anyway.

"Hey, mister!" an angry voice challenged from the ring of spectators. "What gives you the right to wallop our pard like that?"

Hickok turned leisurely, nothing about his casual stance betraying his suddenly heightened sense of alertness. Half a dozen roughly dressed, tough-looking men had stepped forward from the crowd. They regarded Hickok and his companions with glares and a belligerent air.

Hickok inclined his head toward Cougar, who continued to move a little and let out a low groan. "I take it you mean this man here?"

"Damn right I do," said the spokesman for the group. He had a sandy beard and wore buckskins. A battered old beaver hat with an eagle feather stuck in the band perched on his tangled thatch of hair. "You didn't have no right to buffalo him like that."

"Your friend was doing his level best to kill my friend," Hickok said, somewhat annoyed by the fact that he was being called on to explain his actions. He was accustomed to doing as he saw fit. "I interceded to save the boy's life. Your friend is lucky I didn't just shoot him like the mad dog he clearly is. I promise you, I considered it."

"If you'd'a shot ol' Cougar, you woulda regretted it, mister." Beaver Hat rested his hand on the butt of the gun at his waist. "We're a mighty salty bunch, and we don't mind provin' it."

Calamity Jane let out a raucous laugh. "You have any idea who you're talkin' to, you stupid asshole?"

Beaver Hat snarled at her. "Shut up, you drunken slut. I know all about you."

Hickok stiffened and moved forward a little. He wished the light was better, but he put that out of his mind and said, "No, you don't know everything about her. You obviously aren't aware that she numbers Bill Hickok among her friends."

Beaver Hat's breath hissed between his teeth. "Hickok?" he repeated. "You're Hickok?"

Calamity Jane stepped forward and jabbed a finger into his chest, causing him to wince from the pain of it. "Fuckin' right he's Wild Bill Hickok! Why do you think I called you a stupid asshole?"

"Calam, you might want to step back," Hickok said quietly. His voice carried easily despite the fact that he hadn't raised it. Silence had fallen over the crowd. Hickok went on. "You're perilously close to being in the line of fire, and I'd hate for you to be wounded if these fellows decide to open the ball."

Grinning, Calamity moved back. She waved a hand and said, "You boys go right ahead. Don't mind me."

Beaver Hat raised his left hand and drew the back of it nervously across his mouth. "Shit, we didn't know you was

Wild Bill Hickok," he said. The men with him muttered agreement and nodded. Their attitude of belligerence had vanished.

Except for one man who said, "Hell, I hear he can't see no more. Think about it, Yoder! You might could be the man who gunned down Wild Bill Hickok!"

"Shut up," Beaver Hat growled with an angry glance over his shoulder. He looked at Bill again and went on. "Sorry, Mr. Hickok. We'll just pick up ol' Cougar and go on back to our wagons. No need for more trouble."

"No need at all," Hickok agreed. Some streak of contrariness made him add, "I'm curious, however. Are you backing down because my argument convinced you that I'm in the right, or because you're afraid that I might kill you?"

Behind him, Colorado Charley said softly, "Bill, there's no need to push it—"

Hickok ignored him and, still facing Beaver Hat, snapped, "Well, which is it? Reason or fear?"

Everyone was quiet now. Cougar had regained consciousness but lay silent on the ground. Jack Anderson sat nearby, flanked by his brother and Silky. The crowd looked on, nerves taut. Nobody wanted to take a breath.

"You, uh, convinced me you were right, Mr. Hickok," Beaver Hat finally said. "Cougar didn't have no right to jump that kid and try to choke him like that."

"So it won't happen again, will it?" Hickok asked.

"No, sir, it sure won't."

Hickok nodded. "All right. Take your friend and get out of here."

Several of the men stepped forward and helped Cougar to his feet. As they led him away, he slowly shook his head like he was still dazed. He went peacefully enough, though.

Jack stood up with the help of his brother and Silky. Steve Utter went over to join them as the crowd began to break up. Colorado Charley and Calamity Jane stayed with Hickok, and Colorado Charley said, "That was an ugly business, Bill."

"You mean the fight? Yes, it was. Young Jack almost met his Maker, I'd say."

"I'm talkin' about the way you humiliated that fella, and you know it," Colorado Charley snapped. "Everybody could see he backed down because he was afraid you'd kill him. You didn't have to make him say it."

"I wanted to be sure he and his friends understood that I would tolerate no further harassment of White-Eye Jack," Hickok said coldly.

"You sure that was the only reason? You didn't make him crawfish a little just because you knew you could?"

Calamity said, "How come you're givin' Bill so much trouble, Charley? You know he's right. He's Wild Bill Hickok!"

Hickok and Colorado Charley looked at each other for a long moment, and then Hickok turned to the woman and said, "I appreciate the confidence, Calam. Now, if this little shindig is over, I think I'll turn in."

"Got a nice soft pallet in my wagon," Calamity offered, unwilling to give up on her dreams.

"I'll have to pass on that generous offer. You see . . ." Hickok leaned closer to her and said in a confidential tone, "I snore."

With that, he stalked off before Calamity could say anything else. But she called after him, "I knew we was friends! You said it yourself, Bill!"

Indeed he had, he thought. And he was a bit surprised to find that it was true.

JACK found himself sitting on a wagon tongue with Silky Jen, just like the night before. She was close beside him, so close that her hip pressed against his and he felt the warmth of it through their clothing. She put a hand on his throat and said, "You poor baby. Are you going to be all right?"

He nodded, and even though it hurt his throat when he spoke, he managed to say in a rasping voice, "I reckon. I don't feel like my lungs are gonna explode anymore."

"I couldn't believe it when Cougar did that. The bastard. If I'd'a had a gun, I would've shot him. I sure would have."

"Then you'd have been in trouble. I'm glad you didn't."

She leaned her shoulder against his, and he felt a shiver go through her. "I thought there was gonna be a gunfight. That Wild Bill . . . well, I just never saw anybody like him before. So big and handsome and dangerous-lookin'."

Well, that was it, Jack thought. Silky was all a-swoon over Wild Bill, so she wouldn't be interested in him anymore. She would probably still bed him if he paid her, but that made him just the same as any other man in this group bound for Deadwood. He had hoped to be something more than that to her. But it had been a crazy hope, he told himself.

His brother Charley had wandered off after being convinced that Jack was all right. He and Silky were alone. The moon and the stars still shone overhead, and the prairie breeze was just as soft and warm as it had been earlier. But everything had changed anyway, Jack thought. He had gotten in a fight and nearly gotten himself killed defending the honor of a whore. A whore! How stupid was that? He had seen red when Cougar started talking about fucking her, but that was exactly what she did. She let men fuck her for money.

She rested her head on his shoulder. He couldn't help but notice how good her hair smelled, but he tried not to think about it. "Of course," she went on, "you're mighty handsome, too, Jack."

"No, I'm not," he said. "I look like some sort of damn freak with this white eyebrow."

She sat up and said, "That's not true. You look just fine."

"You don't have to lie to me. I know you say nice things to all the men you're with. Tell 'em how big and strong they are, and how good they are at what they're doin', but it's just whore talk."

"That's not the way I was talking to you," she said, her voice small with hurt. He heard it, but couldn't seem to do anything about it. He couldn't stop himself.

"Well, we might as well go do it," he said. "I ain't hurt so bad I can't do what I need to do. And I've got money. How much you want?"

Silky shook her head. "I don't know . . . I wasn't plannin' to . . . I never figured on . . ."

"It's simple enough," Jack said. "How much do I have to pay you to fuck you?"

She stared at him for a long moment, and then she breathed, "You son of a bitch."

"Is that any way to talk to somebody who fought for you, who nearly got himself killed for you?"

She pulled away from him, sliding carefully along the wagon tongue. "If you're upset about what happened, I don't blame you," she said. "It must shake a man to nearly die like that. But you don't have to take it out on me."

"I'm not takin' anything out on you. I'm just askin' a simple question—"

"Five thousand dollars," she said.

He stared at her. "What?"

"Five thousand dollars," she repeated. "That's what it'll cost you to fuck me."

"I don't have no five thousand dollars!"

"Too bad. Because the price just went up to ten thousand."

"You think I won't get it? You think I won't strike it rich in Deadwood?" His hands came up and gripped her shoulders. "I will! I'll have ten thousand dollars one of these days."

"Good," she said coldly. "You come see me then. Until then, I'll thank you to let go of me."

His fingers straightened and he lifted his hands sharply from her shoulders. "Fine." Looking away from her, he muttered, "I never thought a whore'd get her feelin's hurt so easy."

She stood up and pulled the lace shawl tighter around her shoulders. "You just never thought a whore would have feelings," she said. Then she turned and walked off, disappearing into the shadows around the wagons.

Jack sat there, wondering what the hell had happened, wondering why he had said those hurtful things to her. She was right: She didn't deserve to be treated like that, no matter what she did for a living. Bill Hickok, that gallant son of a bitch, never would have treated a woman like that. Bill was even polite to Calamity Jane, and you could just barely call her a woman.

Jack touched his aching throat. Maybe Silky was right about something else. Maybe he was just so shook up by nearly dying that he hadn't been capable of thinking straight for a few minutes there.

Whatever the reason for his behavior, he knew that what she might have been starting to feel for him was gone now, and it would never come back. Whatever chance he might have had with her was gone just as surely. Now he was just the same to her as any other man.

It was going to be a long way to Deadwood, he thought with a sigh. A hell of a long way.

Thirteen

~~

"**D**IP your pan like this," Dan Ryan said as he squatted in the chilly waters of Deadwood Creek, near the edge of the stream where the water was shallow and the bottom was mostly flat. He scooped the pan made of sheet iron into the streambed and lifted it half full of water, gravel, and dirt. "Now you start to swirl the water like this. Not too hard, or you'll slosh out too much at a time."

Bellamy Bridges nodded as he knelt on the bank and watched Dan panning for gold. "I thought you were a soldier," he commented. "How did you learn all this?"

"Some of the old-timers in the Seventh had done some prospecting when they were younger," Dan explained. "Most of 'em in Colorado during the boom there, but I wouldn't be surprised if some of them were out in California back in forty-nine. They showed me how, when we were up here in the Black Hills a couple of years ago."

Dan had gotten in quite a bit of practice during that trip, and while he didn't consider himself an expert gold-panner, he knew he was doing it well enough to find the color if it was here.

Patiently, he swirled the water in the pan, moving just his wrists as he did so. With each swirl, a little water lapped over the sides of the pan. The motion made it pick up the sand and the lighter gravel, and that washed away with the water, leaving behind the heavier gravel.

"Do you think you'll find a gold nugget in there?" Bellamy asked, unable to keep the excitement out of his voice.

Dan suppressed the urge to laugh at the young man. Bellamy's inexperience was showing through—but so was his enthusiasm. He would need that, because prospecting was a hard, tedious business. A man needed plenty of patience and determination to make any kind of success at it.

"I suppose it's possible you might scoop up a nugget in a pan like this, but the odds are mighty high against it. What you're a lot more likely to find, once everything else is washed away, are little flecks of gold, what they call gold dust. Some of them are so fine, they mighty near *are* dust."

For nearly ten minutes, Dan washed the gravel in the pan, carefully tilting the pan a little more each time he swirled it, until all the sand and the lighter stuff was gone, along with most of the water.

"What you've got left in here now is called the drag," he told Bellamy. "Once you're down to this point, you're ready to start lookin' for gold."

Bellamy leaned forward eagerly. "How do you do that?"

"Like this." Dan flicked his wrist, as if he were going to toss the pan across the creek. Before doing that, he had gotten the drag concentrated on the side of the pan closest to him, so that when he made the sharp motion, the residue left from the washing spread out across the bottom of the pan. He turned and held the pan toward Bellamy. "Take a look."

Bellamy perched on the very edge of the bank and peered intently into the pan. His eyes widened and he pointed. "Is that . . . is that . . ."

Dan nodded. "There's your first sign of color, kid. I don't reckon you'll ever forget it."

The sun overhead reflected on the tiny bits of gold mixed in with the gravel. Dan set the pan on the bank and took out his clasp knife, along with a small glass bottle that had a cork stopper. He opened the knife and carefully used the very tip of the blade to pick out the specks of gold. One at a time, he transferred them to the bottle, and when he was done he put the cork back in the neck and made sure it was tightly closed. A dozen tiny pieces of gold lay on the bottom of the bottle.

"My God," said Bellamy. "Are we rich?"

This time Dan couldn't keep from laughing. "If we find that much color in every pan we wash and keep it up for a few months, we'll be in pretty good shape. I don't know that we'd be rich, but we'd be doing all right."

Bellamy's face fell a little. "But we won't find this much in every pan, will we?"

"Almost surely, we won't. Too many times, we'll come up empty." Dan waved a hand at their claim, encompassing three hundred feet up and down the creek and stretching from rimrock to rimrock. "But this isn't all. That gold dust came from somewhere. Probably the lode is way upstream somewhere and we'll never see it. But there could be ore around here, too, and we'll look for it, you can count on that. That's where you'll find your nuggets, and the money adds up a hell of a lot faster when you start talkin' about things like that."

"But I'm sure the man who owned this claim before we bought it must have looked for ore like that. Wouldn't he have found it?"

"Maybe, maybe not. Finding gold is a tricky business. You can look for months and not find a blessed thing, and then you trip over a nugget the size of your fist when you're just walkin' along, not even thinkin' about it."

"Do things like that really happen?"

"Been known to," Dan said with a nod. "Or so I've heard. No guarantee it'll happen to us, though. About the only thing you can really count on in life is hard work, and plenty of it."

Despite his cautious words, however, he felt the excitement inside him. He tried to keep it under control, tried not to let it bubble up like one of those geysers over in Wyoming Territory, in the Yellowstone country. But it was there, and he knew in his gut that this was a good claim, even though it had never paid off that much for the previous owner. As soon as he and Bellamy had ridden out here and walked the claim, Dan had known this was meant to be. That was why he hadn't hesitated in making a good offer. He didn't want anybody else to snatch this claim out from under them while he was trying to make up his mind.

For one thing, the geography was right. Upstream, near the upper end of the claim, the creek bed narrowed, making the water flow faster. But down here where Dan and Bellamy were, the stream widened out again and slowed down, and Dan knew that was a prime situation for gold dust to be deposited in the bed. Gold was heavy, so it took a greater force of water to carry it along. Any place where a stream abruptly slowed down, the gold in it would settle rapidly. Also, the streambed was pretty sandy here, which made for easier and more efficient washing. After demonstrating to Bellamy how to pan for gold, Dan started looking around and trying to decide whether it would be better to skip panning altogether and go straight to rocking. That would require building a cradle, a big apparatus that required two men to operate. But there were two of them, he reminded himself, and with a cradle you could wash a lot more sand in a shorter period of time.

Better not get ahead of himself, he thought. He wouldn't want to go to the time and trouble to build a cradle here unless he was sure there was plenty of color in the creek. They would pan it for a while, and if the color held up, then they could consider expanding their operation.

"What are you thinking about, Dan?" Bellamy asked.

A smile stretched across Dan's weathered face. "Why, about how we're gonna get rich, of course."

* * *

THEY had left their wagon parked near the camp with several of the others. The rest of the party had spread out to their claims up and down the gulches. The horses from the wagon team weren't the sort of mounts that Dan was used to from his days in the Seventh Cavalry, but they would do. He and Bellamy rode back into the settlement, Dan explaining along the way that they could move the wagon out to the claim the next day.

"I thought maybe we'd stay here in town," Bellamy said with a frown as they approached Deadwood.

"We can't leave our wagon and all our gear here untended," Dan said. "It was all right today because some of the other fellas were still here to keep an eye on it for us, but in a day or two, they'll all be gone. We'll need to keep our possibles with us."

"I just thought it would be nice to work the claim during the day but come back to civilization at night."

As an outpost of civilization, Deadwood was anything but a sterling example, Dan thought, but he supposed it was the closest they would find in the Black Hills. Dan knew Bellamy wasn't interested in civilization as much as he was in something else. Something soft and warm and pretty named Carla.

"The claim's only half a mile or so up the gulch," Dan pointed out. "You can ride into town any time you want. Hell, you could walk in without any trouble."

"Well, that's true. And I suppose it *would* be safer to have our gear with us."

Dan nodded. "That's right. Anyway, you can't afford to get too distracted, Bellamy. Hunting for gold takes lots of time and energy. You'll probably be too tired most nights to even think about coming into town."

"I wouldn't count on that," Bellamy said.

Dan suppressed a sigh. He remembered what it was like to be young and full of piss and vinegar. Things built up quickly inside a young man until he felt like he was going to explode. That was especially true when there was a girl involved. It was going to be a job in itself just keeping Bellamy's mind on why they had come here and what they were supposed to be doing.

"The General wanted to know what we thought of the claim once we'd had a chance to look it over better," Dan said as they reached the wagon and dismounted. "Reckon I'll walk down to the Grand Central and see if he's around, maybe get some supper while I'm there."

"All right," Bellamy said. "I don't know yet what I'll do."

Dan would have been willing to venture a guess. He figured that before the evening was over, Bellamy would be back at Miss Laurette's Academy for Young Ladies. Just in case, though, he said, "Better steer clear of the Gem."

A visible shudder ran through Bellamy. "You don't have to worry about that, Dan. I'm not going near that place. I'm still not convinced that fellow Dority didn't dope me the other night."

"No need to take a chance," Dan said, even though he didn't believe Dority had slipped anything in Bellamy's drink. As far as he could tell, the young man just couldn't handle that strong rotgut.

Before he headed for the Grand Central, Dan unsaddled and rubbed down the horses he and Bellamy had ridden. Bellamy looked on, not offering to help, which annoyed Dan a little. The youngster's thoughts were too full of that gal. Nothing else even occurred to him. It had taken the sight of gold itself to break through the wall that lust had put up around Bellamy's brain.

Dan washed his face from a basin on the lowered tailgate of the wagon, but he didn't shave or change shirts, figuring he was clean enough to talk to the old General. With a wave to Bellamy, he started walking along Main Street.

He didn't pay any attention to the babble of the Chinese quarter or the music and laughter of the Badlands, which was already growing raucous despite the early hour. A crudely lettered sign in front of the Bella Union Theater advertised that Banjo Dick Brown would be performing there that night. The Bella Union was a slightly higher-class dive than the Gem, at least making a pretense of offering real entertainment other than booze, gambling, and "pretty waiter girls" whose favors were for sale. When you got down to it, though, it was still a whorehouse, just like the Gem and Miss Laurette's and a dozen other places on this end of town.

Dan had been a soldier for quite a few years. He had nothing against whorehouses. If they were evil—and he wasn't fully convinced of that—they were a necessary evil. He had visited quite a few of them himself, in earlier years. But he no longer had any real interest in bedding soiled doves. A man got to the point where he thought more about settling down and finding himself a wife. That wasn't likely to happen here in Deadwood, of course, where nearly all of the respectable women were already married. He had known men who'd taken whores out of the houses where they worked and married them, and they seemed to wind up happy most of the time. That wasn't for him, though, and Dan knew it.

He left the Badlands behind and approached the Grand Central Hotel. As he passed the alley beside the hotel, something caught his eye, and he stopped. As he looked along the narrow space, he saw someone standing at the rear of the building. The light was growing worse as dusk settled down, but he thought the figure was a woman.

Something took Dan's steps along the alley. As he came nearer, the woman heard him and turned toward him. The darkness of her face instantly told him she was Lou Marchbanks.

Dan stopped and lifted a hand to the brim of his hat. "Evenin', ma'am," he said.

"Mr. Ryan," she returned. "What are you doing back here?"

"I might ask you the same thing, ma'am. But since you inquired first . . . I saw you and thought that maybe something was wrong. The way you were just standing out here, I mean."

She smiled. "I'm just taking the evening air," she explained. "Been cooking all afternoon, getting ready for supper, and that kitchen gets mighty hot."

"Yes, ma'am, I expect so. Now that you mention it, you do have a certain glow about you."

"Mr. Ryan, are you trying to compliment me . . . or are you just saying that I'm sweatin' like a nigger?"

Dan felt flustered suddenly. He hadn't meant any offense, and he hastened to say so. "I'm sorry, Miss Marchbanks. I sure wouldn't insult you. I never would."

"You know, I reckon you're the only white man in Deadwood who don't call me Aunt Lou, whether you know me or not."

"Why, I wouldn't be so forward."

"Why not?"

The blunt question caught him by surprise. "Well," he said, "I just wouldn't. Doesn't seem proper."

"Where I come from, a white man treats a nigger any way he wants and don't worry about proper. Especially a nigger woman."

"We come from different places," Dan said stiffly.

"Yes. I reckon we do." She started to turn toward the back door of the hotel, but then she paused and said, "Your given name, it's Daniel?"

"Yes, ma'am, but I go by Dan."

"Mine's Lucretia. You can call me Lou. Just not Aunt Lou. I ain't your aunt, and I sure as hell didn't raise you."

"No, ma'am. I reckon you and me, we're about the same age, come to think on it."

"More than likely." She reached for the door. "I got to get back to it. Good evenin', Dan."

"Good evenin' to you, too . . . Lou." It was a bit more difficult for him to use her first name than it was for her to call him by his. He didn't know why that was, unless it was because of his natural reticence around women.

And there was no question that he regarded Lou March-banks as a woman first, and then an African. He realized that was a mighty odd way for a white man to be thinking, but there it was and there was nothing he could do about it.

He went back along the alley to Main Street, stepped up onto the Grand Central's porch, and walked into the hotel. As he expected, he found General Dawson in the dining room. The General didn't have any family in Deadwood, and when he wasn't working he spent a lot of his time here at the hotel, visiting with friends like Mr. Merrick, the owner of the newspaper.

Dawson raised a hand in greeting. "Hello, Dan," he said as he motioned for the ex-sergeant to come over. As Dan took a seat at the table, the General went on. "Did you have a chance to do some panning on your new claim?"

"I sure did. And just like you said, General, there's color there. I'm thinkin' there might be more than the fella who had it before us believed there was."

The General nodded. "I was hoping that would turn out to be the case. Deadwood needs solid, reliable citizens, and who could display those qualities more than a former cavalry sergeant?"

Dan grinned and chuckled. He said, "Well, to hear some of my old commanding officers tell it, I never was all that solid and reliable."

"Nonsense," the General said with a snort. "I'd put myself up against anyone as a judge of character, and my guess is that your superior officers relied on you constantly to keep things running smoothly in the outfit. George Custer was a fool to let you leave the Army." In an undertone, he added, "Of course, Custer is a fool in many other ways, too."

"Bein' a former member of the Seventh, I'll pretend I didn't hear that, General," Dan said stiffly.

Dawson waved a hand. "Politics, my boy, politics. As bad in the Army as anywhere else, I sometimes think. Why don't you have some supper and tell me all about your claim?"

"I'd be honored to do that, sir."

"Where's that young partner of yours this evening?" the General asked.

"I'm not sure," Dan said, slowly shaking his head. "I reckon I could make a pretty good guess where he is right about now . . . but I'm not sure I want to."

Fourteen

BELLAMY slicked himself up as best he could. He even put on clean clothes. That killed some of the time, but he still had to just sit and wait impatiently for night to fall. He supposed he could have gone on down to Miss Laurette's, but it seemed wrong somehow to enter a place like that while there was still light in the sky. Darkness was better if a person was going to be sinning.

God sees you, boy. You cannot hide your sin and your shame. His heavenly light reaches into the dark places, into the darkest place of all, the heart of a sinner.

Bellamy could hear his father's voice. And it wasn't like Thaddeus Bridges was even a preacher. He was just a farmer. But God and the Devil, Heaven and Hell, good and evil, were always in the forefront of his mind, and even when he and Bellamy had been plowing the fields or pulling up stumps or digging a well, the talk about sin and shame had gone on and on. His mother had been the same way.

Growing up on a farm, Bellamy had figured out at an

early age just what had to happen between male and female to result in a baby. The way his folks harped about how evil such things were, it was a wonder he'd ever been born, he had thought more than once. He might have figured that his pa had just rolled over wrong in the bed one night, but he had younger brothers and sisters. That meant that his parents must have sinned quite a bit, because he knew not every time resulted in a pregnancy.

That made him worry that he might have gotten Carla in the family way, but surely not. Girls like her—girls who worked in places like that—they had to have some way to keep the seed from falling in a fertile field. Otherwise they'd be popping out babies right and left and whorehouses would be full of squalling brats.

Bellamy closed his eyes and scrubbed his hands over his face. There were some things he just didn't even want to think about.

Maybe what he ought to do, he told himself, was to climb up in the wagon and dig through his gear until he found the Bible he had brought along. He could light a candle and sit and read the Good Book for a while instead of going down to that so-called Academy for Young Ladies. That was the way to deal with temptation.

But then the sun dipped below Forest Hill to the west, and darkness descended on Deadwood Gulch, and almost before he knew what was happening, Bellamy found his footsteps leading him eagerly toward Miss Laurette's.

As usual, the street was clogged with people on foot and on horseback. Bellamy felt like every single one of them was watching him as he made his way toward his destination. It was bad enough to have the disapproving Eyes of God on him; did everybody else in Deadwood have to be minding his business, too?

Of course, they weren't watching him. Logically, he knew that. Everyone was just going on about his or her own business and not paying the least bit of attention to a nervous young man on his way to a rendezvous with sin.

A hand suddenly clamped down strongly on his arm, pulling him to a stop. Bellamy let out a yell and twisted around, ready to fight if he was about to be robbed.

Instead of a ruffian bent on thievery, Bellamy saw the thin, bearded face of the preacher who had greeted him and Dan when they first rolled into Deadwood. "Peace, brother, peace," the man said, letting go of Bellamy's arm and holding up his hands as if to ward off a blow.

"What do you want?" Bellamy asked.

"Do you remember me, my young friend? Preacher Smith?"

"Yeah. Yeah, I remember you. What do you want?" Bellamy asked again.

"I saw you coming along the street. . . ."

And I know what you were going to do. Bellamy finished the thought. He had been right: Someone had been watching him. And a preacher, a man of God, at that. The sense of shame that went through Bellamy was almost overwhelming.

"Will you help me?" Smith reached out and clasped Bellamy's right hand with both of his.

"H-help you do what, Preacher?"

"I need to move this box." Smith let go of Bellamy's hand and pointed to a crate of some sort that stood at the edge of the street. "It's not all that heavy, but it's awkward for one man to handle by himself."

Bellamy relaxed a little. The preacher didn't know what he had been about to do after all. He just needed a hand with a chore.

"Of course, Preacher. I'll be glad to help you."

"The Lord bless you, brother."

Bellamy went over to the crate with Smith, and together they hefted it. Smith was right: The crate wasn't heavy. The two of them were able to handle it without much trouble. Smith backed down the street, saying, "Let me go first. I know where I'm going with it."

Bellamy concentrated on what he was doing instead of

where he was. So when Smith said, "This is it," and started to lower his side of the crate, Bellamy did, too. Then surprise went through him as he straightened, looked up, and saw that they were in front of the Gem Theater. The Bella Union was right across the street, with Miss Laurette's next to it.

"Thank you, brother," Smith said with a smile. While Bellamy stood there open-mouthed, the preacher climbed up onto the crate, his long legs making the task an easy one. He reached under his coat, took out a small black book that could only be a Bible, and spread his arms. "Hallelujah!" he shouted in a voice that cut through the hubbub of Deadwood's Main Street. "Brothers and sisters! Gather ye all around and attend ye to the Word of the Lord!"

Not everyone paid any attention to Smith, but as he continued to exhort them at the top of his lungs, more and more people gathered in front of the crate. Bellamy edged away, slipping through the crowd that was forming.

Smith launched into his sermon when he judged that he had enough of a congregation. "My friends, just as Our Lord and Savior drove the moneylenders from the holy temple, we must drive the purveyors of wickedness and debauchery from the streets of Deadwood!" He waved his Bible toward the front of the Gem, just to make sure that everyone knew who he was talking about. "These dens of iniquity must be closed and shuttered, boarded up so that their evil may no longer spill out and contaminate the souls of the good citizens who have come here to make Deadwood their home!"

Not that many people figured on staying in Deadwood, Bellamy thought as he worked his way across the street. They had come to the Black Hills to get rich, and when they had accomplished that, they would go back to wherever they had come from. Deadwood wasn't home. It would never be home. It was just a temporary stopover on the road to either riches or ruin.

Smith continued preaching as Bellamy stepped up onto the porch of Miss Laurette's. At that moment, the front door of the academy opened and the tall, lean, black-clad figure of Fletch Parkhurst stepped out.

"Bellamy," Fletch said, extending a hand. "Good to see you again." As the two young men shook, Fletch added, "I take it you've recovered from your little misadventure the other night?"

Bellamy nodded. "Yes, and I learned my lesson. I'm not going anywhere near the Gem again."

"That's probably wise," Fletch said with a grin. "If you want a drink, Miss Laurette has some fine wine that won't have the same effect on you as Swearengen's rotgut."

"Yes, I thought I might come in and, uh, have a drink."

"And pass some pleasant time with one of the young ladies, too, eh?"

Bellamy shook his head. "Not just any of them. One in particular."

"Oh, ho. Carla, I'd wager. She took good care of you when you were recovering."

Bellamy felt his face get so hot, he worried that it was shining in the dark. "She seems like a very nice girl."

"She is, at that."

Bellamy didn't know exactly what Fletch meant by that, nor did he want to know. If Fletch had gone to bed with Carla, Bellamy didn't even want to think about it.

Fletch clapped a hand on Bellamy's shoulder and said, "Go on in. Get away from all the caterwauling." He nodded across the street toward Preacher Smith.

For some reason, Bellamy felt like he ought to defend the preacher. "He's just trying to do what he thinks is right."

"Yes, I know, but he's never going to succeed in cleaning up the Badlands, no matter how hard he tries. People are too dedicated to sinning. It's what they do. They drink and gamble and lust after gold and flesh."

"People are weak," Bellamy said. "And not everybody does those things."

"If they don't, they do something else. Take my word for it, Bellamy. Everybody has their vices. Some are out in the open and some are secret, but they're always there if you look hard enough. What's it say in the Bible? 'For all have sinned, and come short of the glory of God'?"

Bellamy's eyes widened in surprise that somebody like Fletch would be quoting Scripture.

"Thank God for sin," Fletch went on. "Without it, folks like me would be out of business." He gave Bellamy a gentle push toward the entrance. "Now go on with you. I've got business of my own to be about. The cards are calling, and somewhere in this town men are just waiting to give me all their hard-earned gold dust on the turn of an ace or a king."

Fletch sauntered away, and Bellamy hesitated only a moment longer on the porch of Miss Laurette's. He looked across the street at Preacher Smith one more time. The preacher was waving his arms around as his words thundered out, and his face shone with sweat in the light of lanterns hung here and there around the settlement. Despite his enthusiastic preaching, however, the crowd that had gathered in front of him was now beginning to thin. People had indulged their curiosity and listened for a spell, but now they were bored and ready to go do something else.

Bellamy felt a little bad, and for a second he considered postponing his visit so that he could go back across the street and listen to Smith for a while longer. But then he decided he couldn't wait any longer, and he grasped the doorknob and turned it and went in.

FLETCH Parkhurst sat at a table in the rear of the No. 10 Saloon, next to Miss Laurette's, playing cards with several men. The saloon was narrow and dimly lit. Unlike the academy next door and the Bella Union beyond it, no women worked here. Other than a few gamblers, the men who came here were intent on drinking. The No. 10 dealt strictly in intoxication, not fornication.

Carl Mann, who owned the place along with Billy Nuttall, was behind the bar, along with the part-time bartender, Harry Sam Young. The front door was open, and the strident voice of the preacher was clearly audible as Smith declaimed across the street in front of the Gem.

"Somebody oughtta shut that damn preacher up," one of the prospectors at the bar growled. "All that yappin' gnaws at a man like a damn toothache."

Another of the drinkers said, "That there's a man of God you're talkin' about, Riley. Best not be bad-mouthin' him."

"He's a man just like any other man," Riley insisted. "And he's annoyin' the hell out of me."

Carl Mann continued polishing glasses with a half-clean cloth. "It's a free country, last I heard," he commented. "Man's got a right to say what he wants to say, even if he's makin' a jackass of himself by preachin' to folks who don't want to hear it."

At the poker table, Fletch discarded two cards and picked up the two that the dealer slid his way. He had just filled an inside straight, but no one would ever know it to look at him. The expression on his face never changed.

Harry Sam Young said, "You ought to hear how Al Swearengen talks about the preacher. I swear, Al hates him worse'n anybody. You know how Al feels about anything that threatens to cut into his profits. If one man listens to the preacher and decides not to go into the Gem to get drunk or dally with the whores, Al's gonna take it mighty personal."

As if to prove the bartender right, another voice was suddenly raised in the street outside. This one was profanely angry, though, not exhorting people to righteousness. Carl Mann leaned forward so he could peer out the door and said, "Looks like Swearengen's gettin' in on it now, boys."

Fletch laid down his cards and drew in his winnings, then said, "Why don't we take a break for a few minutes? I think I want to watch the show."

He stood up, slipping the money into his pocket, and strolled toward the door of the saloon. Some of the other men followed him, but most continued to concentrate on their drinking. Fletch stepped out into the street and leaned a shoulder against the building. Across the way, Preacher Smith still stood on the crate that Bellamy Bridges had helped him place there. Al Swearengen, the owner of the Gem, stood beside the crate, yelling obscenities up at the preacher and demanding that he shut up and get down off of there. Smith ignored him, raising his voice so that he could continue preaching over the saloon keeper's tirade.

Fletch watched Swearengen closely. The man's face was livid with rage. He shook and trembled with the depth of the anger that filled him. His hands lifted and hooked into claws, and Fletch knew he wanted to drag Smith down from the crate and beat the hell out of him. But not even Al Swearengen, who thought he was a law unto himself in Deadwood, would dare to lay hands on the preacher. Smith was a good carpenter, like the Galilean whose teachings he followed, and he was quick to help out anyone in town who needed assistance, whether it was building a house, carrying water, chopping firewood, tending to the sick, or any other chore. Deadwood wouldn't stand for it if Swearengen were to assault the preacher.

Swearengen finally threw up his hands, spit out a few more oaths, and turned to stalk back into the Gem. Fletch watched him go.

"Hey, Parkhurst," one of the poker players said. "Are we gonna get back to the game?"

Fletch shook his head. "I think I've had enough for tonight, gents."

"But you've got most of our money!" another man protested. "You gotta give us a chance to win it back."

"Tomorrow night," Fletch said with an easy grin. "You've got my word on it."

There was some grumbling, but no one tried to stop him

as he left. They knew he was handy with the short-barreled Colt he wore in a black holster under his coat.

He went back to Miss Laurette's. Across the street, Smith continued to preach, but Fletch didn't pay any heed to him now.

Fifteen

⌒⌒

Miss Laurette had met Bellamy just inside the door, in the foyer of the house. She smiled, took his hands in hers, and said, "My, my. The prodigal returns."

Bellamy could have done without the Biblical reference, and it wasn't really apt, anyway, since by no stretch of the imagination was this bordello his home. But he told himself not to be nervous, and returned the madam's smile.

"Good evening, ma'am," he said. "I hope this evening finds you well."

"Aren't you the polite one? Come on, come in. Do you want a drink, Mr. Bridges? Or would you rather just pick out your companion for the evening?" She waved an elegant hand toward the parlor, and when Bellamy looked in there, he saw several young women sitting around on divans and overstuffed chairs. They all wore scandalously short gowns that left their legs bare to the knees. The garments were sleeveless, too, exposing their smooth, round arms. Some of them smiled at Bellamy while others ignored him.

But none of them were Carla.

"I . . . I spoke to Fletch outside," Bellamy said. "He mentioned something about fine wine. . . ."

"Of course," Miss Laurette said without hesitation. "A drink to relax you after a long day's work. Have you located a suitable claim yet, Mr. Bridges?"

"Yes, ma'am. My partner and I—you remember Dan Ryan from the other night, I expect—we've got Number Eight above discovery. Looks like it's going to be a good claim, Dan says."

"Well, that's excellent. Come along. Let's get you that glass of wine."

She linked her arm with his and led him into the parlor. He tried not to stare at the girls. The gowns they wore were so thin, he could almost see their bosoms through the fabric. He could definitely see the hard nipples poking out. There were all kinds of girls, too: short, tall, skinny, plump, blondes and brunettes and redheads. There was even a black one. And at the bar on the other side of the parlor, a Chinese girl with long, straight hair the color of midnight and the smoothest golden skin Bellamy had ever seen poured the drinks for him and Miss Laurette. Miss Laurette said, "Thank you, Ling," and the Chinese girl smiled.

Miss Laurette sipped her wine and then leaned close to Bellamy. "You seem quite taken with Ling. Would you like to spend the next hour with her in one of the rooms? I assure you, it would be a very pleasurable hour."

Bellamy drank some of the wine, gulping it rather than sipping. It was a lot smoother than the whiskey he'd gotten in the Gem, but it had a fiery quality of its own that kindled a warmth in his belly.

"No offense to Miss Ling," he said, "but I thought I might see Miss Carla again."

"Ah," Miss Laurette said, as if a great light had dawned. "I'm afraid Carla's occupied right now. But if you'd care to wait . . ."

Occupied. That meant some other man was having carnal knowledge of her, Bellamy thought, right at this very minute, more than likely. Well, Bellamy told himself sternly, he had known she was a whore. That was what whores did. He felt himself nodding. "Yes. I'll wait."

"You just set yourself right down, then. Ling, you see to Mr. Bridges' needs until Carla is free, you hear?"

"Yes, missy," Ling said, and the singsong quality of her voice told Bellamy that she most likely hadn't been speaking English for very long. She was probably the daughter of one of those laundrymen down the street.

A bell set over the front door jingled, and Miss Laurette left to greet the newest gentleman caller. Bellamy kept his eyes cast toward the floor and slowly drank his wine as Miss Laurette led a roughly dressed miner into the room and let him have his pick of the girls there. The man chose a plump blonde, and off they went toward the back of the house, laughing together.

There was still time for him to get out of here, Bellamy thought. He could leave right now, go back to the wagon, and never return to this place. That would be the right thing to do. . . .

"Hello again," a soft voice said.

He looked up into deep brown eyes and was lost.

Carla stood there wearing the same sort of short slip as the other girls. She went on. "Miss Laurette tells me that you've been waiting for me, Mr. Bridges."

"B-Bellamy," he said. "Call me Bellamy."

She sat down beside him on the divan, so close that her thigh pressed warmly against his. "You look a lot better than you did the last time I saw you, Bellamy," she said. "And if I recall correctly, you did all right by yourself even then." She laughed softly.

Bellamy flushed again and wished his face would stop turning red like that every time somebody mentioned what had happened before. He said, "I . . . I've been thinking about you a lot since then."

"And I've been thinking about you, too."

That was probably a lie, a part of his brain told him. She probably hadn't thought of him at all. How could she, when she was . . . busy . . . with all those other men?

She leaned closer. "You're really sweet, Bellamy," she whispered in his ear. "You want to go back to one of the rooms with me?"

She smelled good. She must have just splashed on some lilac water, he thought. There was a faint scent of sweat about her, but not so bad that he couldn't ignore it. Anyway, it might not be her sweat he was smelling, he told himself, but somehow, that thought didn't help all that much.

She took his hand and stood up. "Come on," she urged. "I know you want to."

"Yes," Bellamy said honestly. "Yes, I do."

Before they could leave the parlor, however, Fletch Parkhurst came in. All the scantily clad girls sat up straighter, and Bellamy saw the interest on their faces as they looked at Fletch. Bellamy was hardly an expert on such things, but he supposed that Fletch was a pretty handsome gent. Clearly, even these whores thought so. From the looks of it, he could have had any of the girls he wanted, even if that hadn't been their business.

Fletch didn't pay much attention to them, though. Instead he went right over to Miss Laurette and spoke to her in a low voice. She nodded and turned, leaving the parlor and heading toward her private quarters at the rear of the house. Fletch followed her.

"Sort of odd, isn't it?" Carla said beside Bellamy.

He looked over at her. "What?"

"Sort of odd," she repeated. "I mean, the way Fletch doesn't have anything to do with us girls. The only one he spends any private time with is Miss Laurette." She shrugged smooth bare shoulders. "I guess he just likes older women."

"I guess so."

She tugged on his hand again. "Forget about them. Come on, honey. I'm gettin' tired of waiting. I need what you can give me."

Money? Bellamy thought. Then he decided it was unfair for him to be so cynical. He ought to give Carla the benefit of the doubt. Sure, she would expect to be paid for her efforts tonight. It wouldn't be like the other morning, when she had done what she did out of the goodness of her heart. But still, she seemed to like him, and until he saw proof to the contrary, Bellamy was going to assume there was some truth to that feeling. He stood up and let her lead him out of the parlor, and even though his heart was hammering a mile a minute and he couldn't quite seem to get his breath, he knew he was doing the right thing. Sinful it might be— there was no doubt about it, actually—but sometimes the need for comfort, for closeness, was just too overwhelming to be denied. When two people reached out for each other, it couldn't be *that* bad, now could it?

And the best thing about it was that once they got in the room and the door closed behind them and Carla pulled that slip up and over her head, Bellamy stopped asking himself questions. He stopped thinking about anything except what the two of them were doing.

Too much brooding and pondering were bad for a fella. Bellamy was sure of that now.

IN Miss Laurette's room, Fletch took off his hat and coat and hung them carefully on hooks. He pulled off his string tie and opened his collar, then sat down in an armchair and put his booted feet up on a brocaded ottoman. At a small table across the room, Laurette poured drinks for both of them. She carried the glasses over to Fletch and handed him one of them. He tossed back the whiskey and sighed in satisfaction. The stuff was expensive. It was freighted in from St. Louis. But it was the real thing, not the homemade panther piss that most of the men in Deadwood were satisfied with, at least until it made them go blind.

"I saw something interesting tonight," he said.

Laurette took her drink and sat down on a stool in front of a dressing table. She kicked off her shoes, sipped the whiskey, and then picked up a brush to run it through her thick, dark red hair.

"What's that?" she asked.

"Preacher Smith was standing on a crate in front of the Gem, telling all and sundry what a cesspool of evil it is."

Laurette gave an unladylike snort. "The preacher was telling the truth about that."

"Yes, but Swearengen came out to rail back at him. I thought for a moment that he was going to pull the preacher off his box and start whaling the tar out of him."

Laurette lifted her glass and looked over the top of it at Fletch. "Al might have found himself tarred and feathered if he had done something like that."

"My thought exactly," Fletch agreed.

Laurette downed some more of the whiskey. "What's that got to do with us?"

"You've been complaining because the preacher interferes with the businesses at this end of town. This isn't the first time he's come down here and started preaching. Some of the men are too ashamed to walk past him into this place, or into the Gem or the Bella Union."

"Smith's a damned busybody," Laurette snapped. "He thinks that just because he's a preacher, he's got a right to cause trouble for us."

"Yes, but as long as he has his sights set on Swearengen, he's playing right into our hands."

"How do you figure that?"

"Because Al Swearengen is a lunatic," Fletch said. "If Smith keeps preaching in front of the Gem, sooner or later, Swearengen will break. He'll attack the preacher or maybe even haul out a gun and shoot him."

A smile of understanding spread across Laurette's face. "If he does that, he's liable to get strung up."

"Thereby ridding us of not only the annoyance of the preacher, but also one of our leading competitors as well."

"I like that idea," Laurette said slowly. "I like it a lot. How are we going to make sure it comes about?"

"The preacher will talk to anyone," Fletch said. "I thought I would drop a few hints to him about how the Gem is the worst place in the Badlands and how the rest of the businesses might change for the better if the Gem was gone."

"That's bullshit."

"Yes, but it's the sort of bullshit the preacher will want to hear."

Laurette drained the rest of the whiskey in her glass and reached for the bottle. "I was thinking about being a little more aggressive."

"How do you mean?" Fletch asked.

She looked squarely at him and said, "I was thinking you could kill the preacher yourself."

Fletch took a sharp breath. "What?"

"You could kill the preacher," Laurette said. "Just don't do it here in Deadwood. You know how he wanders around the countryside, looking for somebody to help or some fresh meat to preach to. He's lucky the savages haven't got him already. But if you were to get rid of him, and somehow make it look like Swearengen was responsible . . ." Her voice trailed off as she smiled at Fletch.

He sat back in the armchair, blinking rapidly. It had never occurred to him that she might suggest he murder the preacher. Egging on the situation so that the friction between Smith and Swearengen finally erupted into violence was one thing; killing a man in cold blood was another.

Laurette must have seen what was on his mind. He might have a great poker face, but she had always been able to see right through it. "What's the matter?" she asked. "You've killed men before. Three that I know of, not counting Indians or greasers."

"I never shot anybody who wasn't trying to shoot me first," Fletch said. "That makes a big difference."

"The hell it does." She stood up and took a step toward him. "Listen, don't you go getting cold feet on me. You showed up here and horned in on this place, remember? I didn't ask you to be my partner. You forced me into it. Well, if you're gonna rake in your share of the profits, you've got to carry your share of the load when the time comes."

"I just don't know. . . ."

She moved closer to him, and her hand flashed out to crack sharply across his face in a slap. The blow rocked Fletch's head to the side. The imprint of Laurette's hand turned white as the rest of his face flushed red with anger. But he stayed where he was, hands tightly clasping the arms of the chair.

"You puling little pissant," she said in a low, savage voice. "We had a deal. We were going to work together to take over this whole end of town. The Badlands were going to be ours! Getting rid of Swearengen is just the first step, but once he's gone, the rest will fall over like a row of dominoes. You know that, damn you!"

"You never said anything about murder."

"I never said it wouldn't come to that." Laurette looked down at him and shook her head in contempt. "I thought I raised you better than this, boy."

"You didn't raise me at all . . . *Mother*." Scorn dripped from the word as Fletch spoke it. "You abandoned me when I was just a boy, remember?"

"You did all right for yourself. But you can do a lot better if you'll just listen to me and do what I tell you."

"Like murdering the preacher."

"Two birds with one stone, Fletch. The preacher and Al Swearengen."

Fletch sighed. "I'll think about it. I can't make any promises . . . but I'll think about it."

"Don't think too long," Laurette said. "I might get tired of waiting."

"What are you going to do? Kill Smith yourself?" Fletch shook his head. "You're a lover, not a fighter, remember?"

"You don't really know what I'm capable of, now do you?"

Fletch had to admit that he didn't. And as that realization hit him, he felt a cold ball form in his stomach.

Laurette was his mother, but truly, he didn't know her. They had been apart for too long.

But as he looked at her now, standing over him with her

eyes flashing fire and her breast heaving with the depth of the emotions coursing through her, he thought that she was probably capable of anything.

Anything at all.

Sixteen

For the next few days, Dan and Bellamy worked hard on the claim, both of them panning along the creek and accumulating a small store of gold dust. Dan was satisfied with the color they were finding, but Bellamy often expressed his disappointment when he picked only a speck or two out of the drag after he was finished washing it.

"At this rate, we'll be old men before we're rich," he said one day when he had washed three pans in a row without finding any gold.

"Move on down the creek a ways," Dan suggested. "Could be we've worked that spot out."

"Could be there's not near as much gold here as we thought," Bellamy said gloomily. "That fella was willing to sell out for a reason, Dan."

"Reason was, he didn't have enough faith."

"Faith won't buy you a drink or a good meal."

Dan shrugged. Bellamy either understood what this life was like, or he didn't. He would either learn, or he wouldn't. There wasn't much Dan could do to force the issue.

"Just keep panning," he said. "You never know what you'll find next time."

Bellamy grumbled, but he kept working. After a while, he said, "You know, they're having a dance at the Grand Central."

Dan's head was down as he peered into the pan of gravel he was washing, but it came up at Bellamy's comment. "A dance?" he repeated.

"That's what I heard in town last night."

Bellamy had been walking into Deadwood every night since they had started working the claim, and he usually didn't return until late, sometimes not until the next morning. Dan didn't care for that, because it made Bellamy even more tired and grouchy, but Bellamy didn't seem to be able to stop himself. He was going to see that girl at Miss Laurette's, Dan knew. Youth and lust was a potent combination, too potent for age and wisdom to counteract it. Anyway, Dan told himself, he might be old, but he wasn't all that wise. Never had been.

"I didn't know there were enough women in Deadwood to have a dance," he said. "Leastways, not respectable ones."

"Don't be too quick to judge," Bellamy snapped.

"I wasn't. Just sayin' I'm surprised they're havin' a dance. To tell you the truth, kid, I don't care who they invite to it, either."

Dan didn't want to argue with Bellamy. He was too busy thinking about the fact that the dance was going to be held at the Grand Central Hotel. There would probably be refreshments, and that meant Lou Marchbanks would be involved. Surely she would be there, and if Dan attended, he might have a chance to talk with her again. He might even—

With a frown, he stopped that thought in its tracks. Her being an African and all, he couldn't dance with her. The community would never condone that. Not that he gave a rat's ass what folks thought of him. He didn't. But he would never do something to embarrass Lou.

Just seeing her and talking to her would have to be enough. He said, "I reckon I'll go."

"To the dance, you mean?"

"That's right."

"What about the claim? You said somebody has to stand guard on it all the time."

"It ought to be all right for one evening. Now that we've been here for a while, I can see that there's not much thievery around these parts, except when the Indians sneak in. Most men know that miner's justice is pretty quick and final. Nobody wants to get strung up from a tree limb over a piddling little robbery."

"Well, if you say so," Bellamy said. "I know I'm going to the dance. I'm gonna ask Carla to go with me, and I don't care what anybody thinks. They'll keep a civil tongue in their head, or there'll be trouble." He reached down and patted the butt of the revolver he had taken to carrying. Dan had shown him how to use it and supervised a few sessions of target practice. Bellamy had demonstrated some natural skill at gun-handling, but he was still raw.

"You don't need to be gettin' in a gunfight," Dan told him. "You'd wind up gettin' shot to pieces, and then I'd have to work this claim by myself."

"Maybe I'm better with a gun than you think I am," Bellamy said confidently. "Maybe I've been practicing some on my own."

"As long as you're payin' for the bullets, you can practice all you want, kid."

Dan had mixed emotions about the way this conversation had gone. He found the news of the upcoming dance intriguing, but he didn't like Bellamy's talk about using a gun. More than one young man on the frontier had gotten it into his head that he was a fast gun, and most of them didn't live very long after that. A kid just naturally had to prove himself. His pride wouldn't let him do otherwise. When a gun was involved, too, it was bad.

You couldn't talk to a youngster like that, though. The words went in one ear and right out the other. All you could do was hope for the best.

Dan dipped up another pan full of sand and gravel and

water and began to swirl it around. He thought about the dance instead. The dance, and Lou Marchbanks . . .

DAN bit back a curse as his thick fingers struggled to tie the cravat at his throat. His fingers felt like sausages. They weren't made for such things. But he managed finally to get the tie the way he wanted it, and when he looked in the broken piece of mirror that was tacked to a tree trunk, he thought he looked reasonably presentable. He licked his fingers and slicked down a clump of his graying dark hair that wanted to stick up.

Bellamy was already gone. They had stopped work early today, and Bellamy had stripped off all his clothes and plunged into the creek for a bath. Dan had been tempted to do likewise, but it seemed like an awfully extreme move to him. He had settled for washing, shaving, and dressing in his Sunday best, the one dark suit and white shirt he owned. His regular boots would have to do.

Before he put on his coat, he strapped his gun belt around his waist. He was no pistoleer; it took him a while to haul the heavy revolver out of its holster. But once he got it out, he could hit what he aimed at, nine times out of ten, even when the target was small and far away. He didn't expect to run into any trouble at the dance, but you never knew. Out here, it paid a man to be prepared for a ruckus, even though it might never come about.

Dan shrugged into his coat, picked up his hat, brushed it off, and tried to curl the brim into a slightly jauntier shape. It didn't want to cooperate very well, so he gave up after a minute. He settled the hat on his head and looked in the mirror again. Not bad for an old ex-cavalryman and current prospector.

The red glow in the western sky was fading fast as Dan rode into Deadwood. He rode past the timbered heights of Forest Hill, looming over the western end of town; past the Big Horn Store and the tin shop and the tailor's place. Main Street was crowded as usual, but tonight the throngs were converging on the Grand Central Hotel. Everybody had heard about the dance, and nobody wanted to miss it. To Dan's surprise as he dismounted, he even saw Al Swearengen entering the hotel, all duded up and looking eminently respectable for a change. Dan looped the horse's reins around the hitch rack and wondered how many other denizens of the Badlands would venture uptown from their usual haunts tonight.

He didn't care if every gambler and whore in the settlement showed up, as long as they behaved themselves and didn't cause trouble at the dance.

Dan went inside and saw that all the tables and chairs from the dining room had been carried out to make room for the celebration. The rough planks of the floor seemed slicker than usual, and when Dan looked down at them, he saw that the floor had been waxed, probably with candle shavings. A dance floor needed to be smooth enough for folks to glide over it, but Dan hoped nobody would slip and fall and hurt themselves.

A couple of men with fiddles tuned their instruments in a corner. More men gathered around the row of ladies who stood along one wall, nine of them in all and not a one from the Badlands, Dan saw. He looked around for Bellamy and didn't see him. That girl Carla must have refused to come with him to the dance, knowing that her kind wouldn't be welcome here.

Dan put those thoughts out of his mind and looked for Lou Marchbanks instead. He didn't see her in the dining room. Dan started making his way through the crowd of men toward the kitchen.

General Dawson stopped him along the way. "Good evening, Sergeant—I mean, Dan!" the General said. "Quite a turnout, isn't it?"

"Yes, sir, General. Half the men in town are here, looks like."

"And every decent woman." Dawson's florid face grew more solemn. "I'm afraid we had to turn away that partner of yours. He tried to bring in one of the girls from Miss

Laurette's place. Wouldn't have bothered me, of course, but the respectable ladies won't stand for it."

"What did Bellamy do when he was told he couldn't come in with her?" Dan asked, worried that the kid might have gotten himself in some trouble.

"Oh, he was upset, of course," the General said with a wave of his hand. "But he calmed down and left with the girl, without making too much of a scene."

Dan heaved a sigh of relief. He had been afraid that Bellamy might have tried to pull his gun and force his way in.

"I'll have a talk with him," he promised.

The General nodded. "Probably a good idea. He's getting a mite too friendly with that crowd down there. If he wants to be a decent, hardworking member of the community, he needs to quit spending all his spare time in that bordello."

Dan agreed, but he didn't hold out much hope that Bellamy would listen to reason. Still, he would have to at least make the attempt to talk some sense into the young man's head.

Dan told the General he would see him later and continued on toward the kitchen. The door was closed, but he opened it and slipped through. Instantly, the delicious smell of warm, freshly baked cake surrounded him.

"What is it?" Lou Marchbanks asked impatiently from the table where she was cutting a cake and putting squares of it on silver trays. She didn't look up from what she was doing until Dan spoke.

"Figured I'd find you in here, cookin' and fixin'," he said.

"That's my job," she told him, pausing in her work. She wore a dark blue gown with white lace at the throat and sleeves. Dan thought she looked mighty handsome. "What are you doin' back here, Mr. Ryan?"

"You said you'd call me Dan, remember?" he reminded her.

"So I did. But you ain't answered my question."

"Why, I came to see you, of course." He was no silver-tongued devil and never would be, but at least he could tell the truth. That would have to be enough. "When I heard there was going to be a dance here at the hotel, I knew you'd be here."

She laughed. "I'm always here, ain't I? Fixin' three meals a day?"

"This is different."

"Not to me, it ain't. Just another job."

"Then why are you wearing that pretty dress?" Dan asked.

"You think it's pretty?" The response came out of her mouth instinctively, before she could stop it. Dan was glad he had gotten an honest reaction out of her.

"I think the dress is pretty, and I think you're pretty, too, Lou," he told her. Again, it was just the truth, stated as simply as he could make it.

She looked down at the table and said sternly, "You're a flatterer, Dan Ryan, nothin' but a flatterer." But he could tell she was pleased, or at least he liked to think that he could.

"Can I give you a hand?" he asked.

"Take these pieces of cake out there and put 'em on the table in the corner. I got another couple of cakes to slice up, but I'll carry 'em out when I'm done. You don't need to be helpin' me so much that you miss the dance."

Dan picked up the tray covered with pieces of cake. "I don't imagine I'd be missin' much. There's a whole heap more gentlemen out there than there are ladies. Tell you the truth, I'd rather be back here where there's only one gentleman and one lady."

"There you go with that flatterin' again. Now take that cake out there." She added more quietly, "But if you want to come back, I reckon I can't stop you."

Grinning, Dan carried the tray out of the kitchen and placed it on a small table in a corner of the makeshift ballroom. The fiddlers began playing while he was there. The women swirled around the floor, each in the arms of one of Deadwood's male citizens. The other men were lined up eagerly awaiting their turns. Some of them clapped in time with the music.

The joyous, spirited rhythms did something to Dan. It had been a long time since he had danced. He had attended quite a few regimental balls during his service in the cavalry, but the Seventh had been so busy in recent years that there hadn't been much time for dances or any other kind of tomfoolery. There was a war against the Indians to win, after all. Dan hadn't really been aware that he missed such things, but now as he went back into the kitchen, the music wrapped around him and seemed to make his feet lighter.

Lou had taken another cake out of the oven and set it on the table. Before she could pick up the knife to start cutting it, Dan took her hand and said, "Miss Marchbanks, may I have the honor of this dance?"

"Are you crazy?" she demanded. She tugged on her hand, but Dan wouldn't let go of it. "We can't dance together, Mr. Ryan."

"Dan," he reminded her.

"Mr. Ryan," she repeated stubbornly. "I'm startin' to think it was a mistake for us to get so familiar. You got ideas in your head that hadn't ought to be there."

"The only idea in my head is that I want to dance with the prettiest woman here tonight," he said. "I want to dance with you."

"You done gone blind?" she asked. "You can't see color no more?"

"Color's not supposed to matter. We fought a war over it, remember?"

She let out a little moan. "I remember, all right. That war changed some things . . . but it didn't change everything."

Dan took hold of her other hand. "Dance with me," he said. "Just dance with me."

"Ohhhh . . ."

She wanted to argue. She wanted to pull away from him. He could tell that. But she came into his arms and put her arms around his neck, and they began to move together in time to the music and the clapping that sounded in the other room. Their dance floor was the kitchen floor, but neither of them cared. They swirled and turned and their faces were only inches apart, their breath warm on each other's cheek, and she felt gloriously light in his arms. What they were doing was scandalous, of course, but at this moment neither of them cared about scandal or propriety or anything else.

The music ended, but they continued swaying together for a long moment afterward. Then Lou leaned her head forward and rested it against his shoulder.

"My God, I wish you wasn't white," she whispered.

"It doesn't matter."

"It *does*." She raised her head to look at him, and he thought her dark eyes were the most beautiful he had ever seen. "You can say it don't from now until doomsday, Dan, but you know it does."

He lifted a hand, put it under her chin, tilted her head back just a little. He wanted to kiss her as much as he had ever wanted anything in his life.

But that was when he realized that the music was still stopped and that there was some sort of commotion going on in the hotel dining room. He heard angry voices.

And one of them, he realized with a shock, belonged to Bellamy Bridges.

Seventeen

"**D**ON'T you worry about it, honey," Carla had told Bellamy as they walked back down the street toward Miss Laurette's. "I didn't want to go to their fuckin' ol' dance anyway."

"You shouldn't talk like that," he said miserably. "If you want to be a lady, you've got to talk like a lady."

Carla stopped short. She wore a rather demure, light blue dress, had her hair pulled back behind her head, and a shawl was draped over her shoulders. Bellamy thought she looked beautiful, and she appeared every bit as decent and respectable as any of the women at the dance. There'd been no reason to turn them away.

"Listen to me, Bellamy," she said. "I'm not a lady. Never been one, never will be one, don't particularly want to be one. What I am is a whore, and that's good enough for me. If it's not good enough for you, then you can just go to hell."

He caught hold of her arms. "Don't ever say that! Don't ever think that . . . that you're not good enough for me. You're sweet, you're beautiful. . . ." He crushed her against his chest. "You're the best thing that's ever happened to me!" he choked out.

They stood there in the shadows like that for a long moment. Carla patted him softly on the back as he trembled. "It's all right," she whispered. "It's all right, Bellamy. You just set your sights a little too high, that's all. Come on back down to Miss Laurette's with me."

"But the dance—"

"We can dance there. We can do whatever you want."

He nodded and straightened, wiping the back of a hand across his mouth. He was still outraged by the treatment they had received, by the looks that those people in the hotel had given Carla, but maybe she was right. Nothing was going to change the way those high-and-mighty bastards thought, so what was the point of fighting it? Maybe it was better to embrace what he really was, to accept all the things he had discovered about himself in recent days. If she was a whore, then he was a whoremonger. So be it.

Because he loved her, and nothing could ever change that.

Arm in arm once again, they went back to Miss Laurette's. Bellamy had paid for the whole night. It had taken every bit of the money he had left, but if necessary he would have used the gold dust he and Dan had panned from Deadwood Creek. Only half of that dust was his, but he would have spent it all if he had to, and paid Dan back later. Luckily, it hadn't come to that.

When they were in her little room with the door closed, Carla sat Bellamy down on the bed and knelt in front of him, still wearing the clothes she had worn to the dance, continuing the masquerade of respectability. As she unbuttoned his fly, she said, "You know those women at the dance, they act so fine and fancy, like butter wouldn't melt in their mouths, but they're just women. When they get behind closed doors with their men, they do the same things I do with you, honey."

Bellamy put his hands slightly behind him to brace

himself. He closed his eyes as she took his stiff penis out of his trousers and began to stroke it.

"They're all whores," Carla said softly. "They all get paid to fuck, just like me, only they ain't so honest about it. Their men buy them fancy clothes and build them nice houses, but when you get down to it, that's just how they get paid to fuck." She leaned over and ran her tongue around the head of his penis. "Some of them probably even do this." She took him in her mouth, closed her lips, and began to suck.

Less than thirty seconds later, he spent, groaning as he spurted in her mouth. Carla gave him a squeeze and smiled up at him, and at that moment she managed to look both innocent and incredibly erotic at the same time.

"What you and me have is a hell of a lot more honest, Bellamy," she said. "Don't you ever forget that."

He shook his head weakly. "I won't. I won't."

She stood up and started to get undressed. "We got all night, honey. Let's see what other kinds of mischief we can get up to."

BELLAMY wore out quickly. Day after day of squatting and panning for gold would do that to a man, sapping his strength and energy. He tried to stay awake, but he dozed off in the bed with Carla's naked form cuddled close to him.

He didn't sleep for very long, however. When he woke up he could tell it was still fairly early in the evening.

And he was mad . . . mad as hell.

Everything Carla had said earlier made sense, but still, how dare they treat her like that? Why, she was just as good as any of them! As she had pointed out, she was more honest than the so-called respectable women. And yet they still looked down on her. It wasn't right. It wasn't right at all.

And somebody ought to tell them that, Bellamy decided. Somebody ought to teach them a lesson.

Carla's deep, regular breathing told him that she was asleep. He slipped out of bed without waking her and fumbled in the darkness for his clothes, drawing them on quickly.

He left his coat off, and left the gun belt for last. He buckled it on and then wrapped his fingers around the butt of the Colt's revolver. The gun was heavy in his hand as he moved it up or down an inch or so in the smooth leather. He was going to march right back down there to the hotel and give those biddies and their stiff-necked men a piece of his mind, and if anybody tried to stop him, there would be trouble. Gun trouble.

He closed the door quietly behind him as he stepped out into the hall. There was no sign of Miss Laurette as he walked past the parlor. She was probably back in her office or her living quarters. Bellamy wondered briefly if Fletch was with her. Fletch was the closest thing he had to a real friend in Deadwood, he thought. Well, other than Carla. Dan had been his friend, but Dan didn't like Carla, didn't like for Bellamy to come here. He was stiff-necked and judgmental, and Bellamy was starting to question the wisdom of going partners with him on the gold claim.

The truth was, Bellamy had begun to question the wisdom of being a prospector in the first place. It seemed unlikely to him that they would ever find enough gold to make all their hard work worthwhile. All they really had to show for it so far were sore muscles and such a small amount of gold dust that he could have made more money clerking in a store or something like that. He was a pretty good cardplayer, he thought. Maybe he could become a gambler, like Fletch.

His anger and resentment forced those thoughts out of his head as he approached the Grand Central Hotel. The doors were open, and he heard the merry strains of fiddle music drifting out into the night. They were having themselves a high old time in there, but that was about to change.

The song came to its end as Bellamy stepped up onto the porch. He went inside, turning to his left into the dining room that had been cleared out for the dancing. People stood around talking while the fiddle players got ready for the next number. The faces of the men and women who had been dancing were slightly flushed from their exertions.

General Dawson spotted Bellamy and came toward him. "Howdy, Bellamy," he said affably. "Glad you decided to come back. You're welcome here—"

"But Miss Wilkes isn't," Bellamy cut in. "That's right, isn't it?"

Dawson's smile disappeared. "I'm sorry, son. The situation was explained to you, and I thought you understood—"

Bellamy interrupted him again. "I understand, all right, General." His voice rose angrily. "I understand that you people are all a bunch of goddamn hypocrites!"

That loud declaration made the conversations in the room come to an abrupt halt. The fiddlers, who had been just about ready to launch into another tune, lowered their bows. Everyone turned to look at Bellamy.

General Dawson took hold of his arm. "Bellamy, if you're going to be like this, you'll have to leave—"

For the third time, Bellamy interrupted the General, shaking off his grip and saying, "I'm not going anywhere, not until I've had my say." He pointed at the women. "Not until everybody understands that they're whores, too, just like Carla. Worse than Carla, because they lie about it!"

That brought angry curses and growls from most of the men in the room, and they started to surge forward as a group, clearly intent on tossing Bellamy out of the hotel and into the street. Bellamy swung toward them, his lips pulling back from his teeth in a hate-filled grimace, and his hand moved toward the butt of the gun on his hip.

"Bellamy!"

The shout came from Dan Ryan, who emerged from the kitchen and hurried toward his young partner. Bellamy shouted, "Stay back, Dan! This is none of your business!"

That black woman—Aunt Lou, that was what she was called, Bellamy remembered—appeared behind Dan in the doorway to the kitchen, a worried look on her face. Charles

Wagner, the owner of the hotel, bustled in from the lobby. The General came at Bellamy from the other side. Suddenly feeling trapped, Bellamy jerked the Colt from its holster. A couple of the women screamed, while men yelled for everybody to take cover.

Bellamy didn't know what to do. Despite his anger, despite his determination to teach the so-called good people of Deadwood a lesson, he didn't want to shoot anybody. And he realized now that by drawing his gun, he had given the other men an excuse to pull their irons, too. A sudden premonition that he was about to be shot to doll rags went through him, turning his guts cold and watery with fear. He had to shoot first, before they could kill him. He jerked the Colt up, his finger tightening on the trigger.

DAN saw the panic and terror in the kid's eyes and knew that in another second Bellamy would start pulling the trigger, and he wouldn't stop until he was either out of bullets—or dead.

So Dan called up all the speed he could muster and struck first, stepping up to Bellamy and throwing a short, sharp punch to the younger man's jaw. At the same time, Dan's other hand closed around Bellamy's right wrist and forced the Colt toward the floor, so that if it went off no innocent bystander would be struck.

The blow landed cleanly, with plenty of power behind it, and Bellamy's head rocked back. He took an involuntary step backward. His eyes rolled up in his head. His knees unhinged, and he fell to them on the waxed floor, his grip on the gun relaxing so that Dan could pluck it from his fingers.

Stunned, Bellamy caught himself with one hand on the floor before he collapsed completely. The room was full of angry shouts. Bellamy shook his head groggily, as if confused by everything that was going on around him. Dan had heard only the tail end of Bellamy's tirade, but he had caught enough of it to know how vile it had been and how outraged the citizens were. They might be mad enough to try a little tarring and feathering, and Dan knew he couldn't permit that, either.

He turned toward the crowd, ready to shout out a command in his best sergeant's voice for them to back off. He didn't blame them for being mad at Bellamy, the way the kid had barged in here and ruined the dance, but he wasn't going to let them take that anger out on him.

Before Dan could say anything, before the menacing crowd could close in any more, the swift rataplan of hoofbeats and a loud, strident voice sounded outside in the street. "Massacre!" a man yelled. "Massacre on the Little Big Horn! Custer's dead! Custer's dead!"

The words went through Dan with a shock so potent that it was almost like a physical blow. Lieutenant Colonel George Armstrong Custer—commander of the Seventh Cavalry, the Boy General, Yellow Hair as the Indians called him—the man Dan Ryan had followed for years—dead? It wasn't possible. It just couldn't be.

But the shouts of alarm outside the hotel continued, and as Bellamy's outrageous behavior was forgotten and everyone who had come to the dance poured outside to find out exactly what had happened, Dan knew it must be true.

Eighteen

"IT happened a couple o' days ago, over in Montana Territory," the rider said. He had come galloping down from Bismarck, spreading the word. It had been a long, hard ride, and both man and horse looked exhausted. The horse hung its head low, its lathered sides heaving. The rider sat on the edge of the hotel porch, his hat pushed back on his tangled hair, his hands trembling a little from weariness. It seemed that at least half of Deadwood was gathered around him: General Dawson, Charles Wagner and Aunt Lou Marchbanks from the hotel, the newspaperman A.W. Merrick, Preacher Smith with a stricken look on his thin face, pudgy comedian Jack Langrishe from the theater, Handsome Banjo Dick Brown, Carl Mann and Billy Nuttall from the No. 10 Saloon, Al Swearengen from the Gem, storekeeper E.B. Farnum, who was also the mayor and justice of the peace, lawyer Eben Martin, James W. Wood, the owner of Deadwood's first bank, local characters such as Slippery Sam and Swill Barrel Jimmy, and dozens of others, many of them prospectors who had come into the settlement for the dance.

The rider had paused to catch his breath. Dan Ryan stood beside him and rested a hand on his shoulder. "Go on, if you can," Dan urged. His voice caught a little as he added, "I used to ride with the Seventh Cavalry."

The rider shook his head and said, "I'm sorry as hell, then, mister, because all your ol' pards are dead. Wiped out to the last man. The way the story reached us, Gen'ral Custer split his command, sent Cap'n Benteen and Major Reno loopin' around as he come up on a big ol' Injun camp on the river they call the Greasy Grass, what we call the Little Big Horn. But the redskins were ready for him, hundreds, maybe thousands, of the devils, and they chased Custer and his boys up on a hill and overrun 'em. Killed ever' one o' them poor soldiers."

Shaken to his core, Dan dragged the back of his hand across his mouth. When he was able to speak, he asked, "What about Reno and Benteen?"

"They had to do a bunch o' fightin', too, but they held out until the Injuns'd had enough. They lost some men, sure, but at least some survived."

They had to be thankful for small favors, Dan thought. Despite the rider's words, not all of the Seventh Cavalry had been killed. It must have seemed like it, though. And Custer had usually kept Dan's company close by, so it was likely that they had died with the general on that lonely, windswept hilltop.

"This is an outrage!" one of the men said. "It's high time the Army wiped out those savages, to the last man if that's what it takes!"

Shouts of agreement came from the crowd. They were angry, Dan knew, but they were scared, too. The Little Big Horn wasn't that far away, only a few days' ride from the Black Hills. The Sioux had killed men around here, in isolated incidents. Now, emboldened by their defeat of Custer, would they move east in force and try to sweep all the white interlopers from the hills that they knew and revered as the Paha Sapa, the navel of the world?

"That ain't all the bad news," the rider from Bismarck

went on. "A few days before Custer got hisself wiped out on the Greasy Grass, the Sioux kicked Gen'ral Crook's ass not far from there at Rosebud Creek."

"My God," Dan said in a hollow voice. "Crook is gone, too?"

The messenger shook his head. "Naw, the Injuns didn't kill Crook, just made him tuck his tail betwixt his legs and run. Ain't no doubt about it, though. . . . Right now, the Sioux are doin' pretty much whatever they want, and there don't seem to be nothin' the Army can do to stop 'em."

Dan still found it hard to believe that Custer was dead. He knew that Custer had been supremely confident, to the point of arrogance, and knew as well that the man was something of a glory hunter. Some of those who had served with him had been blind to Custer's faults as a military commander, but Dan wasn't one of them. Still, luck had seemed to follow Custer ever since the Civil War, and Dan had assumed that it always would.

The General looked around at the crowd and said, "Any man who hasn't been going armed should do so from now on."

"Hell, General!" burst out one of the men. "How's a pistol or a rifle gonna help us if we're set upon by a hundred bloodthirsty savages?"

"Listen to me," the General said. "No man in these hills is truly alone. There are always other men relatively close by. If you're attacked and you put up a fight, someone will hear the shots and come to help you. Likewise, if you're working your claim and you hear shots from a neighbor's claim, go at once to his aid." Dawson looked around at the crowd, his face stern and solemn. "If we all stick together, we won't be driven out of the Black Hills."

One of the men asked, "General, you got that paper written to send to Washington askin' them to take back the treaty with the Sioux and give us the legal right to be here?"

"I'm working on it," the General assured him.

"If that happens, you reckon the Army'll be more likely to run the redskins out?"

"The Army's already doin' all it can," the man from Bismarck said. "Crook and Terry are already back out in the field, tryin' to find the red bastards. They're slippery sons o' bitches, though."

"They can't win," Dan said quietly.

Several men turned angrily toward him. "What do you mean by that, mister?" one of them demanded. "Are you sayin' the Army can't whip those Injuns?"

"I'm saying the Indians can't win. They don't know the sort of resources the Army can muster as far as manpower and supplies go. Think about it." Dan waved a hand as he warmed to the subject. "True, there may be thousands of Indians out there—but there are hundreds of thousands of men in the country for the Army to draw on. The Indians can win a battle. . . ." His voice caught a little as he went on. "The Indians can kill General Custer and a couple of hundred of his men. But General Crook and General Terry are already back in the field with many more men than we lost. It may take some time before they're finally defeated . . . but the Indians can't win."

Few in the crowd seemed to be in the mood to accept Dan's assessment of the situation. They were still too shaken by the news of Custer's defeat, still too angry and afraid to see the logic behind Dan's words. But General Dawson clapped a hand on his shoulder and nodded.

"You reckon I could get somethin' to eat and then find a place to lay my head?" the messenger asked. "I'm 'bout wore out, boys."

"Come on into the hotel," Wagner said. "I'll let you have a room, and Aunt Lou can rustle you up some food."

"I sure will, mister," Lou assured him. "You just come along."

She glanced at Dan, their gazes locking for a moment. Dan wasn't entirely sure what would have happened between them if not for the interruption, but something would have. Dan was sure of that, and judging from the look on her face, Lou was, too.

Thinking of that reminded Dan of Bellamy and the ugly

incident that had broken out at the dance. As the crowd broke up, many of them following the messenger into the hotel to try to dredge more details out of him, Dan looked around and saw Bellamy sitting despondently on a nearby tree stump, one of many that littered Deadwood, marking where trees had been cut down to make room for the settlement.

Lou had gone into the hotel with the others, and while a part of Dan would have liked to follow her, he knew that she would be busy and they couldn't have any privacy, anyway. So he walked over to Bellamy and asked, "Are you all right, kid?"

"My jaw hurts where you punched me," Bellamy replied in surly tones without looking up.

Dan grunted. "You're lucky. If bullets had started to fly, you'd have wound up dead."

"You don't know that."

"Yeah, I do. There were at least fifty men in there ready to ventilate you. It wouldn't have mattered if you were Wild Bill Hickok himself. You'd have been dead in another minute, maybe less."

"Yeah, I reckon," Bellamy admitted grudgingly. "That still doesn't mean they were right to do what they did. They could have let Carla come to the dance." Bellamy's head stayed down, his hands hanging loosely between his knees.

Dan put a hand on his shoulder. "If it had been up to me," he said, "I would have let your gal in, Bellamy. You know things like that don't matter to me. Hell, I nearly—"

He stopped short. He had been about to say that he had almost kissed an African woman, but he didn't figure that was anybody else's business. Besides, he reflected, that was drawing a comparison between being a whore and being black, and that wasn't really fair, either. Carla at least had had a choice in her line of work. Lou hadn't been given any choice about her skin color.

"You nearly what?" Bellamy asked.

"I nearly jumped in the fight with you," Dan lied. "Come

on, let's head back to the claim. I don't figure there'll be any more dancin' tonight."

Bellamy pulled away from him and stood up. "I'm not going back to the claim."

"What do you mean? You plan on stayin' in town tonight?"

"I mean I'm not going back at all. I'm tired of panning for gold. We're never going to find much, anyway."

"Damn it, you don't know that. Don't say such things, Bellamy."

"Why not? It's the truth." He started walking toward the Badlands.

Dan hurried to catch up to him. "What are you gonna do if you give up prospecting?"

"I don't know. I don't care. I'll find something."

"Bellamy, this ain't right. We're partners—"

Bellamy stopped short and turned to look at Dan. "Not anymore, we're not. I'm officially dissolving our partnership."

"But what about the claim?"

"It's all yours." Bellamy waved a hand and then turned toward the Badlands again. "You can work it from now till Kingdom Come for all I care."

"Half of it is yours," Dan said stubbornly. "I'll have to pay you for it, but I can't do that now. I don't have the money."

Bellamy laughed, but there was no humor in the sound. "Don't worry about it, Dan. Pay me when you can. Pay me when you strike it rich, all right?"

Anger welled up inside Dan. "All right," he snapped. "I'll just do that." Bellamy had no right to run out on him this way, and he couldn't help but be mad.

At the same time, there was a certain sense of relief mingled with the anger. Since they had started working the claim, Bellamy had seldom if ever carried his share of the load. If the kid wasn't going to do his part of the work, he didn't deserve any part of the profit. Maybe they would both be better off with the partnership ended, Dan thought.

He hadn't planned on having a partner when he started up here to the Black Hills in the first place. Things had just sort of worked out that way.

Still, there was a feeling of loss inside him, too. Bellamy wasn't a bad kid. He had been brave in the face of danger, when the Sioux attacked the wagon train. And he'd been good company until he got mixed up with that girl at Miss Laurette's. Maybe, just maybe, once Bellamy got that out of his system, he might want to come back and work the claim again. If that happened, Dan wasn't sure if he'd take him back or not . . . but he figured he probably would.

Bellamy walked on without looking back, and finally Dan lost sight of him in the shifting shadows around the saloons and gambling dens and bordellos of the Badlands. He had gone back to Miss Laurette's, Dan thought, back to the arms of Carla Wilkes. So be it. The partnership, at least for now, was over.

But if something had ended tonight, something else had begun. Dan thought about Lou Marchbanks, and even though he was still upset about the rift with Bellamy and the terrible news of what had happened to Custer and the Seventh Cavalry, he managed to smile a little.

Nineteen

EVER since the fight with Cougar and the argument with Silky Jen that had followed, Jack Anderson had stayed away from the girl. He didn't know what she was doing, who she was consorting with, and he told himself he didn't care. He occupied his mind with other things.

Like watching Wild Bill Hickok at his target practice.

Every morning, before the wagon train resumed its trek to Deadwood, Wild Bill walked out a ways from the wagons and set up some targets. He might use rocks or sticks or almost anything that was small and difficult to hit. Clearly, this was meant not as an exhibition but rather a true test, a sharpening of Wild Bill's skills. Jack watched him and after a while even took over the job of setting up the targets, always stepping off exactly twenty-five paces, as Hickok ordered. Then he moved off to the side and watched Wild Bill go to work.

For years, during most of the time when he had achieved his reputation as the Prince of Pistoleers, Bill had carried a pair of cap-and-ball Colt Navy revolvers. Now those guns had been replaced by new-model Colt .38 cartridge revolvers. Jack had gotten a good look at the weapons and had seen that the triggers were filed off. Wild Bill thumbed his shots, which meant he could empty the guns in an astonishingly short span of time, and with dazzling accuracy to boot. More than once, when Bill had been playing poker late at one of the other wagons, Jack had had to help him back to his own wagon because Bill just couldn't see very well after dark. Being moon-blind, some of the boys called it. But in the bright light of day, it was a different story. Then, Bill could see as good as ever. Jack knew that, because he had watched Wild Bill shoot.

Say he lined up half a dozen rocks a little smaller than the size of a man's fist on a low branch of a tree. Wild Bill would stand there, twenty-five paces away, and suddenly his big hands would swoop toward the forward-facing butts of the Colt revolvers and draw them with a twist of his wrists. The draw was so fast it appeared as a mere flicker of motion, even when you were watching for it. Then as the guns came level they instantly began to roar, belching fire and smoke as Wild Bill thumbed off three rounds from each weapon in the time it took a man's heart to beat twice. He was an awe-inspiring figure, tall and sturdy and deadly, with powder smoke drifting around him.

And on the branch, those rocks were all gone, blasted into gravel by the bullets that had come from Wild Bill's guns.

Jack had never seen anything like it.

And Hickok could do that time after time, day after day, such feats of marksmanship that Jack would have deemed them impossible if he hadn't witnessed them with his own eyes. Sometimes on the frontier, the reputations carried around by men were wildly inflated, but not in this case.

Wild Bill Hickok was the genuine article.

A few days after leaving Fort Laramie, the wagon train pulled up to a ranch house on a small, tree- and brush-lined creek. A dozen horses were already there, sporting McClellan saddles on their backs and United States Army brands on their rumps. A few blue-clad cavalry troopers tended to the mounts while the rest of the patrol swam in the creek, grateful for the chance to relieve the summer heat and wash off some of the trail dust.

As Jack reined his mount to a halt, he saw a man in buckskins, with long brown hair and a neat goatee of the same shade, sitting on a stool in front of the ranch house door, whittling and talking to a man in range garb who was probably the owner of the ranch. As the wagons rolled up and stopped, one by one, the buckskin-clad man closed his knife and put it away. He stood up and strolled over to greet them.

Jack swung down from the saddle and turned to meet the man. He thought he had recognized him, and that hunch was confirmed a second later as the man exclaimed, "By God, it's the White-Eyed Kid!" He extended a hand.

As Jack clasped that hand firmly, he said, "Howdy, Mr. Cody. It's mighty good to see you again."

William F. Cody pumped Jack's hand up and down and used his other hand to clap the young man on the shoulder. "It's been a while, White-Eye. Where was it we last crossed paths? Cheyenne? Fort McPherson?"

"I think it was Denver," Jack said as he shook hands with the famous Buffalo Bill.

Cody threw his head back and laughed. "So it was, so it was." As he let go of Jack's hand, he looked along the line of wagons and said, "Is that Bill Hickok?"

"Sure is," Jack replied. "You fellas know each other, don't you?"

"Know each other? Why, we've been friends for years. We even spent a season together treading the boards of numerous theaters back East."

Jack nodded. He had heard Hickok talk about that experience, when he and Buffalo Bill and their fellow scout Texas Jack Omohundro had taken on roles in a traveling stage play called *Scouts of the Plains* or some such. Buffalo Bill had promised that a career as an actor would make Hickok rich, and eventually it might have, if Wild Bill hadn't disliked the whole thing so much that he bolted and went back West after one season in the theater.

Nor were Hickok and Buffalo Bill as friendly as Cody was putting on. Even before the stage play, there had been friction between the two men because of the numerous dime novels written by Ned Buntline about Buffalo Bill. It seemed that Buntline, who was really a fellow named Edward Judson, had first approached Wild Bill in a saloon one night and asked in a rather clumsy fashion for Hickok's permission to feature him in a series of yarns for a New York publishing house called Street and Smith. Wild Bill, not liking Buntline's looks, had refused and told him to get out of town. Buntline, being a scribbler and not a gunfighter, had complied. Later, however, he had made a connection with Buffalo Bill Cody and found him much more receptive to the idea of starring in the stories Buntline proposed to write.

Cody and Hickok had first met back before the Civil War when both young men worked for the firm of Russell, Majors, and Waddell, Cody as a rider for the Pony Express, Hickok as a teamster. They had been friendly enough, and Hickok had for a fact sort of taken Cody under his wing for a while. In the years since, both men had gone on to adventurous careers, enough so that the exploits of either would have filled plenty of pages of close-set type for thrill-hungry Eastern readers.

Buntline's appetite for story material had proven to be insatiable, however, because the man could crank out a yarn in seemingly no time at all and was ready to move on to the next one. As he pressed Buffalo Bill for more true stories of derring-do on the plains, Cody had fallen into the habit of taking some adventure of Wild Bill's and substituting himself for Hickok when he told Buntline about it. Wild Bill might not have discovered this deception if people hadn't told him about reading Buntline's latest opus and described the action to him. Hickok, hearing that Bill Cody was getting credit in the dime novels for things he, Wild Bill, had done, had naturally been a mite irritated. He had been willing to put those ill feelings aside when Cody approached him about performing in the stage play—promises of a lot of money always had the power to soothe quite a few ruffled feathers—but when that hadn't worked out, the possibility of a long-term reconciliation between the two famous frontiersmen had vanished.

At least, that was the way Jack had heard the story, and he tended to believe Wild Bill's version of it.

Now, as Hickok came striding along the wagon train, Cody turned to greet him with an outstretched hand. Hickok took it without hesitation, nodded, and said pleasantly enough, "Good to see you, Bill." Hickok was unfailingly a gentleman, Jack thought, even under somewhat strained circumstances.

"How are you?" Cody asked.

"Tolerable, I expect," Hickok replied with a shrug. "What are you doing here, Bill? I figured you'd be back East somewhere, in the middle of a summer tour with some new play you got Fred Maeder to write for you."

Cody shook his head. "For the time being, I've gone back to doing some real scouting instead of the make-believe sort. The Fifth Cavalry is moving up toward Montana Territory to join up with General Terry. These soldier boys I'm with now are an advance patrol."

"Trouble up that way?" Hickok asked.

Cody frowned. "You mean to tell me you haven't heard what happened on the Rosebud and the Little Big Horn?"

Hickok looked at Jack, who shrugged in ignorance and said, "We've been on the trail for a week or so, Mr. Cody. Ain't got much news in that time."

"What happened?" Hickok asked, tense now as he stood there.

"General Crook tangled with the Sioux on the Rosebud," Cody said. "They chased him back south. That's not the worst of it, though. Custer and the Seventh ran into probably the biggest war party that these parts have ever seen. Except for a couple of smaller detachments that had split off, they were all wiped out."

Jack caught his breath in shock. He had heard about Indian massacres before, had even taken part in a couple of skirmishes with the red men. But as far as he knew, almost an entire cavalry regiment had never been wiped out before.

"Custer," Hickok said quietly. "I scouted for him back in '67, you know."

Cody nodded. "I recall that, all right."

"It's hard to believe he's gone. Luck seemed to follow the man wherever he went. He could do something that seemed utterly foolhardy, and yet it always worked out to his benefit."

"Not this time." Cody turned back to Jack. "Say, where are you bound, White-Eye?"

"Why, I'm goin' to the Black Hills with Mr. Hickok and the Utter brothers and my brother Charley," Jack explained. "We plan on finding gold and getting rich."

"Always an excellent plan, if not always quite safe," Cody said. He looked at Hickok again and went on. "So Colorado Charley is with you?"

Hickok nodded. "He plans to start a freight line and Pony Express between Cheyenne and Deadwood."

"Pony Express, eh?" Jack thought that Cody's eyes took on a touch of wistfulness; his voice certainly did. "I'll never forget those days. Not that long ago, really, but so much has happened since then."

"Things have a habit of happening," Hickok said, and for a moment the two frontiersmen stood quietly, their minds elsewhere, or so it seemed to Jack, anyway.

With a little shake of the head, Cody turned toward him again and said, "I could use another scout on this little expedition, White-Eye. How about coming along with me? You won't get as rich as you probably would in Deadwood, but I think I can promise you a modicum of excitement, as well as one hundred dollars a month and all the Army grub you can eat."

Jack hesitated, unsure how to respond to the offer. He liked Cody, and they had gotten along well enough during the times they had met in the past. And with this news of the Custer massacre, it seemed certain there would be excitement aplenty up in Montana Territory.

But there was gold in the Black Hills, and that was where Wild Bill was headed, too. Over the past couple of weeks, Jack had been tremendously impressed by Hickok, and the famous frontiersman seemed fond of him, too. In fact, as Jack glanced toward Hickok now, Wild Bill shook his head. Cody couldn't see that, and Jack took the gesture to mean that Hickok thought he shouldn't accept the offer of a scouting job.

That was good enough for Jack. He said, "I'm sorry, Mr. Cody, but I reckon I'll go on to Deadwood with the wagon train."

"You won't reconsider?"

"No, I reckon not. I've got my heart set on finding a fortune in gold."

Cody put a hand on his shoulder again. "Well, good luck to you, then. Many men have grown rich searching for gold. I hope you're one of them, Kid."

"You plan on staying here long, Bill?" Hickok asked.

Cody shook his head and said, "No, the patrol and I will be moving out as soon as the horses are rested. We've got a good long ways to go yet."

"Keep your eyes open," Hickok advised. "I suspect there are plenty of Sioux warriors who would just love to lift that hair of yours."

"Oh, ho!" Cody responded with a grin. "You're a fine one to talk, Wild Bill. That pelt of yours would make an even finer decoration for some savage's tipi."

The men shook hands again, and then Cody pulled on a pair of cavalry gauntlets and went to round up the members of the patrol. Hickok watched the patrol depart a few minutes later and said quietly to Jack, "There goes a fine man. We've had our differences in the past, but Bill Cody's one of the few men I'd trust at my back during a fight."

"You reckon the Injuns will wipe him out, too?"

"God, I hope not," Hickok said. "It's bad enough that General Custer has gone under."

Jack thought about it and said, "A big victory like that is liable to make the Sioux even more likely to attack other white men, ain't it? I know this is a big wagon train, but if a war party was big enough to wipe out a cavalry regiment . . ."

"We'll take it as it comes," Hickok said. He peered off into the distance. "When fate calls you to the dance, Jack, all you can do is answer."

Twenty

BELLAMY rolled over in bed and groaned. His head
pounded and his mouth tasted stale and fuzzy. Miss
Laurette had fine wine at her place, as Fletch had promised
and Bellamy had sampled on his first visit, but over the past
few days he had come to prefer the more potent effect of
whiskey. Now that he was used to it, he figured that he
could even tolerate the vile Who-hit-John that Al Swearengen served in the Gem Theater. Not that he planned to set
foot in that place again. Miss Laurette hated Swearengen,
and the feeling was mutual. And since Miss Laurette had
been so kind to him, letting him stay here and all, Bellamy
felt a certain loyalty to her. He hated Swearengen for other
reasons, too.

Beside him in the bed, Carla stirred and muttered something in her sleep. Bellamy didn't know what time it was,
but bright sunlight came in around the flour-sack curtains
over the room's single window. It was probably the middle
of the day or later. Folks who lived in whorehouses didn't
have much use for the morning hours.

Bellamy lifted his head and looked over at Carla. They

had spent a lot of time together over the past few days—
not all the time, of course, since she still had to work—but
enough so that they had talked quite a bit in addition to all
the lovemaking they had done. She had told him how she
had come to wind up in Deadwood.

It was a sad story. Orphaned at an early age, she had
been raised in an orphanage in St. Louis, a hellish place
she had run away from when she was little more than a
child. Forced to fend for herself, she had learned how to
steal and hide from the law and finally had resorted to selling her body. She had been working at a house in Wichita,
she said, when she was kidnapped by a man who was on
his way to the Black Hills to hunt for gold. He had kept her
a prisoner most of the way during the journey, abusing her
at every opportunity, until she had gotten loose at last and
killed her captor with a knife. Alone in the wilderness, all
she could do was continue on to Deadwood, having heard
the would-be prospector talk about it so much that she had
a pretty good idea how to get there. Upon her arrival in the
boom camp, she had gone to work for Al Swearengen at
the Gem, but Swearengen was a brutal man who had a
habit of using his fists on the girls in his establishment
when they did the slightest thing to displease him. Unable
to tolerate that kind of treatment, Carla had left him and
sought refuge with Miss Laurette, who had been kind
enough to take her in and provide a relatively safe place for
her to work. That was one more source of friction between
Miss Laurette and Swearengen, Carla explained, over and
above the natural competition of business rivals. "Al took a
fancy to me," she had told Bellamy, who had sat there
raptly listening to every word of her sordid odyssey. "He
was mad as hell when I ran out on him and took up with
Miss Laurette. I guess he figured he'd have me around to
fuck and beat up until he got tired of me, but he found out
different, didn't he? He's lucky I didn't take a knife and cut
his balls off some night while he was sleepin'."

Bellamy believed the story—after all, Carla had no
reason to lie to him—and when he saw Al Swearengen on

the street after that, he felt a strong urge to pull his gun and blow a hole through the bastard. Bellamy fought down that urge, though. He wasn't a murderer. He might have descended into what his folks would call a quagmire of debauchery and shame, but he wasn't going to gun down a fella in cold blood, no matter how much the son of a bitch might deserve it.

So now, as he watched Carla sleeping, great feelings of tenderness welled up inside him. He didn't know what he would have done if he hadn't been lucky enough to meet her. He couldn't imagine his life without her.

He would do anything she asked him to do. Anything.

"**He's** out there again," Laurette said, her voice tight with anger. "That fucking preacher."

Lazily, Fletch propped open one eye. He had been dozing in the overstuffed armchair in his mother's quarters, his feet resting on the ottoman in front of him. He'd had a late night the night before, as usual, and he was tired. His blood never really started stirring until three or four o'clock in the afternoon.

"It's early," he said. "There's not much business for the preacher to run off. All the miners are out at their claims, looking for gold."

"Not all of them," Laurette snapped. "I was watching out the parlor window and saw a fella coming this direction just a few minutes ago. Before he could get here, Smith grabbed him by the arm and started waving his Bible around and yelling. The fella turned and took off like a cat with a scalded tail."

"How do you know he was coming here? Did he already have his trousers open in preparation?"

"I can tell," she said. "You think after all these years I can't recognize a man who's got pussy on his mind?"

"Elegantly phrased, Mother." Fletch yawned. "I'll bow to your superior expertise."

Laurette put her hands on her hips and glared down at

him. This early in the day, she wore a dressing gown belted tightly around her waist, and her face was unpainted and her hair down. She was starting to look her age, Fletch thought, then chided himself for being rude, even mentally.

"I don't know what in the hell happened to you," she said. "You dress fancy, you talk fancy, you act like a goddamned dude."

He said coolly, "What happened to me is that I was abandoned. A child who grows up with nothing, absolutely nothing, enjoys having something when he's older. I discovered I have a talent with cards and guns, and I put it to good use."

"Yeah, well, if I didn't know better, I'd say you were no son of mine."

"Neither of us could be that lucky," he murmured.

She glared at him a moment longer and then turned away. Without looking at him, she said, "You thought any more about what I said a few days ago? About getting rid of Smith?"

"My answer is the same, Mother. I'm not a murderer." Fletch yawned again and uncurled from the chair like a big cat. He straightened his tie and went to the hooks where his hat and coat were hung. As he shrugged into the coat, he said, "I think I'll go out and circulate a bit. It's early, but I might find a game."

"You do that," Laurette said bitterly. "Leave your old mother here to deal with that fuckin' preacher who's trying to ruin her business."

"It's my business, too, and I don't see that Smith is hurting it all that much."

"You just don't know. You haven't seen this sort of thing before, but I have. If Smith isn't stopped, he'll keep agitating until folks decide to clean out the Badlands. Then where we will go?"

"I really don't know," Fletch said from the doorway as he settled the black hat on his head. "There must be somewhere else in the world where men want to have sex and are willing to pay for it."

He closed the door a second before whatever she threw at him smacked into it.

Shaking his head, Fletch started along the hall toward the front part of the house. The door to another room opened as he approached it, and Bellamy Bridges stumbled out, wearing only long underwear. He was unshaven and his eyes were red-rimmed, and he didn't look anything at all like the innocent, naïve young man Fletch had first met less than two weeks earlier.

"Mornin'," Bellamy muttered. Head down, he started past Fletch, probably on his way to the privy.

"It's after noon," Fletch said.

Bellamy shook his head. "Doesn't feel like it." He winced. "Doesn't feel like much of anything."

Fletch sighed and put out a hand to stop Bellamy. "Look at you," he said. "You're a disgrace. I can see that I'm going to have to take you under my wing, so that I can teach you how to dress and behave."

Bellamy's interest seemed to perk up. "If you can teach me how to shoot better, I'll go along with that. I've heard how you killed three men in gunfights."

"They left me no choice."

"Yeah, that's the way it usually is, ain't it? Next time I don't have a choice, I figure to answer with lead."

Fletch looked at him for a long moment, then gave him a gentle shove. "Go on with what you were doing, Bellamy. We'll talk later."

Outside, Fletch debated whether to turn left toward the Bella Union or right toward the No. 10. He chose the Bella Union. It was bigger and had more gambling tables.

Billy Nuttall, who owned the No. 10 in partnership with Carl Mann, also owned the Bella Union. Mann ran the No. 10 pretty much by himself, since Nuttall was usually at the larger establishment. Harry Sam Young tended bar in both places, going wherever he was needed. It was a profitable arrangement, but Nuttall was always looking for even more profit. More than once, he had made discreet inquiries of Miss Laurette designed to find out if she would be interested in selling the academy, which lay between the two saloons. She had consistently rebuffed those advances, and Fletch knew that his mother had her eye on expansion herself. Instead of Nuttall owning the whole block, Laurette dreamed of turning that situation around and running it all herself.

His mother had never been short on ambition, Fletch mused. That was probably one reason she had run off with a traveling man years earlier, leaving behind a drunken bum of a husband and a little boy who had to pretty well fend for himself after that.

Fletch paused on the boardwalk outside the Bella Union, and unbidden, his fingers went to the watch pocket of his trousers. They traced the outline of the watch he carried there. Inside the watch was a photograph, a picture of his mother as a young woman. It had been all he had left of her, and over the years he had studied it until he knew every line of her face. When he had first drifted into Deadwood and seen her in person, he knew her immediately, even though the years had changed her to an extent. But she hadn't changed so much that he didn't know his own mother.

She hadn't wanted to believe it at first when he confronted her, but he recalled enough details of their life together before she left that she had been forced to admit he was right. When he announced that he was cutting himself in for a part of her operation, she had started to protest, then shrugged and gave in. "I reckon I owe you, after all these years," she had said.

"My thoughts exactly," Fletch had told her.

"Just don't go asking what-all's happened while we were apart or how your old ma came to be running a whorehouse in Deadwood. I'm not talking about it."

"Don't worry, I'm not interested in hearing about it, either," Fletch had replied honestly. Laurette, as he now thought of her, had chosen her own path, and whatever had happened to her along it was her business, not his. He didn't intend to tell her everything that he had done since she abandoned him, either.

So they had struck an uneasy alliance that had grown somewhat more relaxed as the weeks passed. Now, however, Fletch sensed that they were building toward trouble. He didn't draw the line at many things, but he was damned if he was going to kill a preacher in cold blood.

As Fletch went into the Bella Union, Nutshell Bill, a thimblerigger, nodded a greeting without ever pausing in his manipulation of the three nutshells on a board in front of him, one of which concealed a pea. The men who gathered in front of Nutshell Bill's rig wagered on which shell the pea was under. And they were doomed to lose every time, Fletch thought with a faint smile as he walked by. Nutshell Bill looked slow and clumsy in his movements, but somehow the pea always ended up somewhere other than under the shell his victims chose. Every so often, Bill let somebody win, just to keep up the appearance of an honest game.

Fletch checked the tables and saw that no games were going on. He went to the bar and nodded to Harry Sam Young. "Whiskey?" the bartender asked.

"Beer," Fletch said. "I have to keep my wits about me."

Harry Sam drew the beer and set it in front of him. He inclined his head toward the stairs that led to the second floor. "Got a new girl upstairs," he said. "You might want to try her out when she gets through with the fella who's with her now."

"Maybe later," Fletch said, although he knew he wouldn't. If he'd wanted a girl, he could have had any of the ones over at his mother's place. Instead he stood there and nursed the beer and waited for somebody to come along with poker in mind. His fingers missed the feel of the pasteboards if he went too long without shuffling and dealing.

And so another day in Deadwood began, he thought, as outside in the street Preacher Smith's voice rose anew, beseeching the sinful to turn from their wicked ways.

* * *

CARLA was still asleep when Bellamy got back from the privy. He thought about crawling back in bed with her, but he decided he had lain around long enough. He pulled his clothes on and buckled his gun belt around his waist, then wandered up to the parlor. Maybe some of the girls would be there, and he could talk to them for a while. Other than Carla, the whores weren't very smart, except for maybe Ling, and she barely spoke English. But they were better company than nothing.

No one was in the parlor, though, except Miss Laurette, and she stood at one of the windows, the curtain pulled back a little so that she could look out. When she heard Bellamy come into the room, she looked back over her shoulder with a glare.

"Oh, it's just you."

"Yes, ma'am. Something goin' on outside?"

"Just the usual. That damn preacher's going up and down the street scaring folks away." She let the curtain fall closed and turned to look at Bellamy, a suddenly intent expression on her face. "How long are you planning on staying here?"

Bellamy felt a surge of fear. He had been dreading this moment. He had no more money, and Miss Laurette was going to make him leave. That meant he couldn't see Carla anymore.

"I . . . I figured on getting a job," he said, hoping he could persuade her to let him slide a little longer. "You've been mighty generous, Miss Laurette, I know that, and I can't thank you enough—"

She cut in. "You want to stay here, is that it?"

His head bobbed up and down eagerly. "Yes, ma'am, I surely do. You don't know how much—"

"And you want to keep company with Carla while you're here?"

"Yes, ma'am, she's really special, but you must know that already."

Laurette gestured at the gun on Bellamy's hip. "Are you any good with that thing?" she asked.

"Well, I've been practicing," he replied, surprised by the sudden turn in the conversation.

"Show me."

"Ma'am?" Now he was really confused.

"Show me how you can use it," Laurette said. "Come on out back with me."

Bellamy didn't know what was going on, but at least she wasn't threatening to make him leave the academy. She stalked down the hall and out the back door. The privy stood about twenty feet away. One of the planks in the door was a darker shade of pine than the boards around it.

"Hit that board in the middle of the privy door," Laurette said. "The one that's the off color."

"You mean shoot at it?"

She frowned. "Don't go making me think you're stupid. You know what I mean."

Bellamy took a deep breath and blew it out, then faced the door. His nerves were jumpy. He took another second and forced them to calm down a little.

"Get on with it," Laurette snapped.

"Yes, ma'am," Bellamy said, and he drew his gun.

He had taken a lot of target practice, and this was just more of the same, he told himself. Moving smoothly and swiftly, he raised the Colt, earing back the hammer as he did so, and as the barrel leveled, he squeezed the trigger.

The gun roared and bucked in his hand as he fired four rounds. She hadn't told him how many shots to take, but that seemed like enough to him. He lowered the Colt and squinted through the thin haze of powder smoke. Two of the bullets had punched through the board side by side, about the same height as a man's belt buckle. The third one was a little higher, the fourth slightly higher still. But all four holes were fairly close together. This was actually some of the best shooting he had done, he thought. Maybe the added pressure had actually helped him a little.

For a long moment, Laurette stood with her arms crossed and studied the bullet holes in the door. Then she nodded and said, "You'll do."

"For what, ma'am?" Bellamy asked.

"If you're gonna stay here, you'll have to earn your keep," she said. "That means you're working for me from here on out, and you'll do what I say. If there's trouble in the house, you'll put a stop to it. You understand?"

Bellamy did, but he was still confused. "I thought that was sort of Fletch's job."

"He tell you that?"

"No, ma'am, I just thought—"

"Things are gonna be different around here, and if Fletch doesn't like it, that's just too damned bad. Is that a problem for you, Bellamy?"

He thought about Carla and how if he worked for Miss Laurette, he could be around the beautiful young girl all the time. Slowly, he shook his head in answer to Miss Laurette's question.

"No, ma'am," he said. "No problem at all. If you want something done, you just let me know."

Twenty-one

ᐤᐤ

For the first couple of days, the claim had seemed a little empty without Bellamy there, but Dan got used to it after that. He had always been a solitary sort of man, even when surrounded by the other members of the Seventh Cavalry, so he was accustomed to being at ease with his own thoughts. And it wasn't like he was totally alone, either. Men came and went up and down the gulch all day long, either heading out to their claims or back to Deadwood.

Panning in the creek still produced some color, but there were precious few specks of gold in each pan. Bellamy had the impatience of youth, but Dan was starting to feel a little impatient himself. At this rate, it would take a long time to accumulate a decent poke of gold dust.

So Dan started to look around with thoughts of sinking a shaft. Digging for gold was a lot different than panning for it. The risk of not finding anything at all was somewhat higher, but if a man did find something, the payoff would be greater, too. A few nuggets chipped out of the wall of a shaft could easily be worth more than the gold dust a man could take out of the creek in a month. Digging was hard work, of course, but so was panning.

The problem was that Dan was no mineralologist, or whatever such fellas were called. He knew a little about what sort of rock formations he was looking for, but when you came right down to it, he was just going to have to guess where to dig his first shaft. When he had settled on a place on the north side of the gulch, just below an outcropping of rock, he took pick and shovel up there and set to work.

The sun was hot, and he had soon sweated through his shirt. He took it off and kept working, alternating between the pick and the shovel. By the middle of the day he had a good-sized pile of tailings that straggled out below the irregular opening he had made in the side of the gulch.

"That's mighty warm work, looks like!" a voice called up to him. Dan turned sharply. Until this moment, he had been unaware that anybody was around. His Henry rifle was propped against a nearby rock. He put the shovel down and picked up the rifle as a man climbed toward him from the bottom of the gulch.

"You don't need that repeater, friend," the man called as he approached. "I ain't lookin' for trouble."

He was a burly man in late middle age, with a gray-shot beard and a tangle of gray hair under a battered old hat. He wore overalls like a farmer. His left eye tended to wander off to the side, Dan noted as the man came up.

The stranger extended a hand. "Name of Egan," he introduced himself. "I got Number Nine above, so I reckon that makes us neighbors."

Dan shifted the Henry to his left hand and shook with the man. "How come I haven't seen you before?" he asked.

"Because I don't go gallivantin' off into Deadwood ever' day like some of the fellers around here. I stay on my claim and work hard at it. That's the only way to get ahead in this world."

"You're probably right about that," Dan said. "What brings you by today?"

"I'm outta beans," Egan explained. "Figured I'd go in to

the Big Horn Store or Farnum's and buy some more." He patted one of the pockets of his overalls. "My poke's pretty light, but I got enough dust for that, thank God. Man can't work without nourishment, and I don't know of nothin' better than beans." As if to punctuate his statement, he broke wind loudly.

Dan chuckled and said, "Let's see, is your claim upwind or downwind from here?"

"If the wind changes, you'll know it," Egan said with a rusty laugh. "Findin' much color in the creek?"

"Some. Not enough." Dan nodded toward the rudimentary shaft. "That's why I'm diggin' this hole."

"I know what you mean. I found some mighty good pockets of color in the creek when I first started workin' my claim, but they seem to've petered out lately. I been thinkin' about sinkin' a few shafts, too."

"Ever think about sellin' your claim and gettin' out?"

Egan snorted in disgust at the very idea. "A man never gets anywhere by givin' up."

The two men chatted for a few minutes longer; then Egan said that he had to get on about his business. "Stop by for a cup of coffee sometime," Dan told him, feeling an instinctive liking for the older man. "You're always welcome."

"Much obliged. I'll do that."

With a wave, Egan went back down the hill and headed on toward Deadwood. Dan resumed his digging.

That day he got what he considered a good start on the shaft. Egan walked back by late in the afternoon, waving to Dan but not stopping. Dan was tired enough so that he slept like a log that night, but first thing the next morning he was back at it, swinging the pick to gouge out pieces of the hillside, scooping them up with the shovel, and adding them to the pile of tailings. He checked every shovelful carefully, looking for any sign of gold.

It was another hot day, and again Dan peeled off his sweat-soaked shirt. The heat built in the gulch. Not much air stirred between the high, thickly timbered ridges.

"I swear, you about the pinkest white man I ever did see."

Damn it, people kept sneaking up on him like a bunch of Injuns, he thought as he dropped his shovel and lunged for the Henry. About the time he snatched up the rifle, though, his thoughts caught up with his ears and he realized that had been a woman's voice calling out to him.

Somewhat embarrassed, he turned to see Lou Marchbanks standing at the bottom of the slope. "You gonna shoot me, Dan?" she teased.

He set the rifle aside, acutely aware that he was stripped to the waist. "Sorry," he said. "I didn't know anybody was around. Got a little jumpy, I guess."

Lou hefted the wicker basket she had in her hands. "I brought you some leftovers from today's lunch at the hotel. I know how you men are. You get started doin' something and sometimes you forget to stop and eat."

Dan glanced at the sky, saw to his surprise that the sun had moved over a considerable distance to the west. "It's past noon," he said.

"Well past. And you *didn't* eat, did you?"

"Well, no, I reckon I didn't."

"You come on down here," Lou said sternly. "Fella can't keep workin' so hard if he starves hisself."

Dan picked up his shirt and pulled it on, then got the Henry and walked down the slope. He left the pick and shovel where they were, figuring he would be using them again later, after he had eaten.

Lou wore a gray dress and a big bonnet to protect her face from the sun. She smiled at Dan and asked, "Where's your camp?"

"Along here a ways." He led her to the wagon and the tent he had pitched.

The basket contained fried chicken, potatoes, and biscuits. Once Dan started eating, he realized how hungry he was. But even so, he was polite enough to say to Lou, "Why don't you have some of this, too?"

"Lord, I ate a long time ago, and I get enough of my own

cookin', thank you." She was perched on a stool in the shade of the wagon while he sat cross-legged on the ground with the basket in his lap and his back against a wagon wheel. "I'm havin' a fine time just sittin' here watchin' you eat."

"It can't be that entertainin'."

"I like seein' people enjoy what I've cooked."

Dan ate in silence for a few minutes, and then asked, "How are things in Deadwood?"

"Busy and noisy as ever. Folks are still worried about the Indians. Have been ever since the word came about General Custer. Far as I know, though, ain't nobody seen any savages around here lately."

"I imagine the Army is keeping the Sioux busy. The chiefs probably don't want another big battle so soon after what happened on the Little Big Horn, so they'll try to steer clear of General Crook and General Terry."

"Why won't they want to fight? They won the last two battles."

Dan shook his head. "An Indian doesn't push his luck. As long as he believes the spirits are smiling on him, he'll fight. But he doesn't want the spirits to run out of patience with him, either. Still," he added with a shrug, "you can't ever tell for sure what an Indian will do. They fight with their hearts more than their heads."

They were quiet again for a moment. Then Lou said, "I saw that young friend of yours yesterday."

Dan knew who she was talking about, but despite that he said, "Bellamy?"

"That's right. He's stayin' down at Miss Laurette's place."

"You mean he's living there?"

Lou nodded. "Seems to be. Even got him some new clothes. Fancy buckskin jacket and a big white hat."

"Where did he get the money for that?" Dan asked.

"I wouldn't know. Less'n that woman give it to him. Like I said, he's stayin' there. Maybe he works for her now."

"What about Fletch Parkhurst?"

"He's still around. I see him goin' in and out of the

saloons and the gamblin' halls. Not so much at Miss Laurette's, though."

That was puzzling, sure enough, Dan thought. He never had been quite sure what the connection was between Fletch and the Academy for Young Ladies, but there seemed to be one. Fletch was there a lot, and on good terms with the girls and with Miss Laurette. Now, from what Lou was saying, it seemed almost like Bellamy had taken Fletch's place, whatever that was. Dan didn't like the sound of that, but there was nothing he could do about it. And of course, it was really none of his business in the first place.

"You want me to give him any message, I happen to talk to him?" Lou asked.

Slowly, Dan shook his head. "No. I don't reckon there's anything I need to say to him."

Once again, they fell silent. It was a companionable silence, though, and Dan found himself glancing at Lou as he finished the food she had brought him. She was certainly an attractive woman, he thought. He had never been drawn to an African woman before. Back in his days in the cavalry, he had been to whorehouses where one or two of the girls were black, and they had been fairly popular, too, because there were always men who wanted to go with them. Dan hadn't, but he didn't think that was because of their color.

He looked down at the basket, suddenly ashamed of himself. Lou was a fine, upstanding woman, and he oughtn't to be thinking of her that way. She sure as hell wasn't interested in having any sort of romance with him, he told himself. Sure, they had danced together there in the kitchen of the Grand Central Hotel, and he had come mighty close to kissing her, but hadn't she said that she wished he wasn't white? That barrier would always be between them. Wouldn't it?

"There's talk about havin' another dance at the hotel, since the first one got interrupted," Lou said. "You reckon you'll come if they have one?"

"Why, sure," Dan replied without hesitation. "You'll let me know?"

"I can do that." She looked around at the slopes of the gulch surrounding them. "It's pretty out here, and I like to get out of the settlement when I can, so I don't have to smell all the stinks and hear all the racket for a while."

"You're welcome any time," he told her, just as he had extended a similar invitation to the old prospector called Egan the day before. The circumstances weren't quite the same, though. Egan wasn't anywhere near as pretty as Lou Marchbanks.

They stood up, and he handed the empty basket to her. "I got to be goin' now," she said.

"Yeah, and I need to get back to work." A thought occurred to him. "Do you need somebody to walk back to camp with you, just to be sure you're safe?"

She smiled. "There's no Injuns around, and I ain't afraid of anybody else around here, I reckon. No white man would dare bother me. If they did, ever'body who eats at the hotel in town would gang up on him, prob'ly tar and feather him. That is, if they didn't string him up to the nearest tree."

Dan had to laugh, but he knew her logic was right. Decent women were safe just about anywhere on the frontier, except in cases of Indian attacks. And while Lou's color might keep her from being considered a decent woman in the eyes of some, her kitchen skills made her a highly valued member of the community in Deadwood. She would be safe, all right.

"I'll be seein' you," she said.

Dan nodded. "So long."

He wanted to say more than that. He wanted to *do* more than that. It would have been mighty nice to put his arms around Lou and kiss her. But he didn't do it. He wasn't sure how she would react if he did, and he had always been a cautious man. That caution had helped keep him alive during a long and eventful career in the cavalry. The Rebs hadn't gotten him, and neither had the Indians, because he had seldom made a move without weighing it carefully.

Now, though, he sort of wished he could be reckless for a change. As he climbed back to the shaft in the hillside and looked down the gulch to see Lou Marchbanks disappear around a bend in the trail, he told himself he was a damned fool for not telling her how he felt.

But she knew anyway. He sensed that. And she didn't know what to do any more than he did. She was careful, too, with the ingrained caution of someone who knew that most of the people around her considered her inferior. She didn't want to cause trouble, because trouble would always land on her first.

Dan sighed, took up the pick, and swung it. It bit into the rock, and he pulled out another chunk of the hillside. It would be nice to strike it rich, he thought, rich enough to go someplace where the color of a person's skin didn't matter.

He wondered how far that would have to be.

Twenty-two

So far, Bellamy hadn't tired of looking at himself in the mirror in the room he shared with Carla. He stood there quite often, tipping the big hat at different angles, turning from side to side so that he could get a good look at himself. Sometimes he wanted to appear jaunty; at other times, he cultivated a more serious look, as befitted a dangerous gunman. Mostly, though, he just looked at himself in the big white hat, fringed buckskin jacket, tight brown whipcord trousers, and high-topped black boots, and he said to himself—aloud, if he was the only one in the room at the time—"Bellamy, you look like you stepped right off the cover of a fuckin' dime novel."

A small part of him still felt like a naughty little boy every time he uttered that word, but he had fallen into the easy habit of using the obscenity-laced speech of everyone around him. He was hundreds of miles from his ma and pa. They couldn't do a thing about how he talked now. Nobody would ever dare to wash his mouth out with soap again. Anybody who tried, he'd pull iron and blow their fuckin' guts out.

Carla came in while he was preening and stopped to look at him. "I can't get over how handsome you are, Bellamy," she said. "Just looking at you makes me get all fluttery inside."

"I feel the same way when I look at you," he told her. "I'm glad Miss Laurette decided you could just stay with me and you don't have to . . . well, you know."

She came closer to him and slipped her arms around his waist. "I know," she said as she looked up into his eyes. "Ain't it grand?"

Bellamy bent to kiss her. Her lips parted under the insistent caress of his tongue. Her body was soft and warm and enticing under the silk wrapper she wore. Bellamy would have liked to take her to bed right then and there. It was hard to believe that only a couple of weeks earlier he had never even been with a woman. Now he felt as if he were intimately acquainted with every thrilling inch of Carla's body.

But he had responsibilities. Miss Laurette hadn't been so good to him, buying him the new clothes and giving him a place to live, out of the kindness of her heart. She expected him to keep order here in the academy. If any of the customers got out of line, Bellamy dealt with them. He'd had to do that a couple of times already. Once he had pistol-whipped a miner who had gotten drunk and violent, buffaloing the man into unconsciousness. The other time, the troublemaker had backed down and slunk out of the place, rather than face Bellamy's gun. That had made Bellamy feel good, mighty good. He had discovered all sorts of new talents in himself since coming to Deadwood.

The only bad thing about it was that he and Fletch were no longer friends. Fletch spent more time than ever these days in the saloons, playing cards and drinking, but he showed up at the academy some. Whenever he did, he didn't have anything to say to Bellamy. He just went into Miss Laurette's room, and often the sounds of arguing came from in there before Fletch left again, his face cold and hard. Early on, Bellamy had assumed that Fletch and Miss Laurette went into her room to screw, but obviously, that wasn't the case. There was some connection between them, Bellamy was sure of that, but it didn't have anything to do with lust.

He put his hands on Carla's shoulders and moved her back a little. "How's everything up in the parlor?" he asked.

"Quiet. Business has been a little slow this evening, Miss Laurette said. That preacher's at it again, making folks too uncomfortable to come down here. Somebody ought to do something about him. I know Miss Laurette's mighty upset about him."

Bellamy frowned. "Maybe I should have a talk with him."

"You can't talk to somebody like that. They're too crazy."

Bellamy remembered his own parents and nodded in understanding. They had been so focused on their rigid ideas of good and evil that there hadn't been room in their heads for anything else, let alone any sort of logic or reason.

"I'll think on it," he said. "Maybe I can come up with some way to get the preacher to lay off."

"It would be fine if you could do that, Bellamy, mighty fine. It would make Miss Laurette happy, and me, too."

He brushed another kiss across her lips. "I want to make you happy."

"Oh, Bellamy . . ."

As difficult as it was, he forced himself to leave the room and stroll up to the front of the building. He made frequent appearances in the parlor, just so the customers would know that he was there to come down hard on them if they got too rambunctious.

There didn't appear to be any danger of that tonight. Most of the girls were sitting around the parlor looking bored. Only a few were in their rooms with customers. Bellamy chatted with the whores for a few minutes, and then he was about to decide it would be all right to return to his room and spend some time with Carla.

Before he could do that, the front door opened and four men came in. Their unshaven faces and rough garb identified them immediately as prospectors. The girls perked right up at the arrival of potential customers.

Bellamy eyed the newcomers warily. The men were a little unsteady on their feet, indicating that they had already been drinking somewhere. They exchanged loud, ribald comments and hoots of laughter as they looked over the girls in the parlor. One of the men said to Bellamy, "You in charge here, sonny?"

Bellamy didn't like being called sonny, but he didn't know where Miss Laurette was right at this moment, either, so he supposed he *was* in charge. He nodded and said, "You know how it goes, gentlemen. Pick out the young lady of your choice and accompany her to her room. You'll pay her there."

"I want that China doll!" one of the men exclaimed, starting across the parlor toward Ling.

"Hold on there, you son of a bitch!" another miner protested. He reached out and grabbed the first man's shoulder, jerking him to a halt. "I saw her first, damn your hide, and I'm takin' her!"

"The hell you say!"

It didn't take a genius to see that trouble was looming. Bellamy stepped forward and said quickly and firmly, "No disturbances allowed in here. One of you will just have to pick a different girl. Either that, or take your dispute outside to settle it."

That seemed reasonable enough, but these half-drunken gold-seekers were in no mood to be reasonable. The two men who both wanted to go with Ling glared at each other for a second, and then as if they had both realized something at the same instant, they swung fists at each other.

The blows thudded home, knocking the men backward.

They caught themselves, yelled curses, and lunged at each other again. Bellamy tried to get between them, but he was too late. The men grappled and then went over heavily, crashing down on a table and shattering it under their weight. The girls screamed and scrambled to get out of the way.

"Son of a bitch!" Bellamy yelped. He reached for his gun, unsure what he was going to do once he got it drawn. He couldn't just shoot the two brawlers in cold blood. That would be murder, and he'd hang for it.

The decision was taken out of his hands. The other two prospectors howled angrily and jumped into the fray, each of them taking the side of one of the initial combatants. In the process, as the men leaped forward, one of them collided violently with Bellamy, knocking him off his feet. He had the Colt half-drawn as he sprawled on the parlor floor. The gun came the rest of the way out of its holster and slid across the polished hardwood floor.

With crashes and thuds and curses, the four men threw themselves wholeheartedly into the melee, wrestling and punching and knocking over furniture, slamming each other into the walls, running into the fleeing whores and knocking them down, too. The parlor was filled with chaos and destruction. Bellamy tried to get to his feet, but he made it only to his hands and knees before one of the men fell over him and knocked him down again, pinning him to the floor. He looked around desperately for his gun but didn't see it. Even if he had, he probably couldn't have reached it with that crushing weight on top of him.

With a grunt of effort, he heaved himself up and rolled to the side. That threw off the man who had landed on top of him. Bellamy kept rolling and found himself atop the miner, their positions reversed from what they had been a moment earlier. The man shouted a curse in Bellamy's face. Bellamy shut his mouth with a fist, slamming the blow down as hard as he could and bouncing the back of the man's head off the floor.

With that opponent stunned and at least momentarily out of the fight, Bellamy struggled to his feet at last and looked around at the devastation in the parlor. Mirrors were shattered, pictures had been knocked off the wall and had holes kicked in them, sofas were overturned, chairs were broken, and the small bar had been tipped over so that the liquor bottles stored on its shelves were broken and leaking their contents. A small lake of booze had formed on that side of the room. Some of the whores had managed to get out, but others had been knocked down, stepped on, and generally roughed up. Bellamy saw Ling huddled in a corner, crying and cradling her right arm in her lap. The odd angle of the limb told Bellamy that it was probably broken.

The three men still on their feet continued to fight with each other. One of them had a broken chair leg in his hand. He swung it at one of the other men, missed, lost his balance, and fell so that the jagged end of the chair leg ripped a long gash in the upholstery of an overturned sofa. He did even more damage as he got back up.

Bellamy hesitated. If he waded into the fight, the three men would probably turn on him and thrash him. Maybe, if he could find his gun, shooting them wouldn't be out of the question after all. . . .

The deafening roar of a shotgun made everyone freeze. Bellamy looked over his shoulder and saw Miss Laurette step into the room, brandishing the double-barreled weapon. She had fired the first barrel into the ceiling, causing even more damage, but it was obvious she intended to use the second barrel to cut down the brawlers. They were bunched together so that the buckshot would hit all of them.

Unfortunately, Bellamy was in the line of fire, too, and so were a couple of the whores. "Get down!" Miss Laurette shouted to them as she hesitated with her finger on the second trigger.

Bellamy and the girls weren't quick enough to react. Seeing the threat, the three men launched themselves at the front window and crashed through it, spraying glass out into the street. Cut up some, they landed in the mud, rolled over, and came up running. Miss Laurette said, "Shit!" knowing that the men would soon lose themselves in the crowded rat's warren of the Badlands.

Bellamy looked around, thinking that at least they still had the man he had stunned a few moments earlier. But that man was gone, too, evidently having slipped out during the confusion. Bellamy heard the rapid thud of footsteps from the rear hall, then the slam of a door.

"Bellamy!"

He swung around at the angry shout and saw Miss Laurette glaring at him.

"Goddamn it, you're supposed to keep things like this from happening!" she cried.

"I'm sorry," he said miserably. "I tried to break it up, but then those men just went crazy! There was no time—"

"Look at this place!" Miss Laurette wailed. "Just look at it!"

The destruction in the parlor was pretty bad, all right. It would cost a lot to repair and replace everything that had been damaged. And it wasn't just the furniture and fixtures that had suffered. Several of the girls lay around moaning in pain, and a couple seemed to be unconscious.

"I'm sorry—" Bellamy began again, but Miss Laurette silenced him with a fierce stare.

"These girls need medical attention," she said. "Go find Doc Peirce and bring him back here."

Bellamy nodded. "Yes, ma'am!" He hurried out of the academy and started down the street toward the barbershop run by "Doc" Peirce. Doc was also the local undertaker, and had enough medical training so that he could take care of the denizens of the Badlands. The more respectable doctors in Deadwood were often loath to venture down into these parts.

By the time he got back with the portly, mustachioed Peirce, Bellamy had done some thinking. Miss Laurette was still distraught, but she had calmed down enough to listen to him when he took her aside and said, "I don't think this was a common brawl."

She frowned at him. "What the hell do you mean by that? The girls told me two of those drunken bastards started to fight over Ling."

"That's just it," Bellamy said. "They were acting drunk, but during the fight one of them cursed right in my face, and there was no whiskey on his breath. It didn't even smell like beer."

"But if they weren't drunk . . ." Miss Laurette looked around the wrecked parlor, and understanding suddenly dawned on her painted and powdered face. "Son of a bitch! The fight was just a setup. What they really wanted to do was smash up the place!"

Bellamy nodded. "That's the way I figure it, too. When you stop and think about it, they didn't really do all that much damage to each other, but they tore up the parlor and hurt some of the girls bad enough so they won't be able to work for a while. The question is, who would do such a thing?"

Miss Laurette turned and stalked to the front door. She stepped out onto the porch, put her hands on her hips, and glared across the street at the Gem Theater.

"Swearengen!" she spit out. "He hates competition, and he's had it in for me especially since I hired Carla away from him." She glanced over at Bellamy. "She tell you about that?"

"Yes, she did."

"Most of the time, you can't believe much of anything a whore tells you, but that story happens to be true. Swearengen was sweet on her, as sweet as a cold-blooded rattle-snake like him can be on somebody, but he beat on her just like he beats on all his whores. She left him and came over here, and Swearengen's been mad about it ever since, that dirty cocksucker. He's behind this. I'm sure of it."

"You're probably right, but there's no way we could prove it," Bellamy said. "Even if we could, there's no law here, no court. We couldn't hold him responsible."

"Oh, we can hold him responsible, all right." Miss Laurette looked over at Bellamy, and her eyes were like chips of green ice. "The law's got nothin' to do with it. Swearengen did this, and he'll pay for it. I'll bide my time . . . but sooner or later, I swear he'll pay."

Twenty-three

DAN sat in front of the small fire he'd built to cook his supper. Out of habit, he never looked directly into the flames, because that ruined a man's night vision for a while. A fella never knew when he might need to be able to see well enough to shoot. Dan didn't expect trouble, but his Colt was on his hip and the Henry rifle was in easy reach.

He looked up as he heard a crackling in the brush along the creek. Somebody was coming, not that unusual an occurrence. Deadwood Gulch was a busy place, even after dark, as miners left their claims to go into the settlement, or vice versa. Dan set his empty plate and his cup of coffee aside and came to his feet as a couple of men emerged from the brush, leading mules.

The strangers stopped short at the sight of the fire and the ruggedly built man who stood beside it. Dan figured them right away for brothers. They had the same tall, gangling frames, the same thatch of red hair. One was a little taller than the other and had a full beard, while the other was clean-shaven except for bushy burnside whiskers.

"Evenin', mister," the bearded man said in a thick Southern accent. Dan thought he was probably a few years older than the other one. "Hope we ain't intrudin'."

"Not at all," Dan said, although to tell the truth he wasn't looking for any company. Hospitality was just another habit of his, like caution. "I'm afraid there's no supper left, but there's still coffee in the pot."

"Much obliged for the offer, but we ain't got time to do more'n shake an' howdy." The man stuck out his hand. "Ord Galloway's my name. This here is my little brother Clate."

Dan shook hands with both of the Galloway brothers and introduced himself, then said, "I haven't seen you fellas around the gulch before. You have a claim up here?"

"Not yet," Clate said, "but we're plannin' on gettin' us one mighty soon."

"Lookin' for somebody who wants to sell out," Ord explained. "You wouldn't be anxious to get rid o' your claim, would you, Mr. Ryan?"

Dan shook his head. "I'm afraid not."

"You must've found plenty of color, I reckon," Clate said.

"Well, not yet, just enough to be encouraging. I haven't been workin' it all that long. Just gettin' started good, in fact."

"You wouldn't know of anybody lookin' to sell out, would you?" asked Ord.

"No, but I sort of keep to myself, don't talk all that much to the other gents here in the gulch. What you might want to do is to go back into Deadwood and talk to General Dawson. He knows just about everybody and everything that's goin' on around here."

Ord rubbed his bearded jaw. "Gen'ral Dawson, eh? We'll keep that in mind. Prob'ly poke around some ourselves first, though, and see what we can come up with."

"Well, best of luck to you," Dan said. "Sure I can't interest you in some coffee?"

"Naw, that's all right." Ord jerked his head. "Come on, Clate."

Clate laughed for no apparent reason and followed his brother. The two men walked on up the creek, leading their pack mules. Soon they had disappeared into the shadows.

Dan frowned a little as he watched them go. He hadn't felt any great liking for Ord and Clate Galloway. In fact, something about them had rubbed him the wrong way. Their accents marked them as Southerners, and while Dan had never felt any great hatred for Confederates, unlike some of the men who had fought for the Union during the war, he didn't have any sympathy for the Rebels, either. Of course, the Galloway brothers might have been too young to fight in that great conflict, especially Clate. Nor did Dan's dislike have anything to do with the shabby clothes worn by the two men, since he had been poor many times in his life. To tell the truth, he was pretty much poor right now, since coming up here to the Black Hills had taken just about all of his money and he hadn't found much gold yet.

No, it was something else, something vague enough that Dan just put it down to him being tired tonight. And he had been thinking about Lou Marchbanks, too, when the Galloways came up, so he hadn't appreciated the interruption.

He sat down again and picked up his coffee, putting the worry out of his mind. Chances were, he wouldn't see the Galloway brothers very often, if at all. Men came and went up here in the hills, their destinies guided by a capricious golden fate.

DAN hoped that Lou Marchbanks would return the next day, but he wasn't particularly surprised when she didn't. She had a job of her own to tend to, after all, and he couldn't expect her to make the long walk up the creek just to see him, at least not very often.

But the day after that, not long after noon, here she came up the gulch, carrying that wicker basket again. This time Dan spotted her while she was still several hundred yards away, and his heart leaped when he recognized her.

"Hey!" he called out, his voice carrying down the gulch,

and when she heard him she looked up. He waved and then started down the slope from the half-sunk shaft.

They both got to his camp at just about the same time. Lou smiled and said, "I thought you might be hungry again."

"I skipped lunch, just in case you might show up with some more of that good food," he told her.

"You don't need to be doin' that," she scolded, although the smile remained on her face. "Man who's doin' hard work needs to eat to keep his strength up."

"My strength is up just fine."

"Oh, really?" she said.

Dan stammered a little in response to that cool, wry comment. He was glad when she said, "Just sit down and eat, Dan. That is, if you can get your tongue untied enough."

She had brought some roast beef this time, along with the inevitable potatoes and a slab of apple pie. All the food was good, but the pie was so delicious Dan felt like closing his eyes and crying for sheer joy. He settled for saying, "This is the best apple pie I ever ate, bar none."

"Oh, you're just sayin' that," Lou replied.

"No, I mean it." Dan ate the last bite of pie and felt a pang of regret that there wasn't any more. "It's the best I ever had."

"Go on with you. Gimme that basket. I got better things to do with my time than sit round here listenin' to some Irishman spout flattery." She was grinning as she said it.

"It's no blarney," he said as he picked up the basket and started to hand it up to her. Then, trying not to think too much about what he was doing, he reached up with his other hand and took hold of her wrist. "Sit with me for a few minutes before you go."

The grin on her face disappeared, replaced by a look of worry. "Dan, I can't. . . ."

"Ain't nobody around here but you and me," he said. "Ain't no reason we can't do whatever we want to."

Lou hesitated, but after a moment she sank to her knees beside him. He set the basket aside and took both of her hands in his. Quietly, he said, "I still think all the time about that dance we shared."

"So do I," she admitted. "But I shouldn't. Just like I shouldn't be out here alone with you like this. It ain't fittin', even if I am just a nigger wench."

"Don't say that," Dan said with a shake of his head. "That's not who you are, and you know it. I've seen the way you are in town, Lou. You rule the roost around there, and everybody knows it. How come when you're alone with me you start that slave talk?"

"I . . . I don't know. To keep you at arm's length, I guess." She smiled again, but this time the expression was a little sad. "It doesn't seem to be working, does it?"

"Not too well," Dan said, and he pulled her close enough so that he could put his arms around her and kiss her. She didn't resist. Her hands rested on his shoulders, the strong fingers gripping him tightly.

The kiss lingered sweetly, but it had to end. Lou finally pulled back, slid her hands down to his chest, and pushed away from him. Dan didn't try to hold her as she stood up.

"I don't know what you want from me, Dan Ryan," she said in a choked voice. "You know there can't be nothin' between us. Nothin' real, anyway."

"I don't know that," Dan said stubbornly. "Damn it, we fought a war—"

"A war that didn't change nothin' except some words! Folks still feel the same as they always did. North, South, slave, free, it don't make no difference. You're white and I'm black, and that's what it comes down to. That's what it'll always come down to."

"You don't know that," he insisted.

She folded her arms across her chest and took a couple of deep breaths, trying to calm herself. "Maybe it'll be different someday, but not in my lifetime and not in yours." She shook her head. "I ain't comin' out here no more."

"Lou! Don't say that."

"It's the truth."

Dan came to his feet. He didn't try to reach for her,

sensing that she would run if he did. Instead he kept his distance and tried to stay calm as he said, "You think it over, and if you decide you don't want to have anything more to do with me, I'll respect that. But I'm hopin' you'll change your mind and come back to see me."

She bent to retrieve the basket, and as she straightened, she whispered, "I'm sorry, Dan. I really am."

Then she turned and walked away without looking back, even though Dan watched her until the twists and turns of the gulch took her out of sight.

HE dug hard at the shaft that afternoon, taking out his anger and frustration and sense of loss on the uncaring rock and dirt of the hillside. He certainly wasn't in any mood for company, and when somebody hailed him from down below, he felt like ignoring it. But then he looked and saw the rangy figures of the Galloway brothers standing in his camp. Not really trusting them, Dan decided he had better go down and see what they wanted.

"Howdy, neighbor," Ord Galloway greeted him.

"Neighbor?" Dan repeated. "You buy Number Seven above?"

"Nope. Number Nine."

Dan shook his head. "That's old Egan's claim. I didn't figure he'd sell."

"He sold to us," Clate said quickly. "We made him a good price and he took it. Ain't that right, Ord?"

"Yep," Ord said. "We been workin' the claim for a couple days now, and it looks like it might be a good'un." He dug in his pocket and brought out a small rock. "Lookee at that."

Dan stepped closer and studied the small, dull-colored rock, recognizing it for what it was. "That's a nice nugget. You find it in one of Egan's shafts?"

"Our shafts now," Clate snapped.

"That's right," Ord said as he returned the nugget to his pocket. "We're on our way to town to see what it assays out to. Thought we'd do the neighborly thing and stop by to see if there was anything we could fetch you."

Dan shook his head. "Can't think of a thing." Even if there had been something he needed, he wouldn't have wanted to be in the Galloways' debt. "What happened to Egan?"

Ord shrugged his bony shoulders. "Hell, I don't know. We paid him and he left. I'm a mite surprised he didn't stop by here on his way outta the gulch, seein' as how it sounds like you two was friends."

"I only met him the one time," Dan admitted. "We got along all right, but I guess he didn't see any need to let me know he was leaving."

"There you go, then," Clate said smugly.

"If he's still in Deadwood and we run into him, I'll tell him you was askin' about him, how's that?" Ord offered.

"That's fine, thanks." Dan hefted the pick he had brought down the hill with him. "I'd better get back to work now."

"Sure 'nough."

"Be seein' you," Clate added.

The brothers walked on down the gulch as Dan climbed back to the shaft. When he got there, he turned to look at them, since they weren't quite out of sight yet.

Something was wrong. He knew it just as surely as he had known the other day that he didn't like the Galloway brothers. It was purely a matter of instinct, of being able to look at a man and judge his character. Dan had developed that skill in the Army, and he trusted his hunch now. Egan would not have sold out voluntarily to Ord and Clate. They must have pressured him into taking their offer, maybe even threatened him.

Or maybe, just maybe, they hadn't made any offer.

Why pay a man for his claim, after all . . . when you could just kill him and take it?

That was a mighty big leap for his thoughts to make, and Dan knew it. But the longer he considered the idea, the more he feared that there might be something to it. He had seen cold-eyed, hard-faced gents like the Galloways before, and they were nearly always trouble. Scavengers, he thought. Bummers like the trash that had followed General Sherman in his march across Georgia, civilian looters that had laid waste to anything that Sherman's men had left alone. Ord and Clate hadn't bothered him when they came up because they had seen that he was well armed and likely capable of using the Colt and the Henry. But an old-timer like Egan they would regard as easier pickings.

Dan sighed. He couldn't let it go. The possibility would haunt him if he tried to. There was only one thing to do. Ord and Clate would be gone to Deadwood for a while. He could walk up to Number Nine and have a look around, maybe find some sign of what had gone on there a couple of days earlier. He didn't like the idea of poking around on somebody else's claim, but he wasn't going there to steal anything. He just wanted to find out what had happened to Egan.

Leaving the pick and shovel just inside the shaft, he got his rifle and started walking up the gulch.

Twenty-four

THE sun was fairly low in the sky, and Dan knew there was only an hour or so of daylight left. That would still give him plenty of time to reach what he still thought of as Egan's claim, take a good look around, and return to his own camp before night fell.

He followed the creek, and soon he came to the stake that marked the boundary separating his claim from Egan's. The previous owner of Number Eight had put the stake in the ground, and Dan had seen no need to change it since the lines remained the same.

There was not much to distinguish one rugged stretch of gulch from another. Oh, there were occasional landmarks, like a lightning-blasted tree or an outcropping of rock that looked like a woman's breast—called Titty Rock, of course—but by and large there wasn't much difference. The ridges on both sides of the creek were high and steep and heavily timbered, the creek itself narrow and fast-flowing for the most part, usually between banks that ranged from six to ten feet deep. Dan walked along the northern bank, since that was the side of the creek he happened to be on. If he didn't find anything over here, he would cross the creek and work his way back.

He didn't know where Egan's camp had been located. It seemed reasonable enough to assume that the Galloway brothers would have continued using the old-timer's camp, but that didn't necessarily have to be the case.

As he walked along he saw evidence of the work Egan had done, in the form of several shafts dug into the hillside. Dan examined them as he came to them. None extended more than eight or ten feet. They were just wide enough for one man to make his way into them, providing that he wasn't too tall. Dan didn't have to stoop, but he would have if he'd been any taller. Ord and Clate Galloway wouldn't be able to work in the shafts without bending over.

Of course, they probably wouldn't work in these shafts, Dan told himself, because likely there wasn't any gold to be found in them. If there had been, Egan would have dug them deeper into the hillside. These were just exploratory diggings, much like the one Dan was working on now. Egan had gone so far on each one and then stopped. Obviously, his more experienced prospector's eye had told him that he was unlikely to find color in this particular spot and he had moved on somewhere else.

Dan had covered about half the length of the claim on the north slope when he came to the camp. He wasn't surprised to find it centrally located. It was in a clearing in the aspens along the creek bank. Just one tent was pitched. Evidently the brothers shared it. The cold ashes of a cook fire were in front of the tent. Not far away on the bank were the beginnings of a rocker-and-cradle outfit. The Galloways must have started building it before deciding to explore the slopes first. Egan wouldn't have used an apparatus like that, since it took two men to operate it efficiently.

"Anybody home?" Dan called, even though he knew Ord and Clate had gone to Deadwood. He didn't enjoy snooping around like this; it made him feel as if he were doing something wrong, even though he knew he wasn't. If anybody else happened to be around, he didn't want them thinking he was some sort of sneak thief.

No one answered his hail, of course. He moved closer to the tent and used the barrel of the Henry to flick aside the entrance flap so that he could look inside. He saw a couple of piles of dirty, wadded-up blankets. Those had to be the brothers' bedding. There was also a crate with a lantern on it and a few other boxes that probably had food and supplies in them.

Dan was about to let the flap fall closed when he noticed something on the canvas itself, some dark marks. He leaned closer and studied them in the fading light. They were letters, and they looked like they had been scrawled on the tent flap with a piece of charcoal or something like that. They spelled out a name.

Ulysses Egan.

Dan straightened, a frown on his face. This was the old-timer's tent, not one that Ord and Clate had brought with them. That seemed a little odd. He would have expected Egan to take his tent with him when he left . . . unless, of course, Egan intended to give up prospecting and never expected to need it again. Then he might have decided to sell it to the Galloway boys along with the claim.

Dan had come over here thinking that the Galloways might have murdered Egan and stolen his claim. Here was some evidence that might be proof of that, and yet Dan was still trying to find another explanation for it. He wanted to give Ord and Clate the benefit of the doubt, even though he didn't like them and didn't trust them. He didn't want to think that he was living next to a couple of murderers.

Because if that proved to be the case, he would have to do something about it, he realized. He and Egan hadn't been old friends or anything like that, and he wasn't a lawman by any stretch of the imagination, but he couldn't let such an injustice go by. For one thing, if the Galloways had murdered the old man, they might just kill somebody else if they decided this claim wasn't good enough for them. Next time they might come after *him* and try to cut his throat in the night, Dan thought.

But he still had no real *proof* they had killed Egan, he reminded himself. He had only his suspicions, and the fact that they were using the old-timer's tent.

He left the camp and walked on up the gulch, finding several more shafts, including one that had been worked recently. It had occurred to him that if Ord and Clate had murdered Egan, they would have had to do something with the body. The corpse could be buried in one of these shafts. Since this was the first one he'd found that showed evidence of recent digging, Dan examined the end of the shaft carefully. There was enough solid rock there for him to conclude that Egan's body wasn't behind it. The rock would have had to be broken up more in order to hide a body.

He stepped out of the shaft and looked at the sky. The light was going faster than he had expected it would. If he started back now, he would just about reach his own camp by dark, he estimated.

"Hey!" a voice yelled from downstream. "Who's there? Hold it, you motherfucker, or I'll shoot!"

Dan stiffened as he recognized Clate Galloway's voice. What in blazes was Clate doing back from Deadwood so soon? The answer didn't matter, Dan realized. What was important was that he had been caught skulking around someplace where he had no right to be.

Maybe he could bluff his way out of this. As he saw Clate's gangling figure hurrying toward him, brandishing a rifle, he called out in as calm a voice as he could manage, "Take it easy, Clate! It's just me, Dan Ryan!"

Clate came to a stop about fifteen feet away, leveling an old Sharps carbine at Dan. "What're you doin' here?" he demanded fiercely.

Dan didn't see any sign of Ord. He wished the older brother had been here, too, because Ord seemed a little more stable. There was something off about Clate, as if he weren't quite right in the head. Dan wasn't sure if that made him more or less dangerous than his older brother, but he still wished Clate hadn't been the one to catch him.

"I was just on my way up the gulch to one of the other claims. A couple of my friends are working a place about a mile on up."

That was true as far as it went; two of the men who had been members of the party Dan had guided into the Black Hills now owned one of those upper claims. And as long as they weren't looking to get into mischief, miners were allowed by custom to come and go through other men's claims. With the deep, narrow gulches cutting through the Black Hills, there was no way to get around other than following them. Of course, Clate might not understand that, being a newcomer.

"You wasn't just passin' through," Clate said with a sneer. "I seen you come outta that shaft. You figurin' to high-grade us, Ryan?"

Dan heaved an exasperated sigh. "I took a look in your diggin's just to see how it was going and what the rock looks like through here. That's all. I didn't mean any offense, Clate, and if you think I picked up any ore, you're welcome to search me."

For the first time, the barrel of Clate's Sharps lowered a little, and an expression of doubt appeared on his face. "You got to admit, it looks a mite funny," he said, a faint whine in his voice now. "You knew we was gone to the settlement, and here you are on our claim."

"Just coincidence. I shouldn't have gone in that shaft when you and Ord weren't around, though. I'm sorry about that, Clate."

The young man seemed to accept the apology. He lowered the Sharps even more. "I got to feelin' sick," he offered by way of explanation for his presence, even though Dan hadn't asked for one. "Ord told me to come back and lay down whilst he went on to town. I didn't want to, but he made me." A sullen look came over Clate's face. "He'll sell that there nugget we found and spend all the money on whiskey and pussy, and I won't get none. You're a lucky man, Ryan."

"What do you mean by that?"

"You got the pussy comin' out here to you."

Dan felt anger flare inside him. His hands tightened on the Henry rifle.

Clate was oblivious to that reaction, however. He went on. "Course, it's nigger pussy, but I guess that beats no pussy at all. Ord and me saw you kissin' on that wench at your camp. She's comely for a black'un, I reckon. My family never had no slaves, so I never got to try out any nigger gals myself. I hear tell, though, that the fellas what owned plantations used to be a-pesterin' the comely young wenches all the time. I don't know if I'd fuck a nigger gal or not. I'd have to think on it. Does it feel any different—"

"Shut up!" Dan roared, unable to control his temper any longer. He had listened to all of Clate's obscene babbling that he could stand. Clate had lowered the Sharps to his side, and now the Henry came up in Dan's hands until the barrel was pointed right at Clate's surprised, gaping countenance. "Don't you talk about Miss Marchbanks," he said, his voice trembling a little from the depth of his rage. "Don't you even think about her, you son of a bitch!"

"Wha . . . what the hell's wrong with you, Ryan? Put that gun down! I never meant no offense. It's just that we seen that nigger woman—"

"One more word and I'll kill you," Dan said. "I swear it."

Clate gulped and closed his mouth with an audible click of his teeth. He started to back away.

Dan moved to the side, keeping the rifle trained on Clate. "I'm goin' back to my camp," he said. "You and your brother ain't welcome there no more. I won't try to stop you from passin' through my claim, but steer clear of me. You got that?"

Clate's head jerked in a nod of understanding.

"And if you say anything to anybody about me and Miss

Marchbanks, I'll come for you and cut out your lyin' tongue, you hear me?"

Again, Clate nodded.

"Throw your carbine across the creek."

"What?"

"You heard me. I don't trust you at my back with a gun. Throw the carbine across the creek. By the time you get it back, I'll be gone."

"You sure do push a man, Ryan," Clate said.

"When I have to. Now do what I told you!"

With a surly glare on his face, Clate took hold of the carbine by the barrel and slung it across the creek. It landed among some aspens.

"If that gun's busted, you'll have to pay for it," Clate said. "That's only fair."

"I don't give a shit about fair," Dan said as he backed away more.

He didn't turn around until he was a good fifty yards away from Clate. Then he turned and started walking quickly along the creek, pridefully unwilling to break into a run as long as he was where Clate could see him.

Clate didn't seem all that interested in retrieving the Sharps, though. It sounded like he had his hands cupped around his mouth as he shouted after Dan, "You're nothin' but a dirty nigger lover, Ryan! You don't scare me!"

Dan knew good and well, though, that Clate had been scared. He just hoped the young man was frightened enough so that he wouldn't spread any vicious rumors about Lou in Deadwood. Dan felt sick at heart, and his stomach didn't feel any too good, either. He'd had no idea that the Galloway brothers were lurking around when he'd kissed Lou. Just knowing that they had witnessed that private moment made him feel slimy and dirty. If Lou ever found out, she would be mortified.

She couldn't find out, that was all there was to it. He would have a talk with Ord, maybe apologize for losing his temper with Clate, and appeal to Ord's sense of reason and fairness. He couldn't let Lou's name be dragged through the mud.

And he couldn't ever see her again, he realized with a tight, hollow feeling in his chest. Not the way he had during her two visits to his camp. If he ran into her in town, with lots of people around, that was one thing. That wouldn't do any harm. He would be civil, even polite. But he wouldn't ever put her in the position of being gossiped about again, no matter how much it hurt to think that there could never be anything between them.

She had been right. The whole thing was a mistake. He should have kept his feelings to himself. The war had changed things; he believed that with all his heart. But they hadn't changed enough. Not yet.

By the time he got back to his camp, Dan had forgotten all about Ulysses Egan and his suspicions about the old-timer's disappearance.

Twenty-five

~~

"**B**ILL, can I tap your keg?" Calamity Jane asked as she rode up alongside Hickok.

"Help yourself," he said with a casual wave of his hand toward the wagon that rolled along with them, Steve Utter at the reins. "You've just about drunk it dry, you know."

Calamity grinned. "Yeah, but we'll be in Deadwood tomorrow, and you can buy more whiskey there."

"More whiskey for you to drink, you mean?" Hickok asked.

"Hell, Wild Bill, you know I'll pay you back any time you want. All you got to do is ask." She leered at him and wiggled her eyebrows.

Hickok held up a hand and said, "No, that's quite all right. I've no objection to sharing my whiskey with you. Drink all you want."

"I'm obliged," Jane said. "I purely do enjoy a little dram from time to time."

That was quite the understatement, Hickok thought. The woman drank like a fish. At times she smelled a bit like one that had been out in the sun for too long, as well.

Calamity reined over next to the wagon and stepped right from the saddle into the back of the vehicle. Hickok called out to Steve to let him know that it was all right. He leaned over and caught up the reins of Calamity's horse so that he could lead the animal.

Jack Anderson rode up on Hickok's other side. "Mighty pretty country, ain't it, Bill?" he asked as he looked around at the timber-covered hills. "Sort of rugged to travel through, though."

"Yes, it is," Hickok said, agreeing with both of Jack's comments.

"Folks are talkin'. They say we'll be at Deadwood tomorrow."

"Should be," Hickok said.

"Fella back there on one of the wagons said he figured you'd take over as marshal once we got there."

Hickok's head jerked toward Jack. "What?"

Jack pointed over his shoulder with a thumb. "One of the fellas said—"

"I heard what you said," Hickok cut in. "But it's a lie. A damned lie, even."

The boy looked a little crestfallen. "I swear, Bill, I heard him say it."

Hickok shook his head impatiently. "No, no, I believe the fellow said it. But if that's the rumor going around, there's no truth to it. My days of wearing a badge are over."

"But it makes perfect sense," Jack protested. "You were the law in Abilene and Dodge and cleaned up those places with no trouble."

No trouble, Hickok thought. As if gunning down a friend of his was something that happened every day and was nothing to worry about. For a moment he was so angry that he almost lashed out at Jack, verbally if not physically.

But the boy meant no harm, and Hickok knew that. Like everyone else, Jack sometimes believed a little too much in the whole legend of Wild Bill.

At times during his life, Hickok thought, he had believed too much in the legend himself. . . .

"I won't be the marshal," he said quietly. "I've no interest in law enforcement. I'm going to Deadwood to look for
gold, remember?"

"Yeah, but—"

"But me no buts, White-Eye. But you can do me a favor."

"Anything, Bill."

"If you hear anyone else speculating on the idea that I
might pin on a badge ever again, disabuse them of the no-
tion, will you?"

Frowning, the White-Eyed Kid thought it over for a moment, and finally, with a sigh, he nodded. "Folks are going
to be disappointed to hear that, though. They expect a
whole lot where Wild Bill is concerned, you know what I
mean?"

"I know," Hickok said. "Believe me, I know."

CALAMITY Jane sat in the back of the wagon, leaning
against a crate with a tin cup in her hand. The motion of the
vehicle made her head rock back and forth, and that made
her sleepy. So did the Who-hit-John that she had tapped
from Wild Bill's keg. She supposed she ought to be
ashamed. He had brought that keg from Cheyenne for himself, and here she had drunk nearly all of it during the trip
up to the Black Hills from Fort Laramie. She was too
snockered to be ashamed, though. She giggled instead.

Leaning over, she pulled up the canvas cover where it
came down over the wagon's sideboards. When she put her
eye to the little opening she made by doing that, she could
look out to the side of the wagon and see Wild Bill riding
along. Lord, he was handsome! His long hair brushed his
broad shoulders, and his big hands held the reins so gently.
Calamity imagined those hands would be just as gentle
when they touched a woman. Even though he was dressed
rather plainly, his regal air made even simple duds look
fancy somehow. Charley Utter's clothes were a lot more
gaudy, but Charley was just a popinjay. He couldn't hold a
candle to Wild Bill.

With a sigh, Calamity lowered the canvas and reached over to draw some more whiskey from the keg into her cup. Somehow, she knew in her heart that she would never have Wild Bill Hickok.

But at least she could drink his fine, fine whiskey.

IN Deadwood, Al Swearengen climbed out of his bed a little past midday and staggered over to the window. He opened it to let a little fresh air into a room that smelled strongly of sweat, piss, and sex. Unfortunately, the air that came in wasn't all that fresh. Instead it was heavily laden with the stink of shit from all the horses, mules, and oxen that plodded along Deadwood's Main Street.

Swearengen forgot about the smell when he looked across the street at Miss Laurette's Academy for Young Ladies. He swore as he thought about Carla Wilkes being in there somewhere. She was supposed to be here in his bed, getting herself fucked whenever and however he goddamn well felt like it. He never should have let her get away from him. He never let anything he wanted get away from him.

The door of Miss Laurette's opened. The bitch herself stepped out onto the walk, dressed up nice and carrying a parasol, of all things. A hat that matched the bottle-green of her dress was perched on her red hair. As if she felt his baleful eyes on her, she looked up, and her gaze locked with Swearengen's. A smile spread slowly across her face as she lifted her hand and raised her middle finger at him.

Swearengen slammed the window shut as a towering rage rose in him. The noise made the blond whore in his bed stir around a little. Swearengen ripped his long underwear open as he stalked over to the bed. He threw the sheet back and slapped the whore on the butt, hard.

"Roll over!" he told her savagely. "On your belly! Now, damn it!"

That redheaded bitch would pay for defying him, for taking Carla away from him. And as he made the whore underneath him cry out in pain, he imagined she was Laurette, and he ignored the whimpers and pounded away that much harder.

FLETCH Parkhurst saw his mother walking toward him, and thought about crossing the street so that he could avoid meeting her. But he knew Laurette had already seen him, and he knew she would be offended if he dodged her. He kept walking, and when they met he nodded politely and touched a finger to the brim of his hat.

Laurette stopped, so he had to as well. She said, "We haven't seen much of you the past few days, Fletch."

"I've been busy," he said.

"You used to never be too busy for your own—"

"Don't say it," he told her, his voice low.

She smiled coldly. "So now you're ashamed of me? Now that the money you made from my house has turned you into a rich man?"

"I'm not all that rich. In fact, sometimes I feel decidedly poorer than most."

If he was trying to rattle her—and he honestly didn't know if that was his intention or not—he wasn't succeeding. She just kept smiling and said, "Al Swearengen paid some men to stage a fight and wreck the academy a couple of days ago."

"I heard something about that."

"You still have a financial interest in the place, even if you haven't been by to collect your share of the profits."

"Why don't you keep them?" Fletch suggested. "I haven't done anything lately to earn them."

For the first time, Laurette's control slipped a little. "That's the fucking truth," she said. "What happened to you, Fletch? There was a time you would've been just as eager to settle the score with Swearengen as I am."

He couldn't really explain it, but he thought perhaps he ought to at least try. "I decided I didn't want to fight the same battles you do," he said. "At least, I don't want to fight them the same way you do."

"You mean you don't want to fight to win?" Exasperation entered her voice. "Is this still about that damned preacher?"

"Not completely. That was just what started me thinking."

"Thinking that you're too good for me and my business? Like being a gambler is so much more high-and-mighty?"

"I don't cheat the people I play cards with."

She leaned closer to him and hissed, "And I don't cheat the people who come to my house. They get the best booze and the best pussy I can give 'em. By God, what could be more honest than that?"

Fletch just shook his head. If she didn't understand, he couldn't explain it to her. He wasn't sure he could explain it to himself.

"Just deal me out," he said. "I don't want anything more to do with it."

"All right. I've got Bellamy to help me now, anyway."

Fletch winced a little. "Bellamy is a greenhorn, and you know it. Sure, you can use Carla to get him to do whatever you want, but he's liable to get killed in the process. Do you want that on your conscience?"

Laurette laughed. "Hell, I haven't been able to afford one of those for years." She stepped toward him, forcing him to move aside. He watched her go on down the street for a moment, and then he turned away with a shake of his head.

Once things changed, they could never go back to the way they once had been. He should have realized that before. But he knew it now, and he would never forget it.

"**FOR** all have sinned," the Reverend H.W. Smith said as he stood on the box he had placed in the street in front of the Bella Union. He lifted the Bible high over his head and looked at the teeming sea of frontier humanity as it ebbed and flowed around him. Why would they not listen to him?

Why did they ignore him and his message? The Word he was trying to spread was so simple, so easy to grasp. "For all have sinned," he cried out again, "and come short of the glory of God!"

Twenty-six

B Y the time Dan woke up the next morning, Egan was on his mind again. The confrontation with Clate Galloway over Lou Marchbanks had shaken Dan to the point that he'd forgotten why he was on the Galloways' claim to start with. But as he fixed himself some breakfast, he couldn't get the old man out of his thoughts.

He was more convinced than ever that Ord and Clate had done away with the old-timer. Egan wouldn't have sold out to them, and even if for some unknown reason he had, he wouldn't have gone off and left them his tent. No, Dan told himself, Egan was dead. It was just a matter of finding his body. That would be the proof he needed against the brothers.

But what would he do with that proof if he found it? he asked himself. The closest law was hundreds of miles away. When you came right down to it, Deadwood was an outlaw camp, smack-dab in the middle of Indian land with no right to be there. There was the Army, with the closest post down at Fort Laramie, but Dan doubted if the commanding officer would take any interest in the murder of one trespasser by two more trespassers.

No, the only justice available was miner's justice. Vigilantes. Dan thought that if he talked to the other men up and down the gulch and in town and presented them with evidence that Ord and Clate were murderers, something would be done about it. A group of men could gather together and mete out their own rough justice to the murderers.

In that case, though, the Galloways would get a chance to talk, and Dan had no doubt they would tell everything they knew—or thought they knew—about him and Lou. He didn't care for his own sake, but he didn't want her to be embarrassed and humiliated.

So he could sit here on his claim and ignore Ord and Clate and hope they would ignore him: an uneasy truce, but one that might hold. Or he could go after them and risk hurting a woman he admired very much.

How the hell had he gotten himself into this mess?

His coffee had gone cold while he was pondering. He drank the last of it now and stood up. He still had work to do. Maybe an answer would come to him while he was digging in that shaft.

Swinging the pick and shovel didn't help, though. After an hour of hard work, he realized that the same dilemma would still be facing him no matter how long he chipped away at the face of the rock at the end of the shaft. He was caught between seeking justice for Ulysses Egan and protecting Lou Marchbanks. Talk about being between a rock and a hard place, he thought. . . .

And then he asked himself what Lou herself would want him to do if she knew about this problem. How would she solve it?

Dan lowered the pick and straightened from the crouch in which he had been working. He hadn't known Lou for that long, and he supposed he didn't really know her all that well. But he knew her well enough to believe that she was honest and practical and a good woman. Would she want a couple of murderers to get away with their crime just so she wouldn't be embarrassed? Dan tried to convince himself that she might.

But in his heart he knew the answer. Just like he knew now what he was going to have to do.

WITH the Colt belted at his hip, the Henry in his hands, and his cavalry field glasses slung around his neck, he crossed the creek and climbed to the rimrock on the southern side of the gulch. From here he had a good view of the creek far below and the twisting gulch it had created. Dan began working his way to the west, keeping low and using the trees for cover so that he wouldn't be skylighted.

He left his claim behind and moved onto the one now being worked by the Galloway brothers. He moved carefully and as silently as possible, stopping often to listen. If Ord and Clate were working in one of the shafts, he ought to be able to hear them, he thought.

During his years in the cavalry, he had talked with many of the scouts, both white and Indian, who had ridden with the Seventh. He knew how to move so that he could see and not be seen, hear and not be heard. He wasn't as good at it as those scouts had been, of course, but he took his time and did the best he could.

He spotted a tendril of smoke climbing into the sky, and moved along the rimrock until he reached a spot where he could look down at the Galloways' camp. Raising the field glasses to his eyes, he peered through them and saw that the brothers weren't at work yet. They sat by the fire, having a late breakfast. Ord looked a little green around the gills, Dan thought. Clate must have been right: Ord had sold the nugget and gone on a bender the night before, and now he was sick and hungover. That explained why the brothers were getting a late start on the day's work, if they intended to work at all.

Dan waited until they finished breakfast. Then, taking a pick and shovel with them, they walked down the gulch to one of the shafts and disappeared inside it. A few minutes later, Dan faintly heard the clink of the pick against rock and knew the brothers had started digging.

As long as they were in the shaft, Dan had a free hand in searching the claim, especially here across the creek on the southern side of the gulch. He got busy, quartering back and forth across the rough landscape, not sure what he was looking for but hoping that he would know it when he saw it.

He didn't find any shafts on this side of the stream. Egan must not have gotten around to prospecting over here, Dan thought. He kept one ear cocked, listening to the sounds of digging that came from the shaft on the other side of the creek. Any time it stopped, Dan went to ground, finding himself a good hiding place in the brush and timber, but each time the digging resumed after a spell, telling him that the Galloways had just taken a break.

He estimated that he had just about reached the western boundary of the claim when he came to a narrow, brush-choked ravine cut into the side of the gulch. A tiny trickle of water came out of it and merged with the creek. Dan walked on past the mouth of the ravine and then abruptly stopped and turned back to look at it. He had seen something from the corner of his eye, something that didn't seem right somehow.

After a moment of study, he figured out what it was that had caught his attention. The leaves on several branches of the thick brush were turning brown, as if they were dead, but the brush around them was green and vital. Dan moved closer and saw that the branches he had noticed were all broken, as if they had been bent back until they cracked. They had sprung back into place to a certain extent, so that the wall of brush appeared intact, but now that he'd had a closer look, Dan knew that something had forced its way through there. A bear, maybe, he told himself.

Or two men, carrying a corpse?

There was only one way to be sure. Dan pushed through the branches and into the ravine.

It was about forty feet deep and less than ten feet wide.

Brush grew from both sides and weaved its branches together into an almost impassable barrier. Dan's clothes were torn and his skin scratched before he had gone more than a few steps. This was crazy, he told himself. Ord and Clate wouldn't have hidden Egan's body up here.

And yet, what better place could they have found? Nobody would ever claw through this brush unless he had a mighty good reason.

Dan wished he had an ax. He could have used it to hack some of the branches out of his way. He pushed the brush back with the barrel of the rifle as much as he could and slid through the narrow openings he created that way. It was slow going, but finally he reached the end of the ravine and found nothing there but a sheer wall with a tumbled pile of rocks at the base of it.

He sniffed and caught the scent of something dead. His eyes went to that pile of rocks, and he moved closer to it. The smell got stronger.

Swallowing a curse, Dan went to his knees and began moving the rocks aside. Most of them were pretty big, causing him to grunt with the effort. Two men could have handled them without much trouble, though, he thought. His nose wrinkled as the bad smell grew even more pronounced.

He wasn't at all surprised a few minutes later when he uncovered part of a bare arm. He found the elbow and followed the arm on up, lifting rocks out of the way. Even knowing what to expect, he was still taken aback when he rolled a rock aside and saw the bearded face of Ulysses Egan. The old-timer stared up sightlessly, his features battered and misshapen. His wandering left eye had been forever stilled. There was a black-rimmed hole just above it where he had been shot.

Dan closed his eyes and leaned on one of the bigger rocks. A shudder went through him. He had seen violent death before, plenty of times, and he had known when he began his search that there was a good possibility Egan had been murdered. Knowing that, and seeing the grisly evidence right in front of him, were two different things, however.

Breathing as shallowly as he could because of the stink, Dan began replacing the rocks, covering up Egan's corpse. He didn't want animals to get at it before he could deal with this. Later, he could bring a group of men up here and they could take the body back to Deadwood for a proper burial. The other miners would probably have to see the corpse for themselves before they would take action against Ord and Clate. The Galloways might deny that they'd had anything to do with Egan's death, but the evidence was clear. Clear enough for frontier justice, anyway.

When Dan was satisfied that Egan was covered up well enough, he began working his way back out of the ravine. He was soaked with sweat from all the effort he had put into the last half hour when he pushed his way out of the brush and stumbled onto the bank of Deadwood Creek.

Twenty feet away from him, Ord Galloway stopped short, eyes widening in shock. Ord had a new Winchester in his hands, and he suddenly lifted it, trying to bring the barrel to bear on Dan.

Dan had no idea what Ord was doing here. Judging from the expression on his face, Ord hadn't expected to find anybody at the ravine. But Ord had to know that Dan had found Egan's body, which meant that he couldn't allow Dan to leave here alive. Dan grabbed the butt of his Colt, knowing he wasn't any kind of a fast draw but knowing as well that his life depended on summoning up all the speed he could.

Ord got the first shot off, firing while Dan was still drawing the revolver. In his hurry, though, Ord rushed his shot and it missed, whipping past Dan to the right. Ord started to lever another round into the Winchester's chamber as Dan brought up the Colt. He couldn't risk a shot from the waist. Too big a chance he would miss. He had to aim, if only for an instant . . .

The revolver boomed and bucked in Dan's hand. He saw cloth and flesh and blood fly from the upper part of

Ord's right arm. Ord was just grazed, but the impact of the heavy slug was still enough to knock him back a step and make him drop the rifle. He screamed in pain and then yelled, "Clate! Clate!"

Dan fired again. This time his bullet knocked the battered old hat from Ord's head and sent it spinning into the creek. Ord was reaching for the fallen Winchester, but that close call changed his mind. He spun around and ran instead, hunching his shoulders and pumping his arms. Dan took one more shot, aiming at Ord's legs in hopes of bringing him down, but Ord ducked to the side and started to zigzag. Dan's bullet chipped bark off the trunk of an aspen.

Somewhere down the gulch, Clate Galloway was yelling. Dan knew if he tried to fight both of them, they would probably kill him. If he'd been able to capture Ord, he could have used him as a hostage against Clate. Now, faced with the possibility of both brothers coming after him, he knew it was time for a tactical retreat.

He jammed the Colt back in its holster and ran up the slope, hoping to lose himself in the thick timber. He had to get away from the Galloways and find some help. The shots would bring other miners in the area to see what was wrong. Everybody was still nervous about Indian attacks. Dan knew that if he could dodge Ord and Clate for a while, the odds would likely swing in his favor.

He climbed high on the slope, wanting to stay above them, and began moving down the gulch toward his own claim. He reloaded the Colt, replacing the rounds he had fired, and then clutched the Henry tightly in his hands, ready to use it if need be. He didn't see or hear any signs of pursuit, though, which came as something of a surprise. The Galloways had to know that they couldn't afford to let him live.

When he reached the spot above their camp, he paused and peered down, seeing movement around the tent. He frowned in confusion as he watched Ord and Clate saddling up their horses. They couldn't hunt him down in the gulch on horseback. Using his field glasses, Dan studied them and saw that a bloodstained rag was tied tightly around Ord's wounded arm. The two brothers swung up into their saddles and grabbed the reins of the packhorses.

They were running away, Dan realized with a shock as he lowered the glasses. Rather than trying to hunt him down and kill him, they were taking off for the tall and un-cut. Talk about a couple of craven, low-life cowards . . .

But he had known that already from the way they had murdered Ulysses Egan and stolen his claim.

Dan started to run along the rimrock. The Galloways ap-peared to be headed for Deadwood, hoping maybe they could pick up some supplies and be well on their way before Dan reached the settlement and spread the news of their crime. He had to stop them. If they made it out of Dead-wood, they could disappear into the Black Hills or leave the area entirely and light a shuck for somewhere else. The fron-tier was a mighty big, lonesome place, and men had dodged retribution for their crimes many times in the past.

But not this time, Dan swore to himself as he hurried over the rugged landscape. Not this time.

Twenty-seven

***

DEADWOOD nestled in the hills like a jewel in the folds of a deep green cloth. Well, not exactly a jewel, Wild Bill Hickok thought as the wagon train wound its long length down the trail into the settlement. That was giving the squalid boom camp entirely too much credit. Perhaps one day Deadwood would be the crowning jewel of the Black Hills, but not now.

From the wagon seat, Colorado Charley called, "There she is, Bill! I was beginnin' to wonder if we'd ever make it!"

Calamity Jane rode alongside Hickok. She said, "Hell, it don't look like much."

"It's the biggest town we've seen since Cheyenne," Jack Anderson put in from where he and his brother Charley were riding behind Hickok and Calamity. "I'm glad to be here."

So were the other members of the group. Whoops of excitement went up from nearly all the wagons. The whores in one of them started singing a bawdy song about what they were going to do when they got there. The White-Eyed Kid dropped back a little, until he could see Silky Jen among the bunch that was singing. She stopped as their eyes met for a moment, and then she pointedly looked away. She had never forgiven Jack for his atrocious behavior after the fight with Cougar. Most of the time, he had been able to force her out of his thoughts, but not always. When he dwelled too much on what might have been, he got first angry, then maudlin.

Maybe things would be different now that they were all here in Deadwood, Jack told himself. He wasn't sure what he was going to do or how long he would stay in the camp, but surely there would be a chance for him to see her again. He had talked to some of the other girls and knew that Silky planned to go to work with them for a man called Swearengen. Jack hoped the place wouldn't be too bad.

Up ahead, Calamity turned to Hickok and said, "Come on, Bill, let's go take a look at this fuckin' burg." She kicked her horse in the flanks and sent the animal galloping ahead of the wagons.

Hickok lifted the reins and hitched his mount to a faster gait, although Calamity pulled ahead of him, too. He didn't want to be too far behind her when she reached the camp. There was no telling what sort of trouble she might get into. Hickok sighed as he wondered just when it was that he had appointed himself Calamity Jane's keeper. Lord knows she needed one, though.

Just before Calamity and Hickok reached the edge of town, two men came galloping into Deadwood on a different trail, one coming from the gulch to the west. They were leading a couple of packhorses and seemed to have no regard for anyone who might be in front of them. Several men had to leap out of the way to avoid being ridden down. They yelled curses and shook their fists at the two horsebackers, but the riders never slowed or looked back. Hickok saw them haul their sweating mounts to a stop in front of a building farther along the street. They left their saddles in a hurry and rushed inside.

With a little shake of his head, Hickok put them out of

his thoughts. The two men didn't have anything to do with him.

BELLAMY and Carla were sitting on one of the divans in the parlor, which had been fixed up as much as possible after the brawl a few days earlier, when two men came into the academy, their muddy boots stomping heavily on the floor. Bellamy had seen them a few days earlier, he recalled. They had come here and talked to Miss Laurette, then spent some time with a couple of the girls before leaving. But that was all Bellamy knew about them, except that one of the men seemed to be injured. The taller one had a bloody bandage tied around his right arm.

"Where is she?" the wounded man demanded loudly. "Where's the woman who runs this place?"

Bellamy stood up. "Take it easy, mister," he said. "It's too early in the day for this much ruckus. Most of the girls are still sleeping."

The other man yanked a gun from its holster and pointed it at Bellamy. "We didn't ask about the whores, you dumb cocksucker!"

From the divan behind him, Carla gasped. Bellamy's eyes widened in a mixture of surprise and fear as he stared down the barrel of the revolver. Those emotions went away and were replaced with anger. He didn't like being threatened like that. Not here, in front of Carla.

"Put that gun up," he said coldly, "or somebody's going to get hurt."

"Yeah, you, you fuckin' idiot!"

"Clate," the wounded man snapped. "Take it easy." To Bellamy, he went on. "Where's Miss Laurette?"

"I'm right here," the madam said from the door between the hall and the parlor. "What do you want?"

The wounded man turned toward her while the one called Clate still menaced Bellamy with his gun. "You remember us?" the wounded man said.

Bellamy saw Miss Laurette's face harden into an

unreadable mask. "I remember you," she said. "Come on back to my office."

"You gotta help us," Clate babbled as he backed away. "You got us into this, you gotta help us."

The two men disappeared down the hall with Miss Laurette. Bellamy stood there, feeling vaguely cheated. That man had pointed a gun at him and gotten away with it.

But they were still in the house. He might still have a chance to satisfy his wounded honor, Bellamy told himself.

"**HE** knows what we done!" Clate Galloway said frantically. "He found that old bastard's body, Ord said! And it was all your idea to kill him!"

With his left hand, Ord grasped his brother's shoulder and squeezed hard. "Shut up, Clate," he said. "It won't do us any good for you to panic."

From behind the desk, Laurette regarded the two men coldly. "What happened?" she asked, directing the question at Ord. She knew that Clate was too walleyed to make any sense.

"We did what you said," Ord replied curtly. "We went out to that claim a few days ago and tried to get the old man to sell it to us. When he wouldn't do it, we killed him and hid the body."

"I never told you to kill him," Laurette said.

"You might as well have," Ord shot back at her. "You said after you saw the size and quality of that nugget he had, you wanted that claim, no matter what it took to get it. You gave us the money to try to buy it from him and said we could keep it if the old man wouldn't sell. Hell, that's the same thing as payin' us to kill him!"

"But now that son of a bitch Ryan knows," Clate said. "You got to give us more money so's we can go on the run."

"Ryan," Laurette said quietly. The former soldier was a damned nuisance, first with Bellamy and now this. He was going to ruin everything.

She almost wished that old prospector had never come into the academy for a quick dalliance with one of the girls. He'd had a little gold dust in a poke and tried to make out like he wasn't finding much color, but the girl had gotten a glimpse of the nugget the old-timer had wrapped up in a dirty bandanna. She had tipped off Laurette, who had given the old man a drink and contrived to get a look at the nugget herself. If he was finding nuggets like that, the claim had to be worth a fortune, and suddenly Laurette wanted it for herself.

Fate had delivered the Galloway boys into her hands the very next day. She knew them from Wichita, knew they were up for just about any sort of dirty work if it paid well enough. Laurette had enlisted them in her plan. They were the only ones who knew about it. If things had been different, she might have told Fletch, but not now, not since he had gotten all holier-than-thou on her. And she didn't trust Bellamy enough yet, even though he was quite a promising boy, to tell him about something like this.

She placed her hands flat on the desk and said, "All right, settle down, both of you. You say Ryan knows about the old man?"

"He must," Ord said. "Clate told me he was over there snoopin' around yesterday, and today I got nervous about the place where we hid the body. So I went up there just to have a look, to make sure nobody had disturbed it, and who do I see comin' out of the ravine but Ryan himself, damn his eyes. I tried to blow his fuckin' head off—"

"But you missed," Laurette finished for him. "And then, instead of hunting him down and finishing him off, you lost your heads and ran."

"We'll swing if the camp finds out about this!" Clate said. "You know we will!"

"Just give us some money," Ord said, "and we'll head for the high lonesome. I know some places we can hide out where they'll never find us."

"If you don't help us get away, we'll tell everybody about your part in this!" Clate threatened.

Laurette's lips pressed together until they formed a thin line. "All right," she said. She opened a drawer in the desk and took out a small stack of greenbacks. Pushing it across to Ord, she said, "Take it and get out of here. Don't ever let me see your faces again."

Ord scooped up the money. "This ain't hardly enough, but with what you gave us before, I reckon it'll have to do."

"Damn right it will."

They turned to start out of the office. Clate jerked the door open and then stopped short.

Bellamy Bridges stood there, his face pale except for a spot of angry color on each cheek. "You and me have got some unfinished business, mister," he said.

BREATHING hard from the exertion of running all the way to the settlement, Dan almost collided with a man who was dismounting from a horse in front of the Grand Central Hotel. He had already spotted the Galloways' saddle mounts and packhorses in front of Miss Laurette's. As he dodged the tall man, Dan glanced up at his face and felt a shock of recognition.

"Wild Bill!" he exclaimed.

Hickok looked at him calmly. "Do I know you, friend?"

"Dan Ryan. I used to ride with the Seventh. You did some scoutin' for us, back in '67 or '68."

"Of course," Hickok nodded. "Sergeant Ryan. I remember you now. How are you?" Looking Dan up and down, Hickok added, "You look like you've been fighting with a mess of wildcats."

"A couple of killers is more like it." Lord, this was a stroke of luck, Dan thought. "Mr. Hickok, I know it's a lot to ask, but would you mind givin' me a hand bringin' some murderers to justice?"

Hickok frowned. "I don't wear a badge anymore, Sergeant."

"And I ain't a sergeant no more, either, sir, but these bastards killed a good man and stole his claim."

A short, ugly man in buckskins who had ridden into Deadwood with Hickok punched the famous gunfighter on the arm and said, "Come on, Bill, it sounds like it might be fun!"

When he heard the voice, Dan realized the person in buckskins wasn't a man at all, but rather a woman. The only woman he could think of who might look like that was Calamity Jane. Dan had never seen her before, but he had heard plenty of stories about her, most of them rather unbelievable in their sordidness.

Hickok glanced at a line of wagon trains just entering the town. He shrugged as if acknowledging that trouble was going to greet him no matter where he went. "Lead the way, Sergeant," he said. "Perhaps after the long journey I've been on, I could use a little excitement."

"**BELLAMY,** get the hell out of the way!" Miss Laurette ordered. He thought he heard a hint of hysteria in her voice.

He stood his ground anyway, his hand hovering over the butt of his Colt. Glaring at Clate, he said, "I told you, we have some unfinished—"

"Shit," Clate said, and hit Bellamy in the face.

Bellamy didn't see the blow coming. It caught him squarely and knocked him back. He hit the wall on the other side of the hall, bounced off, and fell to one knee. While he was down, the two men rushed past him, heading for the front of the building.

Before they could get there, the front door was thrown open, and a voice Bellamy recognized shouted, "Ord! Clate! You might as well give it up!"

Dan? What the hell was Dan doing here? What was going on? Those questions flashed through Bellamy's brain as he struggled to his feet. Miss Laurette was beside him, grabbing his arm, but he threw her off and rushed after the two men.

Clate yelled, "That's fuckin' Wild Bill Hickok!"

Then two things happened, two sounds that Bellamy would never forget.

Guns began to boom, and Carla screamed.

DAN ducked back out of the doorway as bullets whined past him. Behind him, Hickok and Calamity spread out, drawing their guns. Ord Galloway appeared in the doorway, his wounded right arm looped around the neck of a frightened young woman. Dan recognized her as the whore called Carla, the one Bellamy was so fond of. He held his fire.

"Back off!" Ord shouted as he came out onto the boardwalk, holding the terrified Carla in front of him as a shield. Behind him came Clate, a gun in either hand now. Ord went on. "Give us our horses, or we'll kill the girl!"

They had the attention of everybody on the crowded street now. With his guns pointed down, Hickok said, "You kill the girl, mister, and you'll have a hundred rounds in you before you can go five feet. Let her go, and at least you'll live."

Ord's face twisted in a sneer. "Yeah, until we hang! Now get back, damn it—"

"That's Hickok," Clate said again, his voice filled with awe. "Fuckin' Wild Bill. If I kill him, I'll be the most famous gunman in the West."

"Clate," Ord warned. "Don't—"

Clate ignored his brother, stepped out from behind him, and started to swing his guns toward the tall, long-haired figure.

Dan had already drawn a quick bead. He fired.

The bullet slammed into Clate's chest and jerked him halfway around. His fingers clenched involuntarily on the triggers of the guns he held. They both roared, and then Clate staggered and fell.

The bullets struck Carla Wilkes in the midsection as Ord held her, ripping through her body and on into Ord. He stumbled backward and let go of her. She fell, but Ord stayed on his feet. His head jerked toward the door as Bellamy and Laurette rushed out. "You don't know—" he said.

"Kill him!" Laurette shrieked.

Bellamy already had his gun in his hand. He fired twice, the slugs pounding into Ord and slamming him off his feet. He spun around once in the air and crashed facedown into the street, obviously dead.

Clate lay on the boardwalk, equally deceased. A few feet away, Carla lay in a crumpled heap with a pool of crimson spreading around her. When Bellamy saw her, he shrieked her name, dropped his gun, and fell to his knees beside her. He grabbed hold of her, pulled her up, and cradled her against him. Her head lolled lifelessly on her shoulder. The heart just about went out of Dan when he saw that and heard Bellamy's sobs.

Hickok holstered his guns. He had drawn them but hadn't fired them, hadn't even really lifted them. He said to Dan, "Sergeant, would you mind explaining just what this is all about?"

Dan looked at the sprawled bodies of the Galloway brothers and listened to Bellamy's choked sobs and said, "Justice, I guess. Justice . . . of a sort."

Epilogue

NIGHT had fallen over Deadwood, and on this evening, even the normally raucous Badlands seemed subdued, after the violence earlier in the day.

Dan Ryan had explained about the murder of old Ulysses Egan and had taken a group of men up the gulch to recover the body. Nobody doubted his story; after all, there was Egan's corpse for evidence, and Dan was an old acquaintance of that illustrious new arrival in the camp, Wild Bill Hickok his own self. The consensus of opinion was that Ord and Clate Galloway had been no-good, murderin' skunks and had gotten what they deserved. Better than what they deserved, really, because they should have swung from a good sturdy tree branch.

Damn shame about the whore, though, folks said. She'd been in the wrong place at the wrong time. . . . But that was the story of many a whore's life, wasn't it?

Wild Bill was in the Bella Union, playing cards and drinking and putting up with the people who came up to him and surreptitiously touched him for luck. He acted like he never noticed. Colorado Charley and Steve Utter were with him, and Charley was talking about the freight line and mail delivery service he was going to start. That had folks excited, especially the part about the Pony Express. The news wasn't as exciting as having the famous Wild Bill in their midst, but still.

Over in the No. 10 Saloon, Calamity Jane sat at a table in the corner and took an occasional swig from a bottle of Who-hit-John. She knew that Bill was surrounded by well-wishers and admirers over in the Bella Union, and she didn't want to intrude. He basked in that glory. He might deny it, but she had seen it in his eyes. He was a legend, and his fame was well deserved. He wouldn't want to have anything to do with a drunken slattern like her. She couldn't blame him for that. So she sniffed and took another hit from the bottle and told herself that her vision was blurry because she was drunk on her ass, not because her eyes were wet with something that might be tears.

Across the street, the White-Eyed Kid went into the Gem Theater and looked around, but he didn't see Silky Jen anywhere. He spotted some of the other whores who had just come into town on the wagon train, but not the one he was looking for. He bought a beer from Dan Dority and nursed it along for a while, brushing away the offers from the other whores who came up to him. Eventually, Dority started to glare at him, so he knew he was going to have to either spend some more money or leave. He left, telling himself that he would just have to see Silky some other time.

She wasn't downstairs because she had already caught the eye of someone else. Al Swearengen closed the door of his room and told her, "Get your clothes off and get into bed." God, she was beautiful, he thought, so beautiful she might even be able to make him forget Carla, poor Carla who'd been gunned down in the street like a dog that very day. This one had long brown hair that was smooth as silk, and she had a freshness and innocence about her that was intriguing. She smiled shyly at him as she moved naked to the bed. Al Swearengen smiled back at her, and at his side his hands clenched into fists. This was going to be a good night.

In the kitchen of the Grand Central Hotel, Lou Marchbanks kneaded the dough for the next morning's biscuits.
She thought about Dan Ryan and wished she could talk to
him. She had heard all about the shoot-out in front of Miss
Laurette's and figured he was probably upset about everything that had happened. He was a tough man, no doubt
about that, a tough old cavalry sergeant, but there was more
to him than that. There was a gentle man inside the rough
exterior, the sort of man who probably thought and felt and
cared too much for this unforgiving frontier that surrounded them. She could picture him alone in his camp, up
that wild gulch, sitting by his fire and sipping coffee and
asking himself what he might have done differently, so that
things wouldn't have worked out in such a tragic fashion.
And he would never know the answer, Lou told herself,
would never know that there was nothing he could have
done. This tragedy, or another. It made no difference. The
world kept turning and didn't care. Lou took a deep breath
and turned her head to the side so the tear that rolled down
her cheek wouldn't fall in the biscuit dough.

Miss Laurette's was open for business, of course. Fletch
Parkhurst stood across the street and watched the miners
trooping in and out of the front door. He had been en-
grossed in a poker game in the Bella Union when the shooting broke out and had missed the whole thing, not getting to
the street until it was over. He had seen Bellamy cradling
Carla's lifeless body, though, and he'd felt sorry for the
young man who had been his friend for a short time. He
could have told Bellamy to stay away from Laurette and
Carla, but it wouldn't have done any good. Everybody had
to make his own mistakes. Lord knows he had made plenty
of his own, Fletch thought as he turned away. But when he
tried hard enough, drank enough whiskey and played
enough poker, he could forget them . . . for a while.

Inside the academy, the door to Miss Laurette's office
opened. She was just sitting at her desk, staring without
really seeing anything. An empty glass was in front of her,
containing the dregs of the laudanum-laced drink she had

swallowed earlier. The drug had calmed her, so that the frenzied violence of earlier in the day no longer worried her as much. Slowly, she looked up and saw Bellamy standing there, his face grim and hard as stone.

"I heard what those Galloways said to you. They killed that old man and stole his claim because of you. Carla's dead because of . . . because of . . ."

She waited for him to draw the gun on his hip and kill her. Right now, she didn't much care if he did.

"Because of Dan Ryan," Bellamy finally choked out. "If he'd just left things alone, Carla would still be alive. It was none of his business. I hate him. I hate him."

Laurette took a deep breath and kept her face solemn, even though she wanted to smile. "I wouldn't have had to get mixed up with that deal if I didn't have so many enemies, like that preacher and Al Swearengen. They drove me to it, Bellamy."

"I know. I know." His façade of control had crumbled. He put his hands over his face and sobbed.

Laurette stood up and went around the desk. She put her arms around him and drew his head down so that it rested on her shoulder. "It's all right," she murmured as he cried. "It's all right, Bellamy." She stroked his hair. "I'll take care of you, and you'll take care of me, and we'll both be all right. They won't beat us. You'll see. Just hush now. It'll all be fine."

Outside in the street, H.W. Smith walked along awkwardly, carrying his crate. A man came up to him and said, "Let me give you a hand with that, Pastor."

"Why, thank you, Mr. Merrick," Smith said to the editor and publisher of the *Black Hills Pioneer.* "Quite a lot of excitement today, wasn't there?"

"Indeed," Merrick said. "Good for the newspaper business, of course, but not so good for the individuals involved."

"No, not good at all. Right here will be fine. Let's set it down."

They placed the crate in the street near the boardwalk.

As they straightened, Merrick said, "Tell me, Pastor, why does the Lord allow such tragedies to happen?"

Smith smiled tolerantly. He had heard that question, and similar ones, too many times to remember. "The Lord moves in mysterious ways His wonders to perform, Mr. Merrick."

Merrick grunted. "Well, pardon my language, Pastor, but those ways seem mighty damned mysterious here in Deadwood." He nodded. "Good evening to you."

"Good evening to you, too, Mr. Merrick."

And with that, Pastor Smith stepped up onto the crate, took his Bible from under his coat, and began once again to spread the Word, whether anyone was listening or not.

Author's Note

MANY of the characters in this novel really lived, and many of the events happened as they are described. Some characters, such as Dan Ryan, are composites of men who actually came to Deadwood in 1876 to search for their fortunes. The purely fictional characters, such as Bellamy Bridges and Laurette and Fletch Parkhurst, are, to the best of my ability, accurate representations of the sort of people who populated that booming camp in the Black Hills. The thoughts, dialogue, and actions of the historical characters are a blend of fact and speculation based on the historical record. Certain minor liberties have been taken for dramatic purposes.

Many references were used in the writing of this book, but the indispensable ones are as follows: *Deadwood: The Golden Years,* by Watson Parker; *Old Deadwood Days,* by Estelline Bennett; *Calamity Jane,* by Roberta Beed Sollid; *Wild Bill and Deadwood,* by Mildred Fielder; and *They Called Him Wild Bill: The Life and Adventures of James Butler Hickok,* by Joseph G. Rosa.

Special thanks to Samantha Mandor and Kim Lionetti, without whom this book and the ones to follow would not exist.

Mike Jameson
Azle, Texas

No one knows the American West
better than

JACK BALLAS

Hanging Valley
0-425-18410-2
Lingo Barnes is on his way to Durango,
Colorado, when he stumbles upon the
kidnapping of Emily Lou Colter.
Now he must save the girl and keep
himself out of the line of fire.

Land Grab
0-425-19113-3
Cord Fain is going to teach his ruthless
former trail boss that when it comes to
stealing land from its rightful owners,
possession is nine-tenths of the law—the
rest is blood.

Available wherever books are sold or at
penguin.com

B303

THE EPIC WESTERN FROM THE AUTHOR OF
THE GUN

JUSTICE GUN

LIVE BY IT. DIE BY IT.

BY LYLE BRANDT

GUNMAN MATTHEW PRICE DID NOT THINK
HE WAS GOING TO MAKE IT OUT OF
REDEMPTION, TEXAS, ALIVE.
BUT AS HE STUMBLES OUT OF TOWN
GUT-SHOT AND DYING, HE IS RESCUED BY A
BLACK FAMILY PIONEERING THEIR WAY TO
FREEDOM. NOW, MATT MUST RETURN THE
FAVOR AND HELP THEM WHEN
TROUBLEMAKERS IN THEIR NEW SETTLEMENT
OFFER UP A NOT-SO-WARM WELCOME.

0-425-19094-3

B678

EDITED BY

ROBERT J. RANDISI

WHITE HATS

BUFFALO BILL CODY, BAT MASTERSON,
AND OTHER LEGENDARY HEROIC FIGURES OF
AMERICA'S OLD WEST GET THE ROYAL
TREATMENT IN 16 STORIES FROM ESTEEMED
WESTERN AUTHORS.

0-425-18426-9

BLACK HATS

A WESTERN ANTHOLOGY THAT INCLUDES TALES
OF BUTCH CASSIDY, NED CHRISTIE, SAM BASS
AND OTHER HISTORICAL VILLAINS FROM
THE WILD WEST.

0-425-18708-X

AVAILABLE WHEREVER BOOKS ARE SOLD OR AT
PENGUIN.COM